"A thin reptilian smile spread across Izbek Noir's face as he watched the CNN report. On screen, the streets were a chaotic, choking mass of wide-eyed and shocked commuters. Noir's war would proceed on all fronts. The distinction between civilian and soldier was now obliterated. As Noir had hoped, the world was now divided between casualties and survivors. Noir played a numbers game, a war of attrition, and he would wait with the patience of a spider before attacking with the speed of a viper."

Praise for *The Prodigal Project* Series

"I strongly urge that you discover for yourself the intrigues found in
The Prodigal Project."

—Terry James, RaptureReady.com

"A must-read!"

—Jeremy Reynalds, *ASSIST News*

THE PRODIGAL PROJECT

BOOK 3
NUMBERS

KEN ABRAHAM
AND
DANIEL HART

A PLUME BOOK

PLUME
Published by the Penguin Group
Penguin Group (USA) Inc., 375 Hudson Street, New York, New York 10014, U.S.A.
Penguin Books Ltd, 80 Strand, London WC2R 0RL, England
Penguin Books Australia Ltd, 250 Camberwell Road,
Camberwell, Victoria 3124, Australia
Penguin Books Canada Ltd, 10 Alcorn Avenue,
Toronto, Ontario, Canada M4V 3B2
Penguin Books India (P) Ltd, 11 Community Centre,
Panchsheel Park, New Delhi – 110 017, India
Penguin Books (N.Z.) Ltd, Cnr Rosedale and Airborne Roads,
Albany, Auckland 1310, New Zealand
Penguin Books (South Africa) (Pty) Ltd, 24 Sturdee Avenue,
Rosebank, Johannesburg 2196, South Africa

Penguin Books Ltd, Registered Offices:
80 Strand, London WC2R 0RL, England

First published by Plume, a member of Penguin Group (USA) Inc.

First Printing, October 2003
10 9 8 7 6 5 4 3 2 1

℗ REGISTERED TRADEMARK — MARCA REGISTRADA
CIP data is available.
ISBN 0-452-28456-2

Printed in the United States of America
Set in Janson Text

PUBLISHER'S NOTE
This is a work of fiction. Names, characters, and incidents either are the product of the author's imagination or are used fictitiously, and any resemblance to actual persons, living or dead, business establishments, events, or locales is entirely coincidental.

For Rhina Smallwood
—D.H.

ACKNOWLEDGMENTS

I thank God for those who work with me and keep me true: Gary Brozek, Ken Abraham, Jane Gelfman, and my family. Always in faith.

—D. H.

"Make yourself two trumpets of silver, of hammered work you shall make them; and you shall use them for summoning the congregation and for having the camps set out. When both arc blown, all the congregation shall gather themselves to you at the doorway of the tent of meeting. . . . The priestly sons of Aaron, moreover, shall blow the trumpets; and this shall be for you a perpetual statute throughout your generations. When you go in war in your land against the adversary who attacks you, then you shall sound an alarm with the trumpets, that you may be remembered before the Lord your God, and be saved from your enemies."

—Numbers 10: 2–3, 9–10

CHAPTER ONE

Cat Early woke in the weak light of predawn in Jerusalem. A momentary sense of displacement had washed over her, induced by the watery light in the room. She burrowed more deeply into the bed covers and curled into a fetal position. Ever since she was a young girl, she loved early mornings. She shared a room with her older sister Carolyn, and always the first in the house to wake up, Cat would whisper her sibling's name. Once she heard the sounds of her sister's stirring, she'd start talking to her, and Carolyn, her voice thick with sleep, would respond.

To Cat those conversations were like lucid dreams. She'd keep her eyes closed and let her mind wander. She'd developed the habit of moving a foot from side to side in a gentle rocking motion, and soon, with Carolyn's voice like a lullaby, she'd drift off again. This morning she tried the same thing, though she knew that Carolyn, dead now for nearly a year, couldn't possibly respond.

She thought of a rafting trip the two of them took just after Carolyn graduated from college. They'd swamped the raft purposely, tumbled over the sides into the warm but roiling water of the New River in southern West Virginia. Cat had come up spluttering, her wide grin an ineffective dam against the rushing waters. But she didn't care; the sensation was exhilarating. She'd done as instructed, pointed her feet downstream, leaned her head back, and let her personal safety flotation device keep her head above water. For years after that she and Carolyn had made a joke of the phrase, wondered what was wrong with "life preserver." In the last few months, she'd come to regret their jokes, wondered if somehow they'd created bad karma for themselves. The disappearances hadn't made it easy to believe in much of anything, but she wanted to believe that it was still possible to laugh, to tumble downstream with the current of whatever life threw at you, and come out of it into a calm eddy whole, refreshed, and eager to do it all over again.

Cat rubbed her eyes and then pulled the sheet over her head, inhaled the pleasant aroma of a fabric softener whose scent she couldn't name but liked anyway. Something fresh, not too flowery, but a reminder of the mountain laurel that grew in the fields outside her childhood home. She let her mind drift, saw herself and Carolyn wandering through the fields toward the orchards that her grandfather had planted in one of his many fortune-making enterprises. He wasn't content to retire to inactivity after a successful career in insurance sales, had to keep his mind and his body active. Fruit trees seemed the thing.

By the time Cat and Carolyn were old enough to be allowed to wander unsupervised, Grandpa Frank had lost interest in the trees. The girls hadn't. They'd climb into the branches of the apple trees and eat the hard, tart, unripe fruit until their bellies ached pleasantly. It wasn't until the fall after they'd returned to school that the fruit matured. Cat would rush home from school on those late September days and head out to the fields, too eager to wait for Carolyn, who had to change into play clothes. They'd gather up as many apples as the creased paper sacks they'd saved from their lunches could hold. Fresh applesauce, pies, or a cored and peeled apple slathered in peanut butter made the wait worthwhile.

After they'd reached adulthood, Carolyn had commented that they'd grown up in a kind of kid heaven. A world of trees and fields, necklaces, bracelets, and headbands made of clover and wildflowers. They'd grown up in an idyllic if isolated environment in a modest home on the sprawling acreage that her grandfather eventually sold to developers. By the time they'd reached junior high, civilization had encroached, and the fields that they'd roamed were parceled out into rectangles of manicured lawns segmented by concrete and asphalt.

Her grandfather had negotiated one deal point, and that was that the fruit trees were to remain. The developer set aside the area for a playground and small park. Cat had experienced her first kiss in the shade of those apple trees. His name was Bobby O'Neil, and his breath smelled of Certs and Red Pop soda. They'd snuck away from the group that had gathered to play a game of touch football. Bobby had been the one she'd had her eye on since the fifth grade when they starred opposite each other in the school play—a watered-down modern-day version of *Romeo and Juliet* that an overly ambitious student teacher from the state university had written herself. All the boys loved Miss Harper, all the girls wanted to be her and wear funky hats and a men's tie and boldly red lipstick. It took three years for Bobby to make real what she'd dreamed about all that time.

Cat stretched and smiled at the recollection. It was on mornings like these that she could believe that all would be normal again. From the warmth of a comfortable bed she could feel hopeful. Cat rolled over and stifled a laugh in her pillow as she remembered why it had taken Bobby so long.

By the time the construction crews had moved close enough to their house that they could see the mounds of dirt piled around like dunes, most of the other homes in the development were occupied. For the first time, Carolyn and Cat had to share their paradise. The first few times the boys in the neighborhood slithered into the field and chased them away, seeking a private domain of their own, Cat and Carolyn had feigned fear and shrieked and ran the way that they'd imagined boys would have wanted them to run away in the face of potential harm. Truth was, they weren't afraid at all. Carolyn had a plan.

Bobby O'Neil led one of the charges. This time, instead of fleeing, they'd stayed in the tree and whipped apples at the boys who could only defend themselves by waving the sticks they'd carried and by shouting the insults using words they'd heard but couldn't have understood. Even at the age of ten, Carolyn was already in possession of the fine and accurate arm that would have her play shortstop for the county champion softball team three years before she gave the game up for good when it became clear that boys wouldn't find her attractive for being accomplished.

Cat could still feel the warm-as-pie sensation in her chest that welled up when she and Carolyn had forced the boys to retreat to safety just out of range of their apple bombardment. She remembered them standing in the shadows of a willow tree, backed up against a creek and the muddy down slope that led to its shallow waters. They'd reminded her of a filmstrip she'd seen in her social science class—early man in a hunting pack, either plotting strategy or about to be ensnared in a saber-toothed tiger's encircling trap. "So dumb," Carolyn had said with a shake of her head. "So sad to be a boy."

Cat was too preoccupied to respond. She wanted to go home. She had to go to the bathroom, but Carolyn refused to let her. She was determined to outwait the boys—make them go home in defeat. Only when the sun angled so low that it no longer set aflame the dusty air and the sounds of mothers calling their children to supper carried on the wind did the boys admit defeat and straggle home, having dropped their sticks in disgust.

Carolyn Early's fierce determination had always been offset by the tender mercies of her compassionate spirit. But she also believed in keeping people off balance, never letting them know what to expect, only hint at which side of her personality she would reveal. Cat had learned that lesson as well, perhaps too well.

She was in Israel. She'd asked to be here, demanded to cover international crises, but had never bargained for all this. Her unprecedented access to Azul Dante. Being a witness to the carnage of the mujahideen's rampage. She didn't know what else was in store for her, but she cherished these early-morning moments when she could transport herself out of this time and into her past.

She climbed out of bed and looked at herself in the mirror above the dresser. If she squinted her eyes just so, the years and the worries they'd brought could slough off of her. Her face could recompose into the softer, rounder features of her younger self. The last to be transformed would be her eyes. She'd seen so much that it took a great act of imagination and a powerful exertion of will to recreate the innocence she once possessed. Recalling the wide-eyed look on her face from birthday party and Christmas morning photos, Cat Early wondered if she'd ever look on anything that way again, not with awe or fear but wonder at the possibilities that life held. More than anything, that's what she wanted. To feel the same sense of comfort and security that she experienced during these morning revels in the bright light of daytime.

Her wake-up call startled her and she felt her pulse

race. A deep breath and into the day. There'd be a time to come up for air at some point, she reminded herself. Just hold on and it'll get here.

+   +   +

A huge orange sun formed an undulating backdrop over the scene of red carnage strewn across the desert stretches of northeastern Saudi Arabia. A firestorm raged, accompanied by the volcanic, full-throated roar of battle. Tanks and other armored vehicles, followed by scattered infantry, hacked and spit at each other with explosives, rockets, grenades, bullets, and cries to Allah for strength and victory. Tracer fire danced and skidded between the clashing units, burning wasps hungry for flesh, ripped in deadly strings by the machine gunners. The very ground shook and rumbled from the treads of the heavy tanks, and when one was hit by a shaped-charge rocket and burst open with a punching guttural cough, the men inside writhed and flailed like mindless animals as the insatiable fire ate them. These tormented souls more often cried out for their mothers than to Allah, wanting in their last agonized seconds of life the one who truly represented love to them. For the infantry, their tread barely left a mark on the earth, their cries of pain and death quickly blown away and lost in the howling, ferocious winds of war.

The mujahideen forces of General Izbek Noir had come boiling up from the gutted interior of Saudi Arabia, thrown north by their leader and emboldened with their many crushing victories, they had carved their war from the Red Sea and Mecca, and in a flanking move ravaged both Riyadh and Medina. The mujahideen were radical fringe Muslims at their core, but their ranks had been multiplied by Muslims of all stripe over time. In the land of Muhammad's birthplace, Sunni and Shia held each other in a stranglehold. It seemed that only when faced with mutual extinction would anyone set aside tribal differences. Moderate Muslim clerics, scholarly leaders, and those who espoused the passages of peace written into the Koran had been quickly silenced by radical assassins all across the Arab world. A few still attempted to argue reason from the relative safety of the United States, but their voices went largely ignored by the unruly hordes more interested in conquest and the spoils of war than in religious speculation.

That so far the mujahideen had warred almost exclusively against other Muslims seemed unimportant to the ranks also. Muslims had a long history of exterminating each other over differences in interpretation and implementation of Islamic law, and the violent, empowered mujahideen saw Muslims who did not agree with them as objects simply in their way. Their general, Izbek Noir, offered little choice to others: Join us and partake of the dominance of the world; resist us and be destroyed. The dark armies of Noir hungered for the chance to destroy Christian armies supposedly forming under the guidance and leadership of Azul Dante and his European Coalition, and those great battles still loomed. The hated Israelis remained on what they considered their God-given slice of Arab soil, and the mujahideen soldiers, well aware of their strength, weaponry, and resolve, chafed at the delay in attacking them. It galled them that their general had ordered Israel bypassed for now. He had his reasons, he had explained. He invited any who wished to go against his orders to speak up. None did. They had seen with their own eyes the swift and brutal death suffered by anyone opposing their leader.

Within the mujahideen ranks all of this was enriched by the recent unexplained global disappearances. Muslims had been untouched. Millions had been "taken," but they were *Christians*. Surely, they thought, Allah has a hand in this. That *all* children had been taken, including Muslim children, caused heartbreak, of course, and fear. But those who explained the workings of Allah for lesser mortals suggested that the merciful and knowing Allah had removed all the children from what would become a world battlefield. Allah expected Muslims to be warriors, and warriors had no time for children.

The Saudi armies, such as they were, collapsed rapidly before the onslaught. The obscenely rich and effete rulers of the country, corpulent and cowardly, had long since fled to safer locales. The Saudis left to face the mujahideen were quick to see the handwriting on the wall, and were largely ineffective in their defense. But from the north, from Iraq, came a Muslim army determined to make a stand. This was a relatively new army, bloodied by skirmishes with its neighbor Iran, with a chip on its shoulder from the bad old days when non-Arab foreigners had humiliated them. They had been trained and equipped by the Western powers, shrugged off the notion they were being sacrificed to buy the mostly Christian European Coalition some time, and took aim on the lead units of the mujahideen. They possessed little finesse. Huge armored units, supported by battalions of infantry, rammed head-on across the regions near the Saudi-Kuwait-Iraq borders. The slaughter was immense.

A column of Iraqi armor, supported by attack helicopters, had found a fissure in the steel wall of the mujahideen army front. They attacked it, planning to punch a hole, then wheel left and rake the mujahideen flanks. Infantry followed to exploit any weaknesses. But it had been a trap. The Iraqis found themselves flanked from both sides, the attack helicopters falling like burning, clattering birds, and the tanks becoming ruptured and charred junk. Billowing columns of black smoke became their pyres, while the hapless ranks of infantry were cut down by scythes of machine-gun fire. Those who could disengage reeled back, north, then east, seeking cover. Some of the mujahideen ground troops pursued them, cutting down those who fought and those who attempted to surrender. The mujahideen knew no rules of war. They were primitives at best, and, caught up in the violent storms of battle, became children of the beast. Their cruelty became fiercer as their victory became more apparent, and their brutality against the vanquished knew no bounds.

A running gun battle developed between the remnants of an Iraqi unit and a company of mujahideen. The movement followed a paved road flanked here and there by damaged buildings. The Iraqis fell back, leaving their dead and wounded. The mujahideen ranks were thinned by those who left the attack to loot and defile the dead and execute the others. In the midst of this chaos, amid the smoke, fire, explosions, and screams, two soldiers from the mujahideen side covertly extricated themselves from the action. They did not flee in retreat, nor did they surrender to the Iraqis. They separated themselves from the battle by moving quickly through several wrecked buildings. One of the two, a large man, dark, a little older than the other, fired short bursts from his AK-47 several times to ward off interference. The younger one, armed only with what appeared to be a camera, did not look back as he stuck with his partner.

Within moments the din of battle was behind them, and in the relative quiet they headed toward Kuwait.

+   +   +

The predawn light was silvery, tinged with pink, and as it illuminated the world surrounding John Jameson, he felt it and opened his eyes. For a brief moment he allowed himself to pretend it was one of those silvery mornings from another lifetime, a morning that brought life and energy to his home. His wife would be up already, quietly fussing in the kitchen, the kids reluctantly accepting their fate and preparing for school, the smells and sounds all signaling a new day for the Jameson clan. As quickly as the picture entered his head and heart, it disappeared, replaced by the reality of what had happened to John Jameson's family, and to the world. They were gone—his wife, his kids, his former life—and the world was a place like none seen in the history of man.

He sat up, his back against a brick wall, his hips stiff from laying on the packed dirt floor of a partially burned-out building on the border of Iraq and Kuwait. He was surrounded by the bundled bodies of the living and the dead. Many slept where they had collapsed, wrapped in robes or loose clothing, bodies jerking fitfully in response to their dreams. The dead did not dream, he knew, but lay with a cold and irrefutable stillness. That the living shared space with the dead, both inside the dubious safety of the wrecked building and on the tarmac and dirt around it, did not surprise him. Man was rapidly becoming a hardened, base animal, each individual desperately clinging to his or her life, accepting it in minute-by-minute increments, fearing that each moment might be his last. There were no children, he reflected, and the loss of that one small but incredibly important ingredient of life had diminished the entire world, and made each day bleak even before it began. War, famine, global unrest, earthquake, the recent rain of burning hail that pocked and scarred the land and destroyed much of the life-giving crops worldwide—these horrors had become a reality. Perhaps the dead, who no longer dreamed, were the lucky ones.

He stretched his arms above his head and turned to look out the broken window. Damaged, wrecked, or burned civilian and military vehicles lay scattered all around. The acrid smoke of burning tires and fuel spiraled into the sky. All man-made surfaces, the walls of buildings, the roofs of vehicles, were dented and torn, blackened by what at first looked like machine-gun fire. A great hand had hurled fistfuls of burning shot across the gracefully curving surfaces of the earth, and the missiles holed and scorched all they impacted. It had come in a hard rain, indeed, and when it was done, rivulets of blood hung like crimson tears to mark the innumerable wounds.

Jameson reached for his AK-47 assault rifle, which lay next to his right leg. He had his weapons, and he had his Dutch passport that identified him as Johann Rommel. He had some U.S. dollars, still accepted almost anywhere in spite of the global ruination of order, a few gold coins, and a glassine envelope that contained five small diamonds. He was stunned by the absurdity of these things, that in the face of such devastation and unrest any material thing could hold value. He reflected that at one time he would have been like those who remained—fighting over parched and spoiled land, believing that oil fields were the key to mankind's salvation. But he knew it was, better yet felt it deeply inside himself, that it wasn't the things he carried that mattered, but what carried him forward—his deepening and abiding faith in God and the Savior, the Lord Jesus Christ.

He wore military clothing and carried a backpack. He also carried two canteens for water, and a few packets of freeze-dried food. He longed for his Bible, but knew that to openly carry one where he had been working would be to invite a quick and brutal death. He was as deep undercover as an agent could get, he reflected, and he had to play the role or die. Worse than dying, in his professional mind, would be failing in his mission. That said, his beloved Bible—left to him by his wife and the instrument of his salvation—was not included in his gear.

Still, he knew he could pretend to be anything he had to be, and by all outward appearances he was a soldier, a Westerner, but one who practiced the Islamic faith. He had traveled for many weeks with the rampaging mujahideen forces, across North Africa, over into Yemen, then up through the vast reaches of Saudi Arabia. He had been a member of General Izbek Noir's personal security unit and had traveled alongside the supreme leader of the mujahideen hordes. He had been accepted by the Muslims as a good fighter, despite his being a Westerner, and had eventually been given a secret, very special assignment by the general.

He sighed and thought, I am caught in a tangled web for sure. He was, first, an American agent infiltrated into the army of Izbek Noir with orders to kill Noir. After one orchestrated attempt to carry out those orders, and after having seen Noir survive other attacks, he had become uncertain if Noir *could* be killed. As he was coming to terms with that unsettling realization, Noir called him to his side and gave him a new assignment: He was to take his Dutch passport, his Westerner looks, his several languages, and he was to travel to Paris, Athens, or the next place Azul Dante showed up. Dante was the charismatic and powerful founder of the Prodigal Project, of course, and the leader of the newly formed European Coalition. Dante had managed to bring the "free" world, or "Christian" world, together to stand against Noir and the Muslims, and many viewed him as a savior in these dark and uncertain times. General Izbek Noir, leader of the mujahideen, had assigned Johann Rommel/John Jameson, a simple task. Find Azul Dante, get close, and assassinate him.

John Jameson, a stranger in a strange land, a soldier of Christ surrounded by the followers of Muhammad, said a silent prayer. Oh, my Lord, Jesus, he prayed, Please watch over me on this day, help me to remain strong and focused, help me to be Your instrument for good. Jesus, hold those I love in Your tender hands, and please guide me in my efforts to bring Your light where I go. Give me the strength to do what I must to help bring righteousness to this land. Thy will be done, Lord . . . Amen.

One of the bodies, wrapped in a frayed blanket and sprawled next to the brick wall a few feet from Jameson, moved. An unruly shock of rust-colored hair showed first, then the lean, sleep-creased face of a sunburned, lanky young man emerged. His bright, inquisitive eyes swept the room and came to rest on Jameson. "Sure, Johann," he said, "Let's make our way to Paris by way of

Kuwait and Baghdad, you said. What could be more fun, you said. We'll stay in only the best places, you said." He sat up, rubbed his face hard with both hands, ran his fingers through his hair, took a deep breath, and added, "Remind me to decline if you ever say it will be a little *rough*."

"Count your blessings, Slim," responded Jameson as he watched the young man automatically reach for his cameras and bag full of lenses and film. "You could still be with the good general, serving Allah by dodging bullets and eating dirt." Jameson had learned the young man's name was Slim Piedmont, a veteran freelance photojournalist who had covered wars and other incidents of import around the world for several years. Slim had accompanied another journalist, Cat Early, when she had managed to arrange an interview with General Izbek Noir, commander of the mujahideen. Noir eventually let Cat Early leave his headquarters and return to the front, but had invited Slim to stay with him, ostensibly to photograph the war from the Muslim perspective. Slim told Jameson he would have signed on to serve the devil if it meant Cat could go free.

That had been several months ago, and since then Slim had witnessed and photographed the horrors of war compounded by what many called the end of the world, the entire experience made surreal by Izbek Noir, who embraced evil, held his fanatically rapacious troops in an iron grip, and seemingly could not be killed. Slim had seen Jameson, knew there were other Westerners who fought with the mujahideen as believers, but sensed Jameson was not like the others. The two had cautiously allowed a friendship to develop as the war carried Noir's headquarters unit across the scarred landscape, and Slim had shared with Jameson his misgivings about the Muslim leader. Noir had sent Jameson, whom he knew as "Rommel," on a secret and deadly mission, and as Jameson had prepared to leave the mujahideen camp, Noir had ordered Slim to go with him almost as an afterthought. The general did not tell the photographer of Rommel's mission, but explained they would be more credible as two Westerners traveling together, and he felt Rommel's chances for success would be increased.

Slim had not hung around to argue the pros and cons of the idea.

Jameson stood, his weapon held in both hands. He looked around the interior of the ruined building, then cautiously stepped outside. Slim followed, both of them quiet. Jameson turned and headed east along a paved road lined with the flotsam and jetsam of war and the refugees who pushed it ahead of themselves. Wrecked cars, trucks, motorcycles, bicycles, wagons, wheelbarrows, and tractors lay at odd angles where they had been abandoned. A few were occupied by the dead, and here and there could be seen the carcasses of horses. Clothing, pots and pans, household items, and all manner of other debris littered the ditches along the road, forlorn, lifeless. The framed photographs they came across saddened Slim the most, each one a captured moment, now lost, one-dimensional testimonials to the vagaries of time. Each time Slim stooped to retrieve one, Jameson held his impulse to do the same in check. No telling who was watching him, looking for signs that he was not who he claimed to be.

"Let's move up the road a bit," said Jameson quietly. "You fire up some of that stuff you call coffee, and we'll plan our day."

"The border is wide open, Johann," replied Slim. He knew Jameson's name was John, but they had agreed to only use the name on Rommel's passport. "We can cross anywhere, then head for Baghdad. I still don't understand why it has to be Baghdad, anyway. We could probably catch some kind of flight out of Kuwait, right?"

"Probably," answered Jameson, "but that won't work for me, okay? And we can't cross the border from here until I take care of one little thing." He gazed down the road, the morning sun already hot and glaring. "We're not far, now. I've got to send a message, then we'll move north."

Slim had grown to respect the way Jameson handled himself in the field. The man was a cold professional, no doubt, and Slim was certain Jameson was more than a simple mercenary. The guy had it together, he was focused, and he was definitely on a mission. "I'm with you, big guy," he said with a grin. "And if you can find a place around here that serves cappuccino, you won't have to suffer with my coffee. Which by the way many people have *appreciated* in the mornings when traveling with me."

Jameson scanned their surroundings and grunted in reply.

A few hours later, Jameson and Slim stood outside a partially destroyed mosque four kilometers west of the Persian Gulf. Much of Kuwait was in shambles, having been ripped apart by rioting mobs after "the day the children disappeared." Adding to the destruction were the flights of missiles fired into Kuwait by Iran, on the other side of the Gulf. The Iranian government, in its never-ending efforts to discredit Iraq and its shaky parliament formed after the death of the last Iraqi dictator, immediately blamed Iraq, but the world had its own problems by then. The destruction of Kuwait was looked at as a "Muslim problem," and no one was worried about destabilization of the region—things were so unstable everywhere that this kind of attack seemed like a welcome reminder of the status quo.

Kuwait City was a ghost town. The residential neighborhoods that ringed the central business district and the capital were in ruins. Kuwaitis with money fled, and those without wandered away in search of food, medical supplies, and shelter. Refugees had taken up residence in the skeletal remains of homes, hotels, and apartment buildings. The general anarchy, incursions from nearby Muslim states, and even the occasional mujahideen attack had turned the area into a huge killing field. There was no nuclear winter, yet, but the skies over Kuwait, northeastern Saudi Arabia, and southern Iraq were cast in the somber, acrid, and forbidding shadows of burning oil wells. The oil that had once been the lifeblood of the region now burned in its veins.

"A mosque?" asked Slim as he glanced around the empty, silent square. "You gonna do some praying before we head for Baghdad, Johann?"

Jameson, sweeping his surroundings carefully as he walked up the four wide steps leading to the two huge wooden doors and the interior, replied quietly, "Are you a print reporter or a photojournalist? Take pictures, don't ask questions." One of the large doors was ripped partially off its hinges and hung canted at an angle. Jameson stepped between the doors, checked the interior, and motioned Slim to follow.

Inside were fifteen or twenty believers in the supplicating posture of prayer, kneeling on small rugs that covered the smooth brick floor inside. The followers of Allah were silent and still, their foreheads pressed to the floor. Slim saw Jameson glance at them as he turned left near the front, then went along the far wall toward the back of the building. It wasn't until Slim stood closer to the back row of Muslims that he was able to see why they prayed so intently. They were dead, every one, each apparently shot in the back of the head. Slim brought his camera up, the 35mm, and using the available light, captured the scene. Then he hurried to catch up with Jameson.

He found Jameson in what appeared to be a small office, kneeling in the corner behind a desk covered with papers and sand. He watched as Jameson scanned the room, apparently taking visual measurements, then pulled out a K-bar knife and used it to dig around the edges of two dun-colored bricks that formed a border around the floor. He lifted the bricks, set them down, reached into the hole, and pulled out a black plastic-wrapped square the size of a notepad. Jameson used the knife to cut the seal on the plastic, and unwrapped a miniature transmitter with keypad and screen.

"Cool," said Slim. "How long has that been buried there?"

Jameson shrugged, fiddling with the instrument. "Since this mosque was rebuilt a few years ago."

"So your unit, or the agency you work for, has these things stashed here and there, and you memorize where they are so you can get to them if needed?" asked Slim, always impressed with forward-thinking government types.

"Yep," responded Jameson as he sat on the edge of the table, hit the power button, and was rewarded with a bright green glow on the small screen. "And look at that—they even remembered the batteries." He didn't bother telling the young combat photographer *he* had cached the transmitter there. "Move around a bit, Slim," he said, "Keep an eyeball around the area while I do this, okay?"

Slim nodded and walked out.

Jameson punched in the codes, pressed "send," and waited. The "received," then "ready" codes appeared, and Jameson typed out this automatically encrypted message on the small keypad:

Jameson to Tsakis:

Insertion and acceptance by muja troops as planned. Eventual placement near target, Noir, successful. Homing signal button attached target headquarters vehicle, and subsequent missile attack completed, but results negative. Repeat, results negative. Target unharmed.

Have witnessed several incidents where target should have, repeat, almost certainly should have been killed, but each time he survived. He shows wounds, and blood, uniform and gear damaged . . . but he still survives.

Target also undaunted by recent strange burning hail.

Not sure of physical nature of target, or of probability of success regarding my mission. I need face-to-face or total secure channel with you about what I have learned regarding the target.

Target has given me orders to leave his headquarters and travel to any location occupied by subject Dante, for purpose of termination. Repeat, I am ordered by Noir to hit Dante.

Accepted assignment from target with no immediate options. Will continue operation in assigned role while awaiting your input.

Options:

- Terminate mission, vacate role, return to base.
- Continue mission, make simulated attempt on new target, return to muja.
- If accepted upon return, make another attempt on Noir.

Subject photojournalist already known with muja HQ now with me. His info on file yours.

Will continue to BD, in role, until advised.

End.

Jameson.

Within seconds he saw "Received—stand by" on the screen. He waited. After three or four minutes that message was replaced with, "Continue in role. Situation being evaluated. Continue periodic contact when possible. Will advise."

"Who did that in there, and why?" asked Slim as Jameson joined him in front of the mosque. Jameson could see the pain in the young man's old eyes. "I looked closely at a few of them," Slim added. "They were all old men. Why kill them like that? Was it some kind of sacrifice?"

Jameson rubbed his mouth with one hand, scanned the far blackened horizon, and answered quietly, "Man embraces the beast during the season of war, and reason is lost." He hesitated, listening, then went on, "But you can bet it wasn't for God's sake."

Slim drank from a canteen, nodded, and said, "Well, what's the good word from home, then?"

"Onward, Christian soldiers," replied Jameson as he slung his backpack over his shoulders and adjusted the strap on his AK.

Slim took another look around the empty square, at the broken doors of the defiled mosque, and said as he followed Jameson, "I love it when you talk like that."

+   +   +

"Sir," said the communications center leader into the phone, "we've received a signal from a Sleeping Beauty." She had called the operations boss as the message was being electronically deciphered. She used the in-house term for the small transmitters, computer identified, that were hidden in various places all around the world. Agents in place, or agents inserted into a specific area, were briefed on the location of the Buried Unassigned Transmitters, to be used as necessary. "The user code identifies the sender as Jameson. I've forwarded the text to your screen." After a pause, the young woman added quietly, "At least he's still alive, sir."

"Yes," replied the operations boss, Mike Tsakis. "Keep me posted." He hung up and turned to his screen. The door to his cluttered office was closed, but he spoke in low tones anyway. "Look at this," he said to Benjamin

Carter, head of the CIA, who was making an unofficial visit to the ops center as he often did. He turned the screen on his desk so they could both read Jameson's message at the same time.

"Jameson," said Carter, "He's the older agent you are keen on, isn't he?" The green glow from the screen frosted his glasses, and he kept his tone cool. He was young to hold his position, and he knew many of the older agents felt he had never really been in the bloodied field. He had been appointed, and not having come up through the ranks of any military or intelligence agency made him fair game for the blood-and-guts troops that staffed the headquarters. The operations agents, and their bosses, the men and women who went out there and *did* it, were the worst.

Mike Tsakis didn't turn his head, but replied, "Yep."

They both reread Jameson's message, and before the operations boss could say anything, Carter said, "Do you trust the authenticity, Tsakis? I mean, do we know if it is your agent and not one of Noir's minions using the transmitter? And what is this stuff about the physical nature of the target? He questions the probability of success? Why does he need a meeting or secure channel to *you*? Sounds like your man might be running scared."

Tsakis, still staring at the screen, said, "This agent, Jameson, he won't run scared." He knew Jameson's record, had actually worked a couple of dicey ops with him back in the bad old days, and knew Jameson had lost everything to the disappearances. "Jameson doesn't scare," he said again. "He got in there, into that nest of scorpions, fought his way in, was accepted, got next to Noir as he was instructed, and even managed to plant the homing button as instructed. We know from the video and satellite feed that the cruiser took that vehicle *out*, but Noir was not harmed. Jameson is simply relaying his observations and evaluations, that's all. We put him in, President Reese approved it, and now we've got to give his input the weight it deserves."

Carter caught the reference to the president, of course, and heard the protective tone in the ops boss's voice. These spooks always cover for each other, no matter how badly they mess it up, he thought. "Well let's consider this, then. Your guy is next to Noir, can't kill him, and now all of a sudden he's skipping off across to Kuwait with some news photographer in tow . . . allowed to leave by Noir. C'mon, what are the chances of *that* happening? Now supposedly Noir has given him a new assignment, to find and kill Azul Dante. Jameson is a busy agent, isn't he? We send him to hit Noir, now Noir turns him and he's off to hit Dante. This doesn't sound like something *I'd* like to explain to President Reese." He paused, then added quietly, "You can't discount the possibility that Jameson has switched sides. Wouldn't be the first time an agent went bad on us, right? Noir offers your guy something we can't, and he owns him."

No way, thought the operations boss. "No way," he said, "Jameson won't go bad." You can't know, Carter, you button-downed, pompous college boy, you can't know what that agent is feeling, what he's experiencing, the very real feeling of walking along the edge of a razor twenty-four hours a day, every second waiting for the bullet in the back of the neck. "He contacted us, he's still viable, still effective. The photojournalist, Slim Piedmont, was already there, and their meeting was encouraged. Jameson is alive, still working, still on the team, still communicating, still trying to do his job." He heard the anger seeping in and took a deep breath. "Look, sir," he said to Benjamin Carter. "Why don't we examine Jameson's options and keep him in the game for now. We can bring him home anytime if we think he's been compromised."

"That transmitter unit is satellite tracked, isn't it?" asked Carter pointedly.

Tsakis sighed again. "Yep. As long as he keeps it with him, we can know his exact location within a meter."

"Excellent," replied Carter as he stood to leave. "Keep me briefed."

Mike Tsakis watched the CIA chief's back as the man walked out. They both knew having Jameson's exact location twenty-four/seven meant the agent could be "neutralized" anytime, anywhere. Tsakis knew Jameson was aware of the BUT's capabilities also, and any agent out there in the wild would keep the transmitter with him precisely so headquarters would have a fix on him. He turned to his computer to begin calling in his "what-if" team. He wanted to formulate a couple of scenarios, possible courses of action for Jameson, and message them back to him quickly so his agent would know the operation was still on, and they were still a working team. Jameson won't go bad, he thought savagely. Jameson won't turn, he won't run, and he won't quit.

CHAPTER TWO ⊕

Cat Early savored the moment. She sat back in her chair, let the morning sun warm her face, and moved her head back and forth as the breeze ruffled her hair. Early-day sounds came to her, shops opening, people greeting one another, an occasional bus trundling past her hotel balcony. She could smell fresh-baked bread, flowers, and the tangy, dry air. It was a moment of peace, a rare thing in her world, and she did not want it to end. She tried to resist the process that had already begun in her own mind, the process of examination and evaluation of her surroundings that would bring her back to a hard and brutal reality. She failed. Her memories of growing up with Carolyn made her realize something was missing.

It was the sweet, melodious, energetic, and promising sounds of children. That was the missing piece of the morning mosaic. A simple thing, but vastly significant, she knew. There were no sounds of children playing because there were no children, of course. They had been taken, each and every child of every race, religion, creed, culture, and country around the entire earth, taken in the blink of an eye, gone from even the tightest embrace. Newborn babies, late-stage still in the womb, even those tiny sparks of life just conceived had been lifted up and freed from the bonds of human form. Immediately following the disappearances, investigations began in an effort to determine the exact age that put a child out of range. Was it when they reached thirteen? When they reached puberty? Worldwide results were inconclusive, rendered fallible by the weight of grief, but most accepted twelve to thirteen years to be the cutoff. Many teenagers of varied faiths who were *not* taken seemed to show the same psychological behavior as one who has narrowly escaped some undefined deadly catastrophe.

Cat sipped from a heavy cup of strong coffee. Her hotel room balcony overlooked a small intersection of streets filled with businesses, offices, and neighborhood restaurants. She was a people-watcher by nature and profession, and enjoyed gazing on the scene below as the area came alive in morning fullness. The bus stop on the same side of the street as her hotel began to get busy. The people waiting for different buses ranged from college students to elderly men and women to young military troops. Some shared quiet conversation, some read newspapers or magazines, and many simply stood, patiently or not, with the resigned expressions of commuters everywhere. Something about one young woman in the group made Cat pause momentarily. The girl was lovely, olive-skinned and slim, with a scarf covering her shiny black hair. She wore hiking boots, blue jeans, and a bulky silver jacket made of quilted material. There was something about the way she stood holding herself, about the way she stared so intently up into the fiercely blue sky. A bus approached from the left and slowed for the stop. Cat looked away, then back, as a commotion broke the morning serenity forever.

The young woman's voice cut through the air like an angry prayer, and as she cried out the crowd of people quickly spread back and away from her. Some were knocked down as others pushed and shoved to get away from the girl, who pounded the center of her chest with her right fist as she screamed. Within seconds she stood alone on the sidewalk, a few yards from the intersection. The driver of the bus accelerated and drove down the street with a roar of straining diesel engine. Now there were other shouts and screams, people pointed, and soldiers came running as they slung their assault rifles off their shoulders and pointed them at the girl. None fired, however, and Cat wondered if it was because the soldiers were themselves young, their eyes wide with fear and alarm, or if it was because there were so many people all around the intersection. The girl, seeing them approach, hesitated a moment, then stumbled into the center of the intersection, still punching her chest, glancing down at the front of her jacket as if to see what the problem was. Must be an electrical-connect detonator, thought Cat as she stared at the scene, mesmerized. She's got the plastic explosives around her waist, and she can't get the thing to go off.

Cat heard someone shouting for the soldiers to shoot, a few more screams, and then the scene became strangely quiet. Cat, like almost everyone observing the terrible episode unfold, was rooted in place, unable to move, to breathe. It was unreal, and too real. The girl, her mission imbedded within her for who knew how long, her heart given over to the certainty of her act, began to make a keening sound of fear, or frustration. She kept striking her chest, and even from up on the overlooking balcony Cat could hear the muted *thud* of her fist against her breastbone. The girl glanced up once or twice, her eyes bright and fixated, her unseeing gaze blazing as it swept the crowd around her. Her jaw was clenched, her olive skin stretched tight across her now unlovely face. The scarf she wore over her long black hair fell away and hung across her shoulders. She turned in a slow circle, a slow and lonely pirouette in the embrace of a sweet morning sun.

Out of the corner of her eye Cat saw a soldier step forward. Another grabbed at his elbow to pull him back, but he pulled free and smiled at his friend. Then he slung his rifle over his shoulder and began walking slowly toward the girl in the intersection. Several people called out, "No!" and "Don't go near her!" but the soldier ignored them. Cat heard the girl's sharp intake of breath as she saw the soldier and saw her point one arm at him and shake her head. The soldier, Cat saw, was young like the girl, darkly handsome, trim and fit in his khaki uniform with the shirtsleeves rolled up. His black hair was curly and full, his back was straight, and he smiled at her with sensuous lips and big eyes topped by arching brows. The soldier called to the girl in a soothing, placating tone. Cat did not understand his words, but understood his intent: "Don't do this, there is no reason for you to do this thing." The girl shouted back, pointing at the young man, pounding her fist against her chest in what had become a sad metronomic litany. *Oh no*, thought Cat. *Oh, no.*

The young soldier closed on the woman in the hushed intersection while all those held by the drama watched. Several of the soldiers had their weapons pointed at the girl, trained to make a head shot if possible, but hesitating because of the actions of their compatriot. None fired. Cat held her breath as the soldier stood before the girl, and from where she watched she saw the beautiful smile he gave her as he reached one hand slowly to her face, and gently brushed the back of his fingers against her soft cheek. If he swept a tear from her face, it could not be seen, and Cat no longer heard the thud of the girl's fist against her heart as the young couple stood and stared into each other's eyes in a forever morning.

Cat took a breath, and at that moment a pinpoint of laser sunlight burst from between the couple in the street, expanding with surreal and inescapable speed, not there, then there, blossoming and erupting into a condensed firestorm that grew with an insatiable ferocity. A huge, unseen fist punched the air out of Cat's lungs even as it lifted her from her chair. Cat saw the searing light cut through the bodies of the young soldier and young woman, lifting them, parting them, enveloping them, until they were consumed. Her ears were slapped with a hard blast, and she felt herself hurled backward as her world turned black.

A roar filled Cat's aching head as she again became aware of her surroundings. She tasted blood and brought one hand up to wipe her nose. She sat up slowly, which intensified the pounding in her head, ran her fingers through her hair, and looked around. She was inside her hotel room, a few feet from the balcony. She saw the tipped chair she had been sitting in, the smashed coffee mug, and the twisted curtain edging the sliding glass door. Bits and pieces of masonry, glass, paper, and other things dusted the carpeted floor. She bent over, her head between her knees, almost vomited, and swallowed hard. She struggled to her feet, tottered to the balcony, hesitated, and looked down to the intersection where the young couple had come together. The pain behind her eyes was fierce, and the fear in her heart a grasping thing, but she looked anyway.

The soldier and the girl were gone. Where they had been was an obscene blackened hole in the pavement, spiderwebbed by cracks and tears, littered with torn cloth, paper, and shoes. Cat could see what looked like one boot on the sidewalk, and a twisted assault rifle a few inches away from it. A small fire burned where a newspaper vendor's kiosk had been a moment ago, and the acrid taste of smoke and explosive hung thick and bitter in the air. But it drifted, the smoke, pushed away from the square by the breeze that still ruffled Cat's hair, and as the smoke drifted away, death drifted away. Life returned. Voices rebounded around the intersection, shouts, cries, names. In the distance sirens howled. The growl of a bus drowned it out, then another. The group of soldiers had recovered, had roped off the scene, and guarded it. Cat saw one of them kneel beside the broken assault rifle, his hands on his face as he openly wept. The hustle-bustle of the morning—haltingly, perhaps fueled by false bravado or cynical acceptance—began again. It would never again be the *same* morning, but it was the morning of this day, and it continued.

Cat stepped into her room and checked herself for injuries. She had the bloody nose, one scraped elbow, and that was all. She grabbed a bottle of headache tablets from her bag, got some water, and managed to swallow four of them without gagging. She had to pull herself together. Within two hours she would attend a press conference held by the prime minister, and there was a chance she might get to interview him one-on-one afterward. She got another coffee mug, poured what was left in the pot, and went into the bathroom to run a hot bath. She let her robe fall and stood naked as she watched the water run, and thought, But did it *mean* anything, *change* anything, the girl's death? Would it make any difference, have any effect? What about the soldier's noble and courageous gesture, his kindness, his effort? Was that in vain? Are *we* in vain? What in heaven's name did the girl think she would accomplish with her act? What made the soldier, a boy really, think he could change her mind? They were both so young and beautiful. What in the *world* does it all mean? She stepped into the hot water and gently lowered herself into its soothing embrace. *Good morning, child of God*, she thought, *welcome to Israel.*

+   +   +

In the early evening of that same day, Cat Early buckled herself into a first-class seat on an El Al flight out of Tel Aviv. She glanced at a few of the quotes from Daniel Pearlman she had scribbled into her notebook, then transcribed onto her laptop.

"Israel, as always, will stand for freedom and democracy in a region bereft of both."

"The world's food supply has been diminished, as you know. First by the massive droughts everywhere, then by this recent strange acid rain. But the crops flourish here in Israel, and we will continue to export all of our surpluses to other countries in need as rapidly as we can."

"Clearly the greatest threat to peace, not only in this region but across the entire battered world, are the fanatical mujahideen forces under the command of Izbek Noir."

"Israel views Minister Azul Dante as a beacon of strength and purpose, a man who has formed a strong coalition of free peoples ready to stand firm against the approaching tide of tyranny. That he has an open and good working relationship with President Clara Reese of the United States only strengthens his ties to Israel. Each of us has a vision of a world, suffering already during these inexplicably troubled times, prosperous, peaceful, and free, and each of us is willing to work together toward that goal.

"Israel stands ready, as always, but not alone."

Her meeting with Prime Minister Daniel Pearlman had been brief, pleasant, and informative. As always, Cat was taken with the strength and focus of attention the man exuded. Better to have him with you than against you, she thought. The prime minister began the interview by mentioning the suicide bombing by the young woman Cat had witnessed earlier. "Even in these mad times, individuals misguided by blind and ignorant hatred are capable of *specific acts* of madness."

Pearlman's small and scarred assistant, Moishe Schimmel, had been there, sitting quietly, his face a mask during the questions and answers. He became animated and personable when the interview was formally concluded, and had invited her to lunch the "next time she was in town." She had enjoyed the exchange that took place between Schimmel and Pearlman as a result. The prime minister shook his head sadly from side to side while he looked at his friend, and Schimmel shrugged and asked, "What? I am not old, like you, Daniel. I can do more than just *wink* at a pretty girl if I want, no? Yes?" They had all agreed it was "yes," even though they all knew the prime minister's lifelong friend and confidant had been happily married for almost thirty years. Schimmel had politely walked her to the door, smiled, and wished her good luck.

From the Information Ministry office, she had phoned her editor in Paris, Simon Blake, and he had told her to get on a plane. Azul Dante was attending yet another conference, Blake advised. It was thought he might announce the beginning of real military action against the forces of Izbek Noir, and perhaps Cat could wrangle another interview with him. She took a cold soft drink from the flight attendant, thanked him, and settled back in her seat. The aircraft was headed for Bern, Switzerland.

+   +   +

Ron Underwood sat on the cold concrete floor of a small jail cell in Selma, Alabama. He held his head in both hands, and with his fingers felt the swollen ridge that had formed along the right side of his forehead. His head ached. He wore slip-on canvas shoes, and a loose-fitting orange jumpsuit. His black hair was flecked with gray, wet and spiky, and his face was dusted with an uneven stubble of beard. He stared at the aluminum edge of the toilet, took a deep breath, reached out with both hands and gripped the hard metal, and tried to will himself to slam his head against it again. He could not. He began to sob, and as he did he thought, Why can't I do this simple thing? Why can't I be man enough to destroy myself? I destroyed my Ivy, didn't I? Shot her through the heart, killed her with my own stupid hand, but now I can't kill myself.

He moved one leg and felt something under it. He reached down and picked up a Bible, brought it up to his face, confused, then remembered the old black prisoner who had pushed it into the cell yesterday through the food slot. "You need this," the man had whispered. Underwood, his mind and heart convulsed with pain and self-loathing, sobbed, "I need this? I need this book of lies and nonsense, this book filled with false promise, false hope?" The words fell from his lips like drips of acid, hard for him to form and say. For so long he had relied on an unstructured and unschooled faith in God, faith that there *was* a plan, even if we couldn't know it, even if our own lives seemed heartbreaking and painful. That's what I always told Ivy, he thought. There is a God, God loves us, Ronnie was born seriously disabled for a reason. Ronnie was born for a reason, we are to love him and raise him and never give up hope, never stop believing in God's love. His wife had come to almost despise him for what she saw as weakness, his living in a state of denial, his grasping at "faith" because there was nothing else to grasp. Ron had never claimed to be a serious reader of Scripture. There were some passages he liked, and he followed along in the rare times he went to church. But the Bible was a symbol, a *book*, a validation for his undefined beliefs. He was ignorant of its contents, but respectful of what they represented. But now he looked at the worn version another prisoner had given him, grunted, and threw it as hard as he could across the cell.

After Ronnie was "taken" right out of his wheelchair, after Ivy had left their small house in California to find the preacher whose voice she had heard on the radio, after Ron had sat in his son's wheelchair for seemingly unending days and nights, he had made a decision. He would find the preacher, too, that lying "man of God" who continued the false promises and lured Ivy away with them. He would find the good Reverend Henderson Smith, and kill him dead.

He pushed away from the toilet, uncoiled his stiff legs, and sat on the edge of the metal bunk with its thin mattress. He looked around at the constantly diminishing space of his gray cell, leaned forward, and held his face in his laced fingers. The policemen who brought him to jail were coldly polite, but distracted on that day, *the day he had shot his Ivy*. There was some emergency, fire engines, ambulances . . . something about burning rain, or burning hail, the city in panic, people on fire, craziness. He remembered one of the cops, perhaps the booking sergeant, saying to him, "We got the skies raining fire, Selma and other towns all over the place burning, and you decide to shoot your own wife right in the middle of it, Underwood? Kind of selfish, don't you think?" His injuries had been roughly treated. He remembered a young guy beating him after he shot Ivy. He had been stripped, given his jail jumpsuit, and taken to a cell. A day or so after his booking, he wasn't sure of time now, he had been taken in shackles to a small office where a young lady in a suit waited with a briefcase. She was a lawyer, Ron knew, but he couldn't make out if she was his lawyer or a prosecutor. It didn't matter. She told him he was charged with attempted murder, but because of the "current turmoil" the judicial system was kind of a mess and there was no way to tell how long before court proceedings began. Did he understand? He knew it didn't matter, nothing mattered, but he nodded politely at her.

It wasn't until hours after that meeting that he remembered the lawyer using the word "attempted." Did that mean Ivy was alive? *Could she still be alive?* He had begun to call for one of the guards, finally screaming, but none came, and he never got an answer from them. But after a while he knew he didn't need their answer. He knew. He had squeezed the trigger of that evil seducer of a gun, the power of life or death in his hand. He had heard the roar of the exploding gunpowder, had felt the heat on the top of his wrist, the kick of the recoil. He—Ron Underwood—had sent that demented lead hornet into Ivy's chest. His eyes had been seared with the image of her contorted face, the horror, the fear and determination, the image of her spasmodic jerk as the bullet slammed into her, the image of her falling, falling. No, he had shot her through the heart, there was no way she was alive.

He tasted blood in his mouth and realized he was chewing his lower lip. He sobbed again and shook his head from side to side. He had not *attempted* to kill Ivy. He had *attempted* to kill the Reverend Henderson Smith.

Smith had stood wide-eyed, staring at the hole in the end of the gun barrel, his sweaty face a petrified mask of fear as Underwood had squeezed that teasing trigger. The bullet would have bored into and through Smith, Ron knew. But then *Ivy* was there, between the gun and the reverend, between life and death. The bullet had found her, and she went down. He remembered being swept up in a vortex of torment and panic, staring at Ivy, at the blood pumping from her as he backed away, before he turned and ran. A young guy had tried to stop him, then tackled him. He remembered trying to get away from the young man, indescribable pain and heartbreak wrenching his mind. But the young man had hit him in the face, and things had become shards and fragments of time until the cops had him and he was pushed into a cell.

He sat back on the bunk, his head and shoulders against the wall. He lifted his face and felt the tears on his cheeks as he said, "Why? Why was our beautiful son born damaged? Why did caring for him twist and embitter my Ivy? Why was my sweet Ronnie taken on the day so many disappeared? Why did Ivy have to come here to listen to the preacher? What made me think I could change anything, or make anything right, by shooting him? What have I done?" He lay down, tucked his legs under him in the fetal position, balled his hands into fists and pressed them against his face, and cried, "What have I done?"

+   +   +

"I've always liked this passage, myself."

Ron Underwood heard the voice, thought it was just one more of those voices in his head, but sensed another person in the cell with him, sitting near his feet at the end of the bunk. Some time had passed since he had fallen asleep crying, but he did not know if it was day or night.

"What do you think, Ron? Pretty nice, huh?"

Underwood looked toward the voice. A man sat there, on his bunk. The man was another prisoner, apparently, but Ron had not heard him being let into the cell. He had the Bible in his hands, and read aloud, "Your hands made me and formed me; give me understanding to learn Your commands. May they who fear You rejoice when they see me, for I have put my hope in Your word. I know, O Lord, that Your laws are righteous, and in faithfulness You have afflicted me. May Your unfailing love be my comfort, according to Your promise to Your servant. Let Your compassion come to me that I may live, for Your law is my delight."

Ron sat up, rubbed his face with his hands, and looked at the new prisoner. The man was about the same age as Ron and wore the same canvas shoes and jumpsuit as all the jail population did. He had dark blond hair, dark eyes, a handsome face, and an easy smile. Ron knew had not seen him before, but he hadn't really been paying attention. "That's my Bible," he said to the prisoner after a moment.

"Yes," answered the man, "it is. I picked it up off the floor, hope you don't mind, kind of bothered me laying there like that. Then, like happens every time I pick up a copy, I begin leafing through it, and the next thing you know I'm all caught up in it. That passage is in Psalms, of course." He grinned at Ron, "The Good Word, and all that."

Ron just stared at him.

"Old Windfield slipped this copy to you, didn't he?" said the man. "Not the first time. He's a softy, that Windfield. *Feels* for others, you know? Sees others hurting, lost, and *worries* about them, *prays* for them. He has been in and out of this place for years, it's actually his home, of sorts. He really cares about the wretches brought into this place, wants to find some help or guidance for them. He tries to get a copy of this Good Book to them if he can—the guards know what he's up to, but they'd never stop him—in the hope they'll begin reading it and find strength, or answers."

"Uh, what did you say your name was?" asked Ron.

"I'm Ayak," replied the man as he put out his right hand, "But you can call me Stan."

Ron felt the man's firm grip as they shook hands. "When did you get thrown in here, Stan?" he asked.

"Little while ago," responded Stan. "Wasn't *thrown*, really."

"So what are you in for?" asked Ron, with jail-cell courtesy.

"For you," answered Stan.

Ron just looked at him sitting there, and said, "No,

no . . . I mean what did you *do?* What are you *charged with?"*

"Oh," replied Stan, nodding his head and smiling. "Well, what I *did* was sort of busywork. I mean, it was okay, and I felt I was a part of the big picture and all, but I kept petitioning my boss for something more *rewarding*, more *substantive*. Times being what they are, something came along almost before I was ready."

"Look," said Ron, becoming exasperated. He wondered if his new cellmate was perhaps a bit slow. "I'm charged with murder. They say it's *attempted*, but I know it's murder. So what are *you* charged with, Stan?"

The man straightened, cocked his head to the side, smiled again, and said, "I'm charged with *you*, Ron. You know, your spiritual well-being, your salvation, if it's to be, and my goodness we certainly *hope* it's to be, don't we?"

Ron Underwood stared at the man. He was searching for a response when there was a clatter at the cell door and a gruff voice said, "Dinner, Underwood."

As the battered plastic tray was pushed into the cell through the slot, Ron leaned toward the opening and shouted, "Hey! Hey! You, guard. I don't want a cellmate. I want to be alone in here. I don't want anyone in here with me!" There was no response. Ron turned and looked at Stan. He shrugged, "No offense, Stan, but I'm kind of struggling right now, my head is totally messed up, I'm not sure if I want to live or die, and I'm just not ready to share this space with you or anybody else. You seem like a nice guy and all, and I'm glad you're concerned about my well-being, but I really just want to be left alone right now."

Ron bent and picked up the dinner tray. He was not hungry, but was already looking forward to the break in the jailhouse's routine monotony that the tasteless meals provided. He sat on the bunk and began to unwrap the plastic utensils on the tray.

"Well," said Stan pleasantly, "I guess we should thank our Lord for this meal, as every time we break bread it is a gift."

Ron glanced to his right and saw Stan had an identical tray balanced precariously on his knees. He didn't remember two trays coming through the slot.

"I don't know which item to try first, Ron, do you?" asked Stan as he poked at the food with his plastic fork. "I was told, of course, that this whole act of nourishment through eating would be one of the more *exotic* aspects of this assignment." He did not look convinced as he added tentatively, "The brown stuff looks interesting, but the green stuff has a nicer texture."

Ron sat and ate his food. He did not trust himself to speak.

CHAPTER THREE

Ivy Sloan-Underwood heard the soft voices around her. They seemed very near, but somehow apart from her, as if a thin veil of gauze hung between their tenuous reality and her distant awareness. The voices were not intrusive, nor did they make her feel uncomfortable, they were simply there, a part of her known world. That it seemed the voices discussed *her* seemed natural, and she waited with dreamlike patience to be called upon to join in. Somehow all seemed as it should, though she did not know how she *knew* how it should be, and she hung there in a golden glow expectant and unafraid. That she was no longer what she *was*, no longer *where* she was, was certain. Again, this was, if she remembered correctly, anticipated and acknowledged. The ethereal weightlessness of her person added validity to her new place and form. The warmth emanating from within her seemed to blend wholly with the warmth and serenity surrounding her, and she recognized the oneness of this new existence.

She *was*. She knew this from her thoughts. She recognized herself, spoke to herself, accepted her own musings on her existence as evidence that she did exist. She was *somewhere*, and knowing this meant the personality, ego, energy, dreams, and memories of Ivy Sloan-Underwood remained in form, remained to be *conscious* of remaining. The voices were there, too, soft bubbles bumping the gauze around her, rippling it like a summer breeze, swaying it from side to side. They came burbling through her consciousness like small loops and whorls in her life's stream, playful, reassuring, inquisitive. She *was*, because *they* spoke of her, and she longed to hear the voice that would alert them to her readiness. I'm here, she thought gently, right here near you. I'm not afraid, and I know it is time. Speak of me and I *am*, call to me and I *will*. But they did not call, really, so she hung suspended in sweet desire, content in repose within the caress of the drifting, eddying, pooling moments.

Then, sweet, pure, and fine like the string of a harp, came a voice tight with emotion and vibration. She had longed for this particular voice, it's true, but still she was not prepared to hear it. She had ached to hear the voice. The still-weeping hole in her heart formed from this absence had never healed, and yet the voice startled her. It was the clarity, perhaps, the vividness of it, the string of words formed into one sentence, driven by love and concern, offered through sure knowledge of *how things were meant to be*. Had the words come to her from *any* other voice she would have simply ignored them even as she recognized that the message they conveyed was wrong. What they told her was absolutely *not* what she wanted or expected to hear, but their source immediately negated any rebellion. They were simple, they were passed to her in love, and she knew—even as parts of her consciousness wanted to resist—that she could only obey and accept.

"*It is not time yet, Mommy*," said the voice of her son, Ronnie.

Ivy Sloan-Underwood opened her eyes. She lay awake in a hospital bed coccooned in white sheets, the walls of the room pale blue, the plaster ceiling dusty white. She heard the gentle brush of air in her nose as she breathed, the rustle of her own hair on the pillowcase. She closed her eyes to see darkness, opened them again to see the room. She lay on her back, with tubes in her arms, two far bumps under the sheet where her feet rested. She felt her chest rise, felt her chest fall, felt a wet tear form at the corner of each eye, then felt the cold tracks of their descent on her cheeks. She heard the voices again, recognized one. Shannon Carpenter was in the room. Another female, a nurse. The deeper voices of two men. One was Shannon's friend, Ted Glenn, she guessed. Perhaps the other was a doctor. She heard the voices through the membranes inside her ears. Vocal chords caused vibrations, these impacted her eardrums, and these resonations were then dispatched and interpreted by her brain. All physical, all part of a physical world's reality. *I'm alive*, she thought, *Praise God, I'm alive.*

"*Ivy*," exclaimed Shannon Carpenter. She had glanced over and seen Ivy's eyes open. "You're awake, you're awake." She came to the side of the bed and took Ivy's left hand in both of hers. "I have been praying, Ivy, praying you'd wake up," she said, tears in her eyes, "And look at you, finally. Oh, praise God, you're alive."

"How long?" Ivy managed to ask. Her mouth felt dry, her lips puffy.

"What? What? Oh, three days, Ivy," answered Shannon, "They took you right into surgery when we got you here. You had lost a lot of blood, they said." She touched Ivy's left cheek with the fingers of her hand, then patted her hair.

"Where is here?"

"Selma General, Surgical Intensive Care," replied Shannon as she glanced over her shoulder at Ted Glenn with a tearful smile. The big man moved beside her, leaned down, and said, "Hey, Ivy."

"Hey, Ted."

"Ivy," added Shannon, "this is Doctor Bass and Doctor, um . . . Spring. Doctor Bass did your surgery, and Doctor Spring is helping with your recovery."

A thin, dark woman in green hospital scrubs nodded at Ivy and said with a grin, "Seems like our nursing staff here was decimated by the disappearances, but the ranks of doctors went largely untouched. As a result, we doctors are taking turns in the nursing role." She shrugged, and added, "I'm kind of enjoying it."

"I'm Doctor Bass," said the portly, balding man next to her wearing the same type of scrubs. "I'm an emergency room kind of guy, but recently we've had to be . . . flexible around here." He saw the question in Ivy's eyes, and added in a businesslike tone, "You were shot. Do you remember?"

Ivy's mind filled with a picture of her husband Ron's face, the twisted hate in his eyes, and the evil black gun in his hand. As she saw the gun and Ron's face she saw herself lunging in front of the Reverend Henderson Smith, and falling, falling. She nodded at the doctor.

"The bullet hit you in the left side," continued Doctor Bass. "It broke one rib, shattered another, cut up some tissue, creased your left lung, missed your heart by an inch, and . . ." He made a face, brought his hands up and moved them in an arc, and went on, "I guess you were moving, turning as the bullet hit you, turning and falling. The bullet's path was irregular, which we think was a good thing." He rubbed one hand over his bald head, "I mean, it didn't take out any major fuel pumps, compressors, or main wiring systems, if you know what I'm saying. Pretty clean, actually, except for the ribs and lung, and loss of blood, of course. It came to rest against the inside of your left shoulder blade, scored it, but didn't break it. All in all, not bad." He looked at Doctor Spring, then at Ivy again. "We kept the exploratory to a minimum and did the surgery to repair the one rib and remove the slug. We have a drain in

place, you'll be very sore for a while, and as soon as our excellent new nursing staff says it's okay, you'll get out of
here."

"Thank you, Doctor," managed Ivy.

The doctor looked at his partner, then at Shannon and
Ted, then at Ivy, cleared his throat, and said, "The day
they brought you to us was . . . crazy. We were extremely
busy, almost overwhelmed, actually. Because of the uh,
nature, of your injury, the police were interested. I sent
them away because of your condition. However, uh, Ivy,
I am now compelled to tell the police detectives you have
regained consciousness, and they'll want to, uh, speak
with you." He made a notation on a clipboard, nodded,
and he and Spring walked out.

Ivy looked at Shannon, and asked, "Ron? What happened to Ron? Is he okay? And the Reverend Smith?"

"They arrested Ron, Ivy. Do you remember the father
and son we met in the cathedral a couple of weeks ago?
Thomas Church and that young cowboy, Tommy?"

Ivy nodded again and discovered she had a headache.

"Well," continued Shannon, "that young guy was just
pulling into the cathedral parking lot, everyone was running around yelling and screaming because of that weird
burning hail. Do you remember *that*?"

Ivy made a face. All she remembered was Ron, and
the gun.

"That's okay, Ivy," said Shannon, "I'll tell you about it
later. But that boy, Tommy, he saw you go down, saw Ron
running with the gun, and tackled him. Then some peo-

ple held him until the police and the ambulance finally got there. They were crazy busy because of small fires and people panicking and everything. They took Ron to jail after you were brought here, and I guess he's been charged with shooting you. One of the detectives told us the whole system is messed up right now, he didn't know about Ron's hearings or trial or any of that."

"Oh, Ron," said Ivy quietly. She began to cry softly. "I should have seen it, I should have seen it coming."

"C'mon now, Ivy," said Ted gently. "We could all tell your husband was kinda stressed out, but nobody would have thought he'd try to *shoot* anyone. You couldn't know either. They'll hold him in jail, where he'll be okay, and eventually they'll work it out. What matters is what you did for Reverend Smith, you flat saved his life by taking that bullet, you saved him."

Ivy could see Ron's eyes, and the gun. She saw the burning hail now, heard the hissing of it. She heard the abject fear in the wailing voice of Reverend Smith, and the pounding of her own blood. She heard someone saying the Twenty-third Psalm. She saw Ron's face as she fell. She looked at Ted, and said, "But Ron will—he'll *hurt* himself because he hurt me. He will. How are they going to keep him safe in jail?"

Ted did not know what to say.

Shannon patted Ivy's hand and said gently, "Ron will be fine, and if you want we can go see him when you are able. What Ted said is true, though, Ivy. You did save Henderson Smith's life."

"He's okay? Does he forgive Ron?" asked Ivy.

Ted and Shannon glanced at each other, and Ted replied, "The reverend ran off when you were shot, Ivy. We heard that nice black woman, Nateesha Folks? We heard she found him up on the pulpit in the cathedral, plenty frightened and confused and all. Nateesha managed to get him up and headed to his room, but he was afraid to go in there we heard. So she took him to another room and got him into bed, and we haven't seen him since. Nateesha is the only one going in and out of that room. Harry, the assistant pastor, he's been doing the services and other church business."

"The reverend was seriously shaken by Ron's act, Ivy," added Shannon. "Perhaps shaken to his core, we don't know. We *do* know you saved his life and so have given him a chance to confront his demons, or whatever he must do."

The word *demons* made Ivy remember the appearance of Thad Night, and the conversation she was having with the reverend when Ron had approached them, something he was telling her or asking her, like he'd had a visit from the same type of dark force or being. She shivered. "I hope he's okay," she said quietly. Then she tried to sit up and said, "The sooner I get out of here, the sooner . . ." But the stabbing pain through her torso wracked her, and she lay back.

Shannon and Ted leaned into her quickly, and Shannon said, "Easy, girl. You just came back to us, give yourself a couple of days to regain your strength. Let them remove that drain, let the wound heal, and then we'll go see Ron and the reverend. Okay?"

Ivy looked at her friends, saw their concern, and managed a small smile. The smile flattened as she asked, "Has the Reverend Smith said anything more about the number seven? Like, how it is important, or what it has to do with *us*?" She looked at Shannon, "Don't you remember me asking you about it before all this happened? And the Reverend Smith was worried about a, uh, dark, sinister . . . person, or *being*." Her mind filled with an image of Thad Night, darkly handsome, his knowing smile emboldened with the sure knowledge he could possess her anytime he wished. She was immediately flooded with feelings of helplessness, desire, repugnance, and shame. Thad Night was her tempter, and she understood how vulnerable she was then, and now. That the Reverend Smith had been somehow tempted, corrupted, was what she suspected he'd tried to tell her just before Ron came with his gun. Smith was frightened, that she had seen with her own eyes, and his fear of death illustrated his weaknesses. If he *knew* God, *believed* in Jesus Christ, *accepted* the word of Scripture, why would he fear death?

"We haven't spoken to him, Ivy," replied Shannon softly. "You and I spoke of the number seven, but the Reverend Smith . . . he has gone into hiding, the poor man." She shook her head. "Doesn't matter now. What matters is you resting and coming back to us." She patted Ivy's left hand and said, "We'll come back this evening." She and Ted walked out of the room.

Ivy rested her head on the pillow and felt another big tear fall from each eye. *I don't want to be here,* she thought. *I want to be with my Ronnie.*

+ + +

Only when it was very, *very* bad would he let her hold him. And it was bad now. She saw it coming, recognized it in his eyes, the way they seemed to stare inward, into a black and bottomless abyss, into his own wracked and abused heart. The taut brown skin of his lean face stretched even tighter, his thin lips compressed, his breath coming in rapid and shallow gulps. When he acted like this she felt compelled to reach out and surround him with her arms, gently pull him to her, and he would not stiffen or resist. She liked it when his face was buried in the side of her neck, his breath warm on her skin, his tears wet. He was a tall and lanky man, bony and hard, with big hands, African American like her, but with darker skin. He had small ears pressed flat against the side of his head, his hair cut tight. He had large, even teeth, a great smile, and a fine laugh . . . when he laughed, when he smiled. Like her, he had lost everything, his wife and their children, to the disappearances. She felt him shudder against her and sang softly, "What a friend we have in Jesus."

Nateesha Folks was a big woman, ample and full. She had always been comfortable with not being petite, however, and this only added to her attractiveness. Her big brown expressive eyes resided in a lovely face. She possessed a pretty smile, a sweet voice, and a saucy wit, each of which she used regularly. She was a woman accepting of herself, with a subtle confidence born of that acceptance. She had liked being exactly this self throughout most of her life, had never longed for boyfriends, and had carried on a strong and loving relationship with the man she eventually married. She had always been strong in her faith, too, until the day not long ago when the very foundation of the earth, and her world, was shaken. The pain of her loss had been exacerbated by her image of herself as a Christian. That she had not been taken with her family, had not been "lifted up" with the other faithful, had been impossible for her to reconcile within a heart crushed by pain and confusion. That is what initially drew her to the side of the man she held in her comforting arms. He had *clearly* been a Christian, a real Christian, a *true* Christian. But his family, like hers, had been taken, and he, like her, had not.

"Nateesha," he said in a voice raw with emotion, "how can I, how can I . . . ?"

She felt his arms around her waist and rocked him back and forth. It was the first time he had done that, put his arms around her, and she could feel his physical strength. She liked it. It's all right, she told herself, it's all right that he's holding you and he feels like a man, and you like it, Nateesha. It's all right to hold him and rock him and let him take from your strength, and it's all right to be a woman and hold a man. You're just comforting a hurting soul, that's all.

"How can you what, Henderson?" she asked softly.

He said nothing for a moment, but continued to hold her. She felt him take a long breath, then he said, "How can I face them, my flock? Those people sitting in those pews, lookin' up at me like I *know*, like I can tell them something that will make them *accepting*, and *unafraid*. They *saw* me, saw me fall in shame and fear, saw me *frightened*. How can I go back to that pulpit and speak to them about the truth, about *anything*?"

"Because you must, Henderson," she responded gently. "It's who you are, it's what you do."

"The people who come here, Nateesha, to find strength in my words, in my interpretation of the Good Book," he said, "They will know I'm afraid."

She held him quietly for a moment, then said, "Henderson Smith, you better go back to that Good Book, just like you tell us. You go back to it, seek answers, everything you need is in there."

He said nothing.

"Psalm 22? Right at the beginning?" asked Nateesha.

After a moment, he responded in a barely audible voice, "*My God, my God, why have You forsaken me?*"

"I've heard it discussed more than once in different Bible studies through the years, whether our Lord Himself felt fear up on that cross. He was a *man* here with us, Henderson, and sometimes a man knows fear." She knew she was not the Bible scholar the reverend was, but she had a pretty good memory for certain sections and passages that had impacted her through the years. "And what do both Matthew and Mark say about His last words as He died?"

Again there was a long, quiet moment. Again the soft voice, "*Eloi, Eloi, lama sabachthani?*" A pause. She felt his arms tighten around her again, "My God, my God, why have You forsaken me?"

"You are a man, Henderson Smith," said Nateesha, gently but firmly, "and a child of God. You draw your strength from *Him*, and you have been given the gift, and the responsibility, to share that strength with the rest of us who are hungry for it. Oh, I know you saw your own death coming at you from the end of that crazy man's gun, and I know you've been somehow harassed by some dark force or evil thing." She rocked him, thinking of how he awoke several times during the night crying out. She slept in the next room with the door open, and heard him speak in his sleep about a "burning man," an "evil laughing man" who "melted" as he taunted him. She had seen for herself the burn marks in the carpet of his old room, where the "burning man" had stood, had seen how he would *not* stay in that room anymore. "Doesn't matter. You go back to that Book, Henderson Smith, strengthen your heart with the breath of our sweet Jesus, *collect* yourself in Him. You are a good man, Henderson, and you can defeat your fears with His help." She smiled, "Then you can help the rest of us work on *ours*."

"I am nothing," he said, his voice muffled as his warm mouth pressed against the skin of her neck.

"You are a preacher," she replied, "And you got to preach."

"I'm afraid," he said, "I'm afraid."

She felt his big hands on her as he shuddered again, and sobbed, and she resumed her singing, her voice a whisper.

CHAPTER FOUR

Azul Dante found the Book to be a pleasing and interesting device, primitive, certainly, but through no fault of its own. He acknowledged that the concept of any book began with a built-in handicap and natural limitations: the use of one of the written languages of man. Man's physical form of communication, vibrations and membranes, sounds formed into audible identifiers, was almost stultifying in its brute smallness. These, transposed into letter identifiers and formed into words, carried with them those same crippling, infantile capabilities. He sipped hot and delicious coffee from a fine and delicate china cup and amusingly gave the Book its due. The words, he mused, crude and small though they may be, taken from the page by the eyes and given to the brain, spark *thought* . . . and even in a primitive being, thought, mental imagery, and speculation can expand with reasonable potential.

Immediately upon *becoming*, of course, he was aware of the vast collected works of man, great thoughts and mean, ruminations, pontifications, explorations, and equations. And questions, always the questions formed through the desire to know, the desire to be assured, questions immense and small, all stumbling toward some truth or another. *Truth, promise, or guarantee*, he thought. He sipped the coffee and stared out the window of his hotel room, just able to see the far Oberland. The hotel was near the Elfenau District, not far from the old city of Bern. With a sigh he acknowledged that when one simply *becomes*, one experiences a sense of displacement at first, one has no *history* to aid in forming a comprehensive self-picture. He shook his head, and a rueful smile distorted his cruel lips for a moment. Self-picture, he thought, what nonsense.

He continued to stare out the window, the Book lying open on the ornate polished wood table beside him forgotten for a moment. Bern was an ancient place, full of man's history, full of stories peopled by souls long transformed. It had great *fog*, and on the bright days there were those Alps, those crags, those wonderful old streets and buildings. He had enjoyed a brief tour through the center, the peninsula mountain fortress, lofty and forbidding—perhaps proud would be a better description—with the river Aare horseshoe shaped around it in a cut that seemed to have been chiseled by a stonemason. Above this beckoning abyss, between the Kornhaus and

Kirchenfeld bridges, stood the Gothic cathedral, and the Platform, a parklike area overlooking the sheer drop to the river below. *Gothic*, he thought, what a fine word. He found it interesting that many of the Swiss, a dour and pragmatic people, spoke four or five languages well, because of their geographic location, and with this multilanguage capability had traditionally and stubbornly clung to their neutrality in world affairs. He wondered if the typical Swiss knew the word for *chameleon* in each of those languages.

He poured more coffee from the pot into the cup, sipped it, and reached for a scone. ". . . I am he that entered through the barrier into the garden and spake with Eve...I am he that caused the angels to be cast down from above and bound them in lusts after women . . . I am he that stirred up Judas and bribed him to deliver up the Christ," he read. "I am he that inhabiteth and holdeth the deep of hell; but the Son of God hath wronged me, against my will, and taken them that were his own from me. . . ." From the same work he had read, "For indeed, I was formed the first angel: for when God made the heavens, He took a handful of fire and formed me first, Michael second, Gabriel third, and other angels of whom I cannot tell the names." He thought the voice rather petulant, and smirked.

He was, of course, intensely interested in the other being of his substance who inhabited this world during these days, and had for some time now. That *he* was infinitely special and unique, he had no doubt. He was mentioned cautiously, circumspectly, in the Bible. John made mention of his eventual appearance before Revelation got into it, but his stature and weight against the other were unclear. He remembered a line from *Psuedodoxia Epidemica*, by Thomas Browne, written in 1646, "Lastly, to lead us farther into darkness, and quite to lose us in this maze of Error, he would make men believe there is no such creature as himself . . . ," and another from C. S. Lewis in *The Screwtape Letters*, "If any faint suspicion of your existence begins to arise in his mind, suggest to him a picture of something in red tights, and persuade him that since he cannot believe in that, he therefore cannot believe in you."

"Ah," he said quietly as he stared out the window, the pastry sweet in his mouth, the aroma of coffee strong in his nostrils, "But *I* believe in you, you poor, miserable, primitive, misunderstood sod." The world, and even the far-flung universes, he knew, were energized with the opposing forces of good and evil—evil being a subjective thing, he reflexively acknowledged, evil representing that which was not of "God," something that began with a self-empowering *philosophy*, one beautiful and powerful creature's desire for freedom. He understood it immediately and was filled with respect for the other—one could say first—being of his substance. He felt, however, that since the "rebellion," Satan had not risen to his full potential. The carpenter from Nazareth, even in his base human form, had limited his impact, had been unmoved by all those rather cunning temptations. The one called Jesus, "Son of God," had in a very short life formed and placed within primitive man's heart a tiny spark of understanding and promise. And for two thousand years the world had grown, and *mankind* had grown, because of it.

But *I* won't be humiliated, or limited, by the "risen" carpenter, he mused. No, there is more to me than a mere dark angel. I am unique in the scope of my power and capabilities, everything that came before me was simply setting the stage, and that other being of like substance, poor Satan, will become as unimportant as all the other creatures of this theater in tumult. He emptied his coffee cup. But I need him for now, him and his misguided Muslim hordes, cavorting on the playground of war. He is actually enjoying himself, he thought, rolling around in the stench of war like a dog, drinking in the bloody nectar like a fine wine. And now, for fun, he has played another hand, a simple gambit based on an assassination he must know cannot happen. He stared out through the hotel's window, not seeing. Ah, he thought, let Satan play while he can. Let them *all* play, while they can.

A sharp knock on the hotel room door snapped him from his reverie. He turned to see his assistant, Sophia Ghent, leaning in with a tentative smile. "Azul," said the tall and lovely young woman tentatively, "Drazic asked me to tell you that your transportation and security are downstairs and ready. Shall I tell him ten minutes?" She wore a tailored charcoal business suit and stylish black shoes. A pair of large-framed glasses were set on the bridge of her nose, and her hair was pulled into a neat chignon. She had very pale and fine-grained skin, and wide, warm eyes that seemed to take on the dominant color in any room.

Azul Dante smiled at her and nodded. "Thank you, Sophia, that would be perfect." He allowed her to call him by his first name, purposely making their relationship less formal, to draw her closer. She had been drawn perhaps too close, he ruefully acknowledged, allowing herself rather sophomoric fantasies regarding their future. Well, he laughed to himself, she *was* only human, and a *female* human, at that. He watched her closely as he added, "Oh, and Sophia, do you remember the nice journalist we met in Paris? Cat Early?"

"Yes, Azul," replied Sophia, "I do." There was another she had met in Paris, but she dared not mention his name.

"She will be here, today, in Bern. She will attend the press conference, with the others. Afterward I would like to invite her for coffee, so she can spend a few minutes with me one-on-one."

"Of course, Minister Dante," said Sophia. She watched his face, his eyes, closely, for some hint of what she had seen there once before. Since their last stay in Paris she saw him in a different light. She could not deny her feelings of wariness when she was around him, certain now the persona he allowed the world to see was carefully constructed and maintained.

That she was still awed by him, swept up in his energy

and power, she reluctantly admitted. It was a trip in the fast lane, working as his personal assistant, watching the power brokers of the world swirl around him in their complex machinations. The globe-spanning trips, the presidential suites, the formal balls and embassy luncheons, it was a heady drink for a young woman. That he was a powerful, respected, attractive, seasoned, and experienced single male, and she was a part of his very small inner circle, only made the whole thing more exciting. Now there was a new element, and it filled her with an undefined foreboding. She had met a young U.S. embassy staffer named James Devane, and they had been immediately attracted to each other. It might have been a mild flirtation, or perhaps it could have turned into a real romance, but it was not given a chance. Dante and Devane had exchanged sharp words, and afterward Devane was told, through channels, not to communicate with Sophia in any way. Both James and Sophia believed the orders were the work of Azul Dante.

The not-so-subtly implied threat worried her. There was a pettiness to it, a *meanness*. She had never once strayed from her strictly dedicated and professional bearing and loyalty to Dante, had made no demands, had not taken advantage of their proximity and workday informal intimacies to try and force a relationship with him. Of course she had occasionally daydreamed, *fantasized*, about him, but what young single woman in her position wouldn't? They remained daydreams. Then she met James Devane, and for some unfathomable reason Azul had become quite territorial and controlling. She had seen something in Azul's eyes afterward that deeply unsettled her.

He waved, "See you in ten, then." Sophia nodded and closed the door.

Sophia had done well, he thought, holding her feelings close like a professional. Other than that brief spark in her eyes, the sudden tightening in her chest he had sensed, she had given no sign that the arrival and special treatment of Catherine Early caused her any angst whatsoever. He sensed also her new watchfulness when she was around him. It wouldn't hurt, he was sure, for her to be a little wary. Good girl.

He sighed, ten minutes, ten bothersome incremental markers in this world of time-space continuum. I am Azul Dante, he mused, that being the name I chose to identify this human form I *became* to begin this New Age, an age preordained and dreaded by the grossly limited entities of this world and those within the universes who should know better. When he allowed small displays of vanity, he admitted to rather liking the name Azul Dante, and knew it was already being whispered in respectful tones throughout the heavens. My being here now is predestined and prophesied, but misunderstood in scope.

He thought of the Prodigal Project. *Perfect.* He, Azul Dante, had formed the Prodigal Project to help save man and his world in what many were calling the "end times." That man was spiritually hungry, spiritually confused and apathetic *before* what they called the "disappearances" had mysteriously ravaged their ranks, was a given. It made for fertile ground for deception, and he *was*, if nothing else, a deceiver. In the form of Azul Dante he was a dynamic leader, charismatic and strong. An air of mystery surrounded him also, born of war and tumult in the Balkan states, a widower who had lost a young wife and child to a bombing. That he was tall, athletic, with a slightly weather-beaten good-looking face, gray hair cut in a schoolboy style, always well mannered and impeccably dressed didn't hurt either. He was a seasoned, well-educated, intelligent, and articulate prime mover, and it was no surprise to those who had seen him at work that so many world leaders decided to join with his European Coalition. The Coalition was political, designed to bring the varied strengths of different countries together to stand against General Izbek Noir and his mujahideen forces. The Prodigal Project appeared to be less so at first glance, more spiritual, more family-of-man supportive. Only he, Azul Dante, knew the real goal of the Project.

He glanced across the room to a recessed bookshelf. There were many interesting works there, and the obligatory Scripture. They call it their *Bible*, he thought. He had known its contents immediately as he was formed, recognized the Book's importance to the scheme of things, and hungrily, combatively, dissected every word, every nuance, every parable, metaphor, admonition, and love song. The mentions of what *he* was prior to what was termed "Revelation" were maddeningly brief and misleading. The words drew him as limited, and far more frustrating and insulting, they drew him as eventually *defeated*. "Bah," he spit into the empty room. "A child's book, written in pleading hope of some promised redemption for these gross and base beings. *Divinely inspired*, what nonsense." There could be no divinity in a book so clearly trampled upon by the hand of man, he argued, and how could any human scribe know the outcome of such a momentous event? "And where are the writings of Jesus Christ?" he asked the far mountains. "Couldn't the poor uneducated carpenter *write*? So many of man's questions could have been already answered if only the supposed 'Son of God' had picked up a celestial pen and written out what man needed to know to find God. His writings would be etched into the hearts of every human being for all time, and there would be no more confusion, speculation, *interpretation*." He stared at the Bible on the shelf, and the Book was immediately consumed by a steely blue fire. The wood of the bookshelf was strangely untouched, but within seconds the Book was gone, leaving only a faint trace of ash. For one uncharacteristic moment he wondered how he could so easily destroy what symbolized the True Word. Somewhere deep within his psyche a part of him whispered that he could reduce the collection of paper and ink to ash because the Truth written there was beyond him. He shrugged it off. "The Word of God," he said contemptuously.

He ran the fingers of his right hand through his hair, pinched the bridge of his nose, and closed his eyes. The number seven appeared to him, written and in numeric form. He shook his head. He did not feel threatened by the number seven, was not frightened by it, but it bothered him nonetheless. It was the incongruity of it, he supposed, the abstract randomness. What it meant escaped him, and he wanted to dismiss it as simply being a minute particle of knowledge and information within the vast resources of his created intellect. He was very *aware* of things here, he had such a total grasp of occurrences, that this tantalizing and bothersome seven was an irritating anomaly. He remembered asking the journalist, Cat Early, if *she* knew what it meant, because it had appeared to him as she approached. She had feigned ignorance, or perhaps really didn't know. His eyes went back to the trace of ash on the bookshelf. The churches? he thought. Ephesus, Smyrna, Pergamum, Thyatira, Sardis, Philadelphia, Laodicea? "Seven," he said to the room. "Seven. Seven *what*?"

Azul Dante, the living Antichrist humanized and personified, rose from his chair, straightened his already perfectly knotted tie, and walked from the room. Behind him hung the faint tang of sulfur mixed with a cupful of confidence born of vanity and lust. Doubt hung there a moment, too, then dissipated like a thread of smoke from a candle.

+   +   +

"How 'bout the number *seven*, Ron, my boy?" asked Stan from the top bunk in their cell in the Selma,

Alabama, jail. "Ever given any thought to *that* meaningful little digit?"

"What in the—," said Ron Underwood quietly as he stared at the torn and stained mattress pushing through the bunk springs above him. He was still uncomfortable with his new cellmate, who had appeared without warning in the cramped gray confines. He had tried to question the guards, had yelled at them again so they'd come and put Stan in another cell, but they acted like they didn't know what he was all bowed up about. It wasn't that Stan wasn't a likeable guy—he *was*. Maybe a bit eccentric, but in a pleasant way. Problem was, Ron really did not feel like company. He was hurting and simply wanted to be alone with his pain. Besides, this Stan, who first said his name was *Ayak*, didn't always make sense to Ron. Like now.

"Seven," said Stan, "S-E-V-E-N." He began to sing in a rich and melodic voice, "Seven . . . I'm in heaven, seventh heaven . . . seventh inning strrrrrrretch . . . seven little fellows singing hi-ho, hi-ho, it's off to church we go-oh . . ."

"Stan," interrupted Ron, "Stan, knock it off. I don't have a clue as to the number seven or what it means and I'd like to get some sleep."

"But Ron Underwood," said Stan, hanging over the side of the bunk, his face upside down, "you are a *part* of the number seven, and it is important in the big scheme of things."

Ron had had enough. He reached out with his left

hand, grabbed the front of Stan's jumpsuit, and pulled. As Stan gave a yelp and rolled out of the bunk, Ron put his glasses on and sat up. He leaned close to Stan, who now sat on the concrete floor.

"Well," said Stan, "now we see the Big Guy was using the old noodle when he designed these human forms with this comfy cushion in the hindquarters." He patted his bottom appreciatively and added, "I did not mean to anger you, Ron, but this is *important*."

Ron made a fist with his right hand, drew back his right arm, and was ready to slam the fist into Stan's face. But he couldn't. The guy seemed so *sincere*, and he had a grin on his face that was invulnerable to anger. Exasperated, Ron brought his fist back and lay it against his own chest. "Look, Stan," he said quietly, "maybe you can't understand or appreciate where I am emotionally or mentally at this point in time. Maybe you are lucky enough to have a personality that is impervious to pain, but listen carefully, please."

He reached out again and grabbed Stan's collar, "I am really *messed up* right now. I mean, I am *lost*, okay?" He shook his cellmate gently, "Have you noticed that the world might be coming to an end, Stan? Have you noticed the children, all the children, are gone, *gone*?" He began to weep and pulled Stan closer to him, "*My* child, Stan, my beautiful, trapped Ronnie. Gone. Then my wife, Ivy, gone, too, but in a different way. Left our home, came here to Selma to hear this *preacher*, this man of *God*, to listen to him *explain* why this had to happen."

Big tears began puddling on the bottom of his glasses before coursing down his cheeks. "Got it so far, Stan? My boy, my wife, gone. Oh, I know others lost loved ones, millions in the blink of an eye, gone. So, is it God's work? *I don't care*, Stan. All I want is my boy, my Ivy, okay? So I come here with a gun and I shoot the preacher." He paused, his eyes went back to that moment, then returned. "Stan, he felt fear, I saw it in his eyes, *the preacher was afraid of death*. If he knows God's promise, how can he be afraid, huh?"

Stan began to speak, then simply shrugged. He wanted to tell Ron he *did* know pain, that it was something those in his ranks were *very* familiar with, having spent most of their existence lovingly trying to allay or deflect as much of it as they could. But he said nothing.

Ron let his hand drop to his side, and Stan immediately missed the sensation of *touch*.

"But it didn't matter, Stan," continued Ron. "The preacher's fear didn't matter because instead of shooting him, I shot Ivy. My Ivy got in the way and the bullet ripped into her and she went down and there was all that blood." He took off his glasses, rubbed his eyes, wiped his cheeks, replaced the glasses and said, "And do you know what *I* did, Stan?"

Stan *did* know, but he waited.

"I ran away," said Ron, "I shot her, saw her blood mixed with the blood from that crazy burning hail, and I ran away." He reached out slowly, grabbed Stan's left arm above the elbow, and squeezed. "I'm charged with mur-

dering my own wife. It's the end of the world, and my son
has been ripped from here anyway." His eyes burned as
he stared at Stan's concerned face. "Now," he added quietly, "do you get it? I'm in prison for the rest of my life,
and it means *nothing*, Stan. All I want to do is die." He
paused and released Stan's arm. "All I want to do is die."

Stan, momentarily overwhelmed with the depth of his
charge's pain, simply looked at Ron's troubled face. Then
he tentatively reached out with his right hand and patted
Ron on one knee. "If you've got nothing, you've got
nothing to lose, right?"

Ron remained silent.

"But you've got everything to gain, Ron, and while
you are gaining, you will help so *many*."

A suspicious look clouded Ron's face, and he said
flatly, "Are you gonna start preaching now? Is that what
this is? You gonna save my soul? You knew that old black
prisoner pushed that copy of the Bible into my cell, and
you started reading scripture to me before I even knew
your name. Is that it, Stan? This whole thing is about
faith, and God, and saving my soul?"

Well, of *course*, thought Stan. But he said, "Actually
this whole thing is about your understanding that your
life is not over. It's not over even when it's *over*, but we'll
save that discussion for another time. What this is about
is you accepting that there is work to be done. We have to
leave this jail, find your wife—who is very much alive by
the way—wounded, but alive. We have to connect you to
a few others who do not know this yet, and go out to do

battle with one *seriously* deranged and lost entity who is here for all the wrong reasons."

Ron just stared at his cellmate. Ivy is *alive*, he thought, and was aware at that moment that he had known it in his heart all along.

"Ron," said Stan. "Ron, are you listening?"

"I am listening," replied Ron. "And I'm hearing you continue to make no sense whatever, Stan."

"Well hear this, Ron-boy," said Stan huffily. "You can't sit there crying when there is work to be done."

Ron shook his head. He could not deny the feeling of strength coursing through his heart, the feeling of hope. But he shook his head, and said, "Tell me again what this is all about, Stan?"

"The number seven," answered Stan as he stood, took the Bible from the top bunk, and smiled, "of course."

"Of course," sighed Ron.

CHAPTER FIVE

The devil made me do it, thought Benjamin Carter, the young director of the Central Intelligence Agency. It was an old and oft-used explanation for evil or hurtful deeds committed by man. As so often is the case, Old Scratch had nothing to do with it, but would have been proud to claim influence. No, Benjamin Carter had not been led astray in this matter by anything but his own aspirations and fears. There was what he perceived to be a loose cannon out there, a rogue player in a complex, dangerous, and global game that would richly reward the winner. He, Carter, did not intend to become a loser because of some wild card careening from point to point with the power and resources to cause serious damage to one or the other contenders in this game. No. He had to ensure that the rogue was eliminated, in a way that would appear to be simply happenstance. He had direct methods at his disposal, too, but with what he had set into play, there would be no chance of backtracking to find a path that would lead to him. The rogue, the wild card, would die, his convoluted mission thus negated, and everyone with access would shake their heads in awareness of the awful capriciousness of this sad and brutal world.

+   +   +

Slim captured the old woman's face in the viewfinder. She was one of almost a dozen women and men riding in the back of a battered old truck stuffed with canned goods, bags of grain, corn, rice, and boxes of dry groceries. When Slim had climbed aboard just as the sun was rising, hours ago, he'd noticed all of the bags and boxes were marked "USA," and the American flag was stenciled on each one. All of these, however, had been hastily painted over, and the words "Democratic Republic of Iraq" were sloppily superimposed. The truck swayed on the road, and Slim's shoulder bumped against John Jameson's, making it difficult to focus the camera. They had climbed onto the truck somewhere south of Ad Diwaniyah, on the road that followed the undulating Euphrates River toward Baghdad. Jameson had spoken with the driver a moment, some kind of deal was made, and they were off. It had been a hot, bumpy, and dusty ride so far, but Slim felt they were making good progress. Next stop, Al Hashimiyah, then the bigger town of Al Hillah, then Baghdad. Slim never thought he'd actually be *pleased* to be in that city, but the sooner they got there, the sooner they would leave Iraq behind.

He concentrated on the woman again. Rembrandt would have done this one, he thought as he studied the woman's long-knowing eyes, the deep crow's-feet, the lined cheeks pulling down to a tightly closed mouth with compressed lips the color of liver. This was a woman of dust, her simple robes and head cover tinted with the hues of the very earth she had come from, the skin of her face and hands sandpapered from the winds of life. He held his breath and took what was probably the first, only, and last photograph of the woman.

Slim still held the camera focused on the woman's face when he felt Jameson stiffen beside him. The big man had been quiet for most of the trip, all business once they slipped across the Iraq-Kuwait border and headed north past columns of mechanized infantry headed south. He seemed to sleep, swaying with the movement of the truck, his eyes opening only when the truck slowed or stopped momentarily for some reason. His hands held the AK-47 assault rifle that never left his side. Now Jameson's eyes were wide open, and he was twisting, his mouth stretched, bringing the AK up even as he used his other arm to slam Slim in the chest, pushing him down toward the steel truck bed. Slim, confused, watched as a line of brilliant, wet red flowers blossomed across the old woman's torso, punching her, causing her to fall even as her arms flailed up and her mouth opened to let out a gasping scream.

The truck lurched, skidded, lurched again, and stopped sideways on the roadway. At that moment Slim became aware of the all-consuming roar of noise that enveloped his entire world. It was a demonic howl of explosions, bullets ripping into metal and flesh, the blasting of grenades, the shriek of rockets. He was on his elbows and knees, and lifted his eyes to see Jameson crouched beside him. Through the deafening noise he concluded that the truck had been hit in the cab or engine area with a mine or rocket of some sort. Then the vehicle was raked with machine-gun fire as grenades were tossed toward it. It was an ambush, but where had it come from? He had the vague thought that there had been a lull in the steady stream of traffic behind, in front, and around them, and that's when Jameson seemed to tense up.

He heard Jameson shout, "Other side!" and followed the big man as he flung himself across the scattered bags of food to the other railing of the truck, the high side. Then Jameson was crouching, firing his assault rifle in a series of short bursts. He could hear shouts and screams, could hear Jameson grunt, and wondered how many bullets his companion had in the AK just as he was clunked in the forehead with an empty magazine. Jameson had flung it out of his weapon before slamming a fresh one home. He heard a soft roar, and the whole world turned orange for a moment. There was a rush of hot air, then a curtain of thick black smoke.

"Shoot, Slim . . . shoot!" yelled Jameson, and for one tilting moment Slim thought the madman with him wanted photos of this terrifying horror for his scrapbook. Then he remembered the .38-caliber revolver

Jameson made him carry around, and he fumbled it out of the leather holster strapped to his lower left chest. It was a cross-draw, which, the first time he'd strapped it on, Slim had thought pretty cool. Thoughts of cool were long gone now, and he held tightly to the pistol, pointed it in the general direction Jameson seemed to be shooting, and squeezed off three quick rounds, then three more. The gun bucked in his hand, and he felt the immediate heat rake the top of his right wrist. He bent over and wretched, then pointed the gun again.

"Roll out, Slim!" shouted Jameson as he threw bags and boxes out of the truck bed. "Roll out, reload, and get *down!*"

Slim looked at the pistol in his hand. *Reload? Already?* He leaped toward the boxes and bags on the ground and heard a pitiful, high-pitched wail behind him. He looked over his shoulder to see a burning man trying to climb over the piles of grain, trying to climb out of the consuming fire. The man faltered and his wail became breathy as he stumbled. Slim saw Jameson shoot the man in the head, and the dead man tumbled loosely to join the others who had already died. He fought back a sob, wretched again, and fumbled in one of his film pouches for his extra bullets. He grabbed a handful and managed to get the cylinder open, then reloaded with his wildly shaking hands. He snapped the cylinder closed, got up on one knee, and looked for a target.

"Other side, now!" shouted Jameson, and Slim flung himself behind a bag of corn, facing the other side of the road. Jameson was firing toward a small truck, two dead men hung out of it, and two more seemed to be trying to hide underneath it. Slim fired his revolver in their direction, once, twice, and saw the men crumple, but he didn't know if they were hit by his bullets. Jameson rose to one knee, and in quick succession flung two grenades at the truck. The explosions jolted Slim and took his breath away. Then Slim heard Jameson yell, "YEEEAAAAHHH!" in a loud and guttural voice and leap up, firing his AK as he ran around toward the front of the truck. Slim got to one knee and pointed his pistol first this way, then that. He saw no movement coming in either direction. The sound of the fire eating the body of the truck was like a live thing, and the smoke hung heavy and acrid with fumes. He got to his feet, aware suddenly of the quiet. There was no more shooting, no more explosions. He stepped a few feet back from the burning carcass of the truck and took another slow three-sixty look around. He forced himself to look into the truck bed for the old woman, but nothing there resembled human form. He glanced down at his 35mm camera hanging on its strap on his chest. He wondered, not for the first time, if the souls of all those whose images he had captured were somehow stored between the lenses. He felt a shiver tap-dance up his spine, shrugged it off, and turned to look for Jameson.

"Classic ambush setup," said Jameson through clenched teeth. Slim found him a few yards in front of the burning truck, standing over a man lying on his back in the middle of the road. Jameson's right boot pressed down onto the man's heaving chest, and his AK was pointed at the man's sweating face. "Slim," said Jameson tightly as the photographer approached, "meet Omar."

Slim, who by this time should not have been surprised by anything Jameson said or did, shook his head. His mouth wouldn't work. Finally he managed, "You, you *know* this one, Johann?"

Jameson's mouth hardened into what might have been mistaken for a grin and nodded. "Take his picture," he said.

"What?"

"Take his picture, I said," responded Jameson without taking his eyes off the heavyset, swarthy bearded man dressed in clean khakis and Russian boots. The man had a flashy gold watch on his left wrist and a .45-caliber automatic pistol in a holster on his right hip. A few feet away, behind another small truck, lay the tube of an expended rocket launcher. "Slim," added Jameson, "I might need his photo to show certain people when I get home."

Slim hesitated a moment, then walked closer to the man on the road, leaned forward, captured him in the viewfinder, and got several shots from different angles.

"John," said the man on the ground, "please."

Jameson looked at him, his face a mask. "Please? Please what, Omar?" he asked. "Please don't take my picture, or please don't put a bullet in my head?"

"Please don't kill me," pleaded Omar. "You and me,

we go back a long way, no? You and me, we have done some good things, some good work, no? You remember who it was that got you hooked into the filthy mujahideen?" He spit, and the effort made his whole body convulse. It was then that Slim noticed the spreading stain of blood that darkened the front of the man's groin. "John, *please* . . ." The man reached up with both hands, grabbing at Jameson's pant leg.

Jameson's face did not change. "You were in the lead vehicle, Omar," he said quietly. "You waited until we were on this long stretch of open road, very little traffic, and you picked your spot. Then you slammed on the brakes, slewed your truck around, and jumped out. The driver of our truck," he said, jerking one thumb over his shoulder in the direction of the burned hulk behind him, "automatically slammed on his brakes, and before he knew what was happening you fired a rocket-propelled grenade into the cab."

Omar's heavy breathing became slightly raspy. Jameson looked all around. Slim did too, and from where he was standing he counted at least nine bodies of those who had attacked them. Jameson had killed them all.

"Then you had your little band of desert scum . . ."

"Leftover Feyadeen," spit Omar. "Freelancers."

"Then you had them come up on either side of us," continued Jameson, "and rake us with automatic weapons and grenades."

Omar shrugged and Slim thought it an eloquent shrug from a wounded man sprawled on a hot, paved road under a glaring sun and the unrelenting gaze of a seriously angry full-combat intelligence agent.

"But they didn't coordinate their fire and maneuver after our truck skidded to a stop, Omar," Jameson went on. "The hotheads on the right, perhaps sensing an easy kill, moved on us before the team on the left. Gave me much better odds, Omar, gave me a chance to deal with an assault from one direction before I had to deal with the one at my back. Just enough time, Omar."

"You were always pretty good, John," said Omar tightly through a clenched jaw. "I told them . . . told them . . ." He licked his lips, and his eyes widened and rolled back slightly. "John," he said, "Maybe you have already killed me." He put both hands on his groin, as if trying to hold the bloody mess together.

"Nah," said Jameson with no smile. "I never got any rounds off in your direction. I was coming for you, but you were already down. Must have been one of your own guys."

"Figures," Omar responded with a downward turn of his thick lips.

"Johann," said Slim, "Maybe we can get him bandaged up, or get him some water or something, I mean, he's . . ."

Jameson just shook his head, and put one hand up to stop Slim. He leaned closer to the man beneath his boot, his voice quiet, but intense. "Omar," he said, "you knew where I was, probably picked me up as I entered Ar Rumaythah, back down the road." He paused, and Slim could tell by the way his shoulders stiffened that his next question was important to him. "How?" he asked. "How did you know?"

To Slim's amazement, the heavyset man on the ground actually chuckled. It sounded like a stuttered series of small dry explosions. "How do you *think* I knew, John?" he answered. He took two deep breaths, then went on, "I felt sad when I learned what I was to do, John, but you know how it is with us independents. We get a job, we must put our personal feelings aside. They offer good incentive, personal feelings get put aside."

"Who, Omar?"

Omar closed his eyes.

"Who made you the offer, Omar?" asked Jameson, his voice husky. "Who gave you my location?"

Omar's eyes opened wide. He grinned, an evil, pale grin. "It wasn't the *bad* guys, John."

"What was your incentive?"

The heavyset, swarthy man convulsed. He drew his legs up and twisted his body so he could lay in the fetal position. A bubble of blood formed on his lips. Jameson took his boot off the man and stepped back, but his AK still remained pointed at the man's head.

"What was your incentive, Omar?"

"America," said Omar, and his mouth turned crimson. "I could go and live . . . in . . . America . . ." Suddenly he arched his back, brought his legs up until his knees almost touched his chest, turned his face toward the fierce and apathetic sun, and died.

Jameson stared at Omar's expression, frozen forever in agony, and waited, as if the answer he searched for would yet fall from the dead lips. It did not, of course, and Jameson turned away. Slim watched as the big man pulled the small transmitter he had recovered in the mosque from inside his shirt. He walked as close as he could to the hottest part of the fire that continued to burn around the truck's fuel tanks, leaned forward, and pitched the device into the white-hot flames.

They drove north in the small truck Omar had used. After almost a half hour, Jameson, behind the wheel, finally spoke. It was in response to something Slim had muttered out loud without thinking.

"What?" asked Jameson, his eyes on the road.

"That little secret transmitter you dug up in the mosque in Kuwait," replied Slim. "That was your lifeline to home base, uh, headquarters, right?" He received no answer and went on. "It was important to your, well, *our* survival, right? But you threw it into the burning truck."

Jameson said nothing for a while. Then he said evenly, "I told you one of the capabilities of that equipment is it constantly beams a signal that is picked up and relayed by satellite." He paused, then added, "So they can locate me."

"*They*, being your guys, the good guys."

"Yep."

Neither man said anything for a few minutes. Slim thought about what the agent had said. He felt fear.

"So now we're back to basically running out here alone?" he asked.

Jameson shrugged, his big hands tightening on the steering wheel. "There are no coincidences in my world, Slim, and Omar being on this road to kill me can't be an accident." Now they'll have my last known sat-nav coordinates, he thought. Maybe they'll get aerial photos of the ambush site with the wrecked trucks and burned bodies. Maybe they'll helicopter a team in to take a closer look. Maybe they'll think they got me, even if they discover Omar bought it. Maybe.

"I'll move forward with my mission," he continued. "I'll communicate with home when I can, and keep the faith." He glanced over at the young combat photographer in the seat next to him and added, "We're gonna be moving fast the next twenty-four to forty-eight, Slim, and it appears I may be in someone's crosshairs. You can travel with me as far as Baghdad, or Switzerland, and then you can peel off and go about your journalistic business. It's okay by me. *Capisce*?"

"We'll see," answered Slim.

They drove on. In a few minutes they saw, far ahead and approaching, what looked like several trucks, an old bus, and a couple of smaller vehicles. Slim figured they must be getting closer to another town. There was something else he wanted to get off his chest.

"Ten-to-one odds, and you beat them," said Slim. "You killed ten men in a matter of minutes when they had it all their way."

"They messed up, gave me a chance . . ."

"I've never seen anyone fight like you in close combat," said Slim, shaking his head, "and I've been around war for a while now."

"I've been around war for a while now, too, Slim," said Jameson. "Mostly it's just reaction, shoot and move, kill or be killed. That, and some luck, I guess."

"Maybe you've got one seriously squared-away guardian angel, Johann," said Slim.

Jameson said nothing, and after waiting a few minutes Slim turned his face and stared out the window. He felt sick to his stomach.

John Jameson drove the dead man's truck alongside the Euphrates River, headed north toward Baghdad. I am a soldier, he thought. A soldier fighting for what he believes is right, and just, fighting for a reason, and cause. Yes, I have killed, and I am prepared to kneel at the feet of Jesus, admit to Him what I have done, and ask for His forgiveness, or at least His understanding. He said a silent prayer, thought about guardian angels, and felt better. Then he turned his mind to the immediate operational problem.

Omar's little ambush told him without a doubt that someone with *access* wanted him out of the picture. Maybe it's because I'm one of *seven*, he thought. He did not know what that meant, but with crystal clarity he knew he would meet another one, another one of seven. He had a small trace of blood over his left eye from a stinging piece of shrapnel. His hands were cut in several places, and the right side of his face was sooty and blackened by gunpowder. His beard, flecked with gray, was dusted with desert sand, and his nondescript uniform was stained with sweat. They had found some bottled water in the small truck, and he gulped half of one bottle down as he drove. He wiped his mouth with the back of his sleeve and thought about death, duty, and treachery. He let the miles pass behind them and thought, *I am one of seven.*

CHAPTER SIX

The Reverend Henderson Smith had a soul as tormented as that of Ron Underwood, but his jail cell of self-loathing he occupied alone. Nateesha Folks was there, of course, and had been there through the terrible hours since he stared at death and fled from it in wild uncontrollable terror. She was strong and loving, talking to him, listening, holding him when the spasms of fear made him weak and helpless as a child. He found warmth and solace in her arms and in the repairing threads of self-confidence she wove by her nonjudgmental, yet somehow still respectful, gaze. She apparently still saw a *man* in him, and he was grateful for it.

"You must do this thing," said Nateesha Folks to Henderson Smith. "You must do it, Henderson, this morning."

"Nateesha, I . . ."

"You must go see Miss Ivy, layin' over there in Selma

General," said Nateesha. "Shannon, Ted, and I will go along. Shannon told me she has asked about you every time they've seen her. They are still members of your flock, Henderson."

"But am I still their shepherd?" he asked, staring at his bare feet on the floor of one of the small guest rooms in the living quarters behind the New Christian Cathedral.

"Yes," replied Nateesha, "and if you are gonna ask next if you are *worthy* to be their shepherd, the answer is still yes."

"I don't know if I'm, uh . . . ready."

"Do you have a Bible, Reverend Henderson Smith?" asked the big woman. "Do you have a shred of faith left, faith in God, faith in yourself?" She stood over him, her fists on her hips. "Yes again, to all four. That woman is alive, Henderson, and you know the hand of God came between you and that bullet, and between her and death. I'm just a simple woman who sings alto in your choir, Reverend, but I know in my heart there is some *reason* for all of this happenin' like it has—you, this cathedral, these people that are comin' here." She knelt down in front of him as he sat on the bed, his elbows on his knees, and she reached for his hands and took them in hers. She looked at him with her big brown eyes, and he thought once again how lovely she was, how female. "You have been scared now, Henderson," she said softly, "and the depth of it has shattered the image of who you thought you were. So now you are *new*, not less, but more. If you know the fear we all have, how frightening this life can be, then you can know the strength it requires to take each day as it comes. You can teach us, your *flock*, about overcoming fear, about puttin' one foot in front of the other, about puttin' your soul in the hands of Jesus, frightened or not."

He sighed and rewarded her with a small smile. "What about my preaching, Nateesha? What about me getting up on that pulpit and preaching about the strength of faith when I have shown everyone here how quickly my faith was melted away?" His smile faded. "And what about the burning man I told you about, the tempter that won't leave me alone? He is *real*, Nateesha, and out there somewhere ready to laugh at me anytime he wants."

"Maybe he's the devil himself," said Nateesha contemptuously. "Don't matter. Is he more real than Jesus Christ? Huh, is he? Huh?"

He looked at her, longing for her simple faith, longing for her strength, longing for her. He shook his head and said quietly, "No, Nateesha, he is not more real than Jesus."

"Okay then," said Nateesha as she stood. "I've laid out fresh clothes for you, Reverend, and your Bible is right there. You should get dressed. We'll go over to the hospital and visit Miss Ivy, then we'll come back here and you can start workin' on your next sermon, which we are all waitin' for."

He stood also. They faced each other, very close. "Nateesha," he almost whispered, "I, thank you. I just

wanted to thank you for standing by with me, for . . .
being here. You, your strength, has done a lot to make me
feel sort of like a man again."

"Oh, Henderson," she responded, "I think by now
you've figured out I'd do anything for you."

He hesitated a moment, took a chance, grinned, and
said with an arched eyebrow, "*Anything?*"

She looked into his eyes for a long moment, saw a new
fire there, saw his grin. "You," she said shyly as she put
her hands on his chest and gently pushed him back. "You
must be startin' to feel better. Now do like I told you to
and get dressed and all. Then we'll see what I might or
might not do for you someday." She turned and smiled at
him as she closed the door behind her.

He had an e-mail from Azul Dante. He saw it was sent
to many of the "new" cathedrals around the world, not directed specifically to him. It was a message of encourage-
ment and promise, a pep talk about the progress of the
Prodigal Project plans. It told of how things were coming
together as envisioned, the one-world currency, the coalition of governments lining up with Dante and the Project.
Dante did not elaborate on the fact that the global conflict
everyone was preparing for was essentially a huge religious battle, Muslim versus Christian, with the Jews sid-
ing with the latter. Dante actually downplayed the
religious aspects of it, apparently trying to be diplomatic
and avoiding a traditional flash point between varied peoples of the world. The Prodigal Project aimed toward a

one-world form, one government, all the peoples of the earth living in controlled peace, all their needs met, all seeds of friction or discontent eliminated. People would not need "faith," he seemed to be saying, because there would be peace on earth. Still, preachers and other religious leaders around the globe were being encouraged to stay with what the people knew for now, teach the Good Word but with the threads of his, Dante's, new theology sewn into it. Be bold, said the e-mail, don't be timid, the time has come for a new dawn, a new day, a new world. Be proud and grateful to be a spokesperson for the Prodigal Project, and help bring the world into a new light.

Henderson Smith turned off the computer on his desk. It felt good to be back in his office, he had to admit. His face clouded as he thought of his private room, just next door. He would not live there again, that he knew. The burning specter, whom he knew as Andrew Nuit, the porcine white man with the beige linen suit and florid cheeks who had first made him an offer he could not refuse, had left burn marks on the carpet as he stood there laughing at him. The same Andrew Nuit had met with him at his old church before the disappearances and told him about this new cathedral and how the Reverend Henderson Smith was the only man who could ascend the beautiful and imposing pulpit in it. His heart told him his dream of being the pastor at such a magnificent church surely came with a price, and it had indeed. He had lost his wife and children on the day of the disappearances, had then ascended to the pulpit of the New Christian

Cathedral as promised, only to be tormented every day and night since.

He stared at his own dark reflection on the dormant computer screen. His eyes looked like two black holes, lifeless, and he asked himself, What have I become? He thought of Azul Dante. Azul Dante . . . why that name? Azul Dante, A and D, AD. He wondered if Dante was in fact Lucifer, then shook his head. No, if these *were* the end times as described in Revelation, then Dante could only be one thing. He knew Scripture scholars speculated and argued over it even to this day. Was Dante *formed* by Satan, *empowered* by him? Who was the bigger junkyard dog, the Prince of Darkness cast down from the heavens, or this new upstart created just for this moment in the time of man? Which one was worse, or did it matter? Traditionally, Satan had beguiled and tricked and led astray humans through the ages. He had no love for God's people and wished all of them only pain and death. Fine. Then, according to Revelation, the new worse-thing-ever arrives not only to torment the souls of man, but to take over and rule the world. He shuddered involuntarily.

Smith took a deep breath and rubbed his eyes with his fists. He checked his reflection again and saw it looked no better. He went over it in his mind once more, one of the sustaining arguments he had formed as a defense against his fear. If the devil is real, he thought, then so is every-thing else in Scripture, so is God, so is Jesus Christ, and if Christ lives, you, you miserable excuse for a man, you still have a chance.

He wondered at Azul Dante's ability to influence so many so quickly and completely. The dark power he held over men and women around the earth didn't come from his coy e-mails, no. Henderson Smith knew without a doubt that the darkness had somehow penetrated his heart. Evil intent and control had found a seam, a crack, in his faith, and like a toxic worm had eaten its way deep inside to cling tenaciously and insidiously to his very inner lining. Perhaps he was truly lost. He thought of Nateesha. Her faith was real and strong, yet it was so simple. He rubbed his eyes again, and thought, Maybe that's it. Maybe I *think* too much.

He wondered about the name Azul Dante again, about AD. The way he had learned it, BC meant *before Christ*. AD meant *Anno Domini*, "in the year of our Lord." Many took it as *after death*, too. After *His* death. From far within the creases of his memory he resurrected another. *Aceldama*. He shuddered again. Judas Iscariot purchased a field with his blood money received after betraying Jesus. In Acts 1:19, Judas falls in this Aceldama, or *akeldama*, this "field of blood," bursts open, and dies, in agony one can assume. Henderson Smith hugged himself, leaned forward until his forehead rested against the cyclopean screen, and thought, BC, AD, no matter. I am worse than Judas, and I won't have an "after death," my death will last forever.

He was jolted back to the moment by Nateesha Folks's

sweet voice calling from the hallway, "We're ready to go, Reverend Smith."

+   +   +

"Ron," asked Stan gently, "Do you want to see Ivy?"

Ron Underwood, leaning against the rear concrete wall of his jail cell, his hands jammed into the pockets of his orange jumpsuit, just stared at his cellmate.

"Ivy is alive, Ron," continued Stan as he ran one hand through his thick blond hair. "She is injured and weakened, of course, but almost ready to leave the hospital, which isn't far from here. See, she *must* get up and get out of there because, like you, she has work to do, *important* work, Ron. Ron? Are you listening to me?"

"Are *you* listening to you, Stan?" replied Ron. "Look around, bright boy, you'll see we're both in a jail, okay? Check the orange jumpsuit, will you? Man, are you thick."

Stan stood near the cell door, barely ten feet from Ron. He placed his hands on his middle, patted himself, and nodded. "I feel solid, that's true," he said. "But I think *thick* carries with it an unattractive connotation."

Ron sighed. He could feel his anger rising.

Stan smiled and spoke again, "Do you mind if I show you something? Look, I'll use this pad of paper and pen the nice jailers gave you." He shook his head and took on an admonishing tone. "You never even wrote down one thought, Ron. All right, no matter." He was busy with the pen and pad a moment, then handed it to Ron. "Look at these names, will you please?"

Ron reluctantly took the pad, adjusted his black-framed Buddy Holly–style glasses, and read:

John Jameson
Catherine Early
Henderson Smith
Ron Underwood
Ivy Sloan
Shannon Carpenter
Thomas Church

"Okay," he said tentatively, "I see this list of names. I see my name, and Ivy's, and the preacher, Smith's. I may have met that Shannon person, but I don't think I've ever heard of the others."

"No matter," replied Stan. "You will in good time." He grinned. "Now. How many names do you see there, Ron?"

"Seven," answered Ron.

"*Seven*," repeated Stan, his grin widening, "Seven. Is that not a totally awesome number, Ron? C'mon, man, give it up for the superbly mystical, lyrical, and totally Biblical number SEVEN."

"Jiminy Cricket," said Ron under his breath. "You are gonna make me crazy with this seven stuff."

Stan, undeterred, pointed at the pad again and said, "C'mon, Ron, stay with me here. Take the pen, come on, take it. Good. Now write down the first letter of each person's first name, then the first letter of each last name. Please? For *me?*"

Ron, scowling, did as he was asked. He stared at the letters he wrote on the pad:

J   J
C   E
H   S
R   U
I   S
S   C
T   C

He grunted and raised his eyebrows.

"The others in my, um, *legion,*" said Stan quietly, "are quite convinced these people, and their names, cannot have been selected without cause, without *reason.* There has been discussion within our ranks as to the relative simplicity manifested in the use of an anagram, like it is almost too, um, *contrived.*" He shrugged, and his lower lip fell, "But like they say, what do *we* know? All things will not be revealed, and all that."

Ron, still looking at the letters, said, "Okay, J. Christ, and Jesus C." He looked at Stan. "What is the last C for?"

Stan grinned, and said, "Well, *Church,* obviously."

"Obviously," agreed Ron. He grinned back at Stan, and said sardonically, "Cool."

Ron stopped grinning and said, "Now let's get back to me seeing Ivy. Again I remind you we are in jail, I'm charged with a serious crime, and there's no way I can simply walk out of here."

"Oh ye of little faith," said Stan.

There was a soft clanging of metal at the cell door, and one of the jailers said, "Lunch, Underwood." The scratched and warped tray was pushed in. This time it looked like some kind of sandwich, some chips, and a container of red Jell-O. Ron went to the tray, picked it up, and turned to find Stan again sitting on the end of the bunk with an identical tray. He didn't even want to think about how that was possible, and sat with his lunch balanced on his knees.

"This," said Stan, poking the sandwich with one finger, "is made with grain, a good thing. What is tucked within I cannot discern." There was a childlike excitement in his expression, and a slight hesitation as he inspected the Jell-O and said, "And this . . . this is like a *postre*, yes? Like dessert? It is an odd sort of nurturer, is it not? But fun, yes?"

"Yes," sighed Ron. He had only taken a few bites of the food and became very sleepy. He glanced at Stan, his eyes heavy, and said, "You can have mine if you want it, Stan." Then he lay back on the bunk, asleep.

One hour later Ron awoke. He was instantly awake, aware of his surroundings, aware of his predicament. He sat up, found his glasses on the bunk, and rubbed his eyes before putting them on. He saw his lunch tray on the floor with the half-eaten sandwich and two empty Jell-O containers. He stood and stretched. At that moment he realized he was alone in the cell. He ran his hands over the bedding on the top bunk, saw no other lunch tray, looked at the secured cell door, and wondered if all of this, *all* of it, wasn't some terribly complex and fearful nightmare. Stan was gone. Well, he told himself, maybe he had a meeting with his lawyer or something, and they took him out while I was asleep. Took him to get his head examined, more likely, he thought. He turned 360 degrees where he stood. Stan was not in the cell. His Bible lay there, open on the top bunk, the pen apparently saving the place. Nothing more. He took the open Bible, glanced at it, and saw that a passage had been circled. It was Romans 3:22–24, "This righteousness from God comes through faith in Jesus Christ to all who believe. There is no difference, for all have sinned and fall short of the glory of God, and are justified freely by His grace through the redemption that came by Christ Jesus."

As he finished reading he heard a key turn in the cell door, and it was pulled open.

"Let's go, Underwood," said a stoop-shouldered, grizzled guard in a wrinkled gray uniform.

"Uh, sure," said Ron. Then he asked, "Where? What's up?"

"This is your lucky day, Underwood," replied the jailer as he turned to walk down the hallway. "Your lawyer is here, and you managed to get one who can actually get things done in this fiasco they call a judicial system nowadays."

"What? That young woman I met?"

"You wanna come with me, Underwood, or do you like it here?"

Ron turned back to the cell, grabbed the Bible, and hurried after the guard. Other prisoners in their cells watched as they passed. Some turned their backs, some whistled, a few made rude noises or reached out to grab at him. He tried to walk in the very center of the corridor, in the guard's footsteps. He saw the old black man, Windfield, sitting on his bunk in his open cell. They made eye contact, and the old man smiled. "God bless you, boy," he said.

Ron stopped, stepped into the open cell, reached out, and shook the man's hand. "Thank you," he said quietly. He held up the Bible, "for this."

Windfield nodded and said, "You are welcome, and may Jesus Christ be your guide in all the days you have left." His smile broadened and he added quietly, "I saw your friend in there with you. Isn't he something?"

"Indeed," responded Ron. He hesitated, then turned and walked to catch up with the guard.

They went out through a series of heavy steel doors, until they came to what Ron remembered was the prisoner intake area. There were offices and visiting rooms. The guard said over his shoulder, "Your lawyer is over there, Underwood, with that other guard. They'll process you." He turned and gave Underwood the time-honored farewell of jailers: "I don't wanna see your face in here again." He walked away.

Ron looked at his "lawyer," and Stan grinned back at him and waved him over. Ron walked slowly across the room until he stood beside the desk. The guard was bent over some papers and ignored him. Stan stuck out his hand and Ron, completely off-balance now, took it. As they shook hands, Stan said pleasantly, "Mister Underwood. Mind if I call you Ron? The young woman whom you first met when incarcerated was tied up with another case, so your file landed on my desk, hope you don't mind."

Ron looked at his former cellmate. Stan looked tall, fit, and handsome in an ash-hued suit over a crisp, white shirt, with a gray tie patterned with muted crosses. His shoes were black, with a mirror shine, and sitting on the desk at his left elbow was a fine leather briefcase, also black, with gold fittings. He felt he was beyond being surprised at this point, and asked, "And you are . . . ?"

"My card," said Stan expansively as he handed a business card to Ron. On it in embossed letters was *Stanley Ayak Sariel, Esq.* As Ron looked it over, Stan leaned away from the guard and whispered in Ron's ear, "Just having a little fun with my boss, you know, with the name."

"Very good, Mister, uh, Sariel," said Ron. "Nice to meet you. Now, why are you here, is something happening with my case?"

"He got a judge's order signed, somehow," said the guard, out of the side of his mouth, as he scribbled on the paperwork. "The judge agrees you are not a flight risk, or something, and the prosecutor's office is waffling about the charges against you . . . might be downgraded." The man shrugged, "Whatever. You are outta here. Mister Sariel, *esquire*, takes you into his custody, since he posted the small bond required. You don't have any property to be returned, except the clothes you had on when you were booked, but they are pretty raggedy."

"Not to worry, my fine man," said Stan. "I have clothing for my client." He pointed to a hanger bag draped across another chair. "Shoes and everything," he added. He smiled at Ron and added, "Why don't you go freshen up and change out of that hideous orange thing. I'll wait right here."

Ron, not sure what was real and what was not, simply nodded, said, "Of course," picked up the hanger bag, and headed for the nearest men's room.

As he walked away, Stan leaned toward the jailer and said politely, "Thank you so much for facilitating this so quickly, sir. Mind if I ask a question?"

The guard leaned back in his chair, the image of patience, and made a beckoning motion with one hand.

"I wondered," said Stan, "where your nurturing providers obtained that delightful red matter . . . *Jell-O*."

Twenty minutes later they were in the sprawling parking lot, and Ron was not surprised to learn that Stanley

A. Sariel was the owner of an immaculate Cadillac Seville. He climbed into the passenger side. The new clothes provided by his new lawyer fit him perfectly, despite his loss in weight. They were casual—shoes, slacks, a shirt, and sport jacket, but of fine quality. His heart thumped as he thought of seeing Ivy again.

CHAPTER SEVEN

The woman who once was Mrs. Thomas Church sat perfectly still in the soft darkness of the kitchen, waiting. She did not want to be there, and wondered if she had agreed to this morning's rendezvous with *Mr.* Thomas Church as a coward's way of admitting she was wrong about her forced-chosen life, and was using it as a convenient escape. She hugged her arms close against her body and felt her heart beating softly within, the steady ticking of a clock the only sound in the house. Six people slept in rooms upstairs. Perhaps they would miss her. They were not bad people, loose or immoral. They professed to like their "unstructured" relationships that melded together, then drifted apart in a sort of harmless way, but had not tried to force their lifestyle on her.

She sighed. She knew she would not be there if Thomas Church had *wanted* her, or wanted *anything* with some passion or clarity. She was beset with the old inner argument. Did she do enough? Was it entirely Thomas's fault? Were the signals of alarm and distress she had given him during the last years of their marriage *strong* enough? She mentally shrugged, accepting the guilt that came with the acknowledgment that perhaps she had simply stood beside him, watching as their ship slowly sank into the waters of apathy. He had drifted away from her in those placid waters of a comfortable, routine, low-expectation marriage, and she had let him.

When Sissy and Tommy had left the house, she and her husband sat night after night, not making eye contact, avoiding meaningful discussion. Their routine was so comfortable it became stultifying, until she wondered if they were even *living* a life. *Divorce*, as a word, as a stir stick, was apparently considered by both of them simultaneously. Their divorce was a mutual shrug between a man and woman who had done all the things one is supposed to do . . . meet, marry, work, have kids, be a family, do family things.

"This isn't it, I guess," she remembered him saying one evening.

"No," she had agreed, "I guess it's not."

"There should be *more*," he had said.

"Yes," she had replied, "perhaps there should."

She sighed again, long and deep. "But I loved him," she said quietly in the empty kitchen. "I loved him." She let her gaze trip and fall over and across things in the shadowed kitchen of the old farmhouse. Milk and sugar containers, one in the shape of a cow, the other, for reasons she couldn't quite figure out, a beehive, sat on the knotted pine table—all purchased at some estate or another. Odd, she thought, how you could buy pieces of another family's life, cobble a life together from discards and chipped ceramics. She shook her head, ashamed of thinking this way. After all, this place was at one time her refuge, what she'd sought as an escape from that previous life.

After the divorce, she went searching. She searched for life, for adventure, for meaning, for God. Her first tangible act of defiance and identity was to formally change her name. She left her old name behind, knew it was a symbolic changing of skin, and became a single woman with a new name, in search of self. She had found adventure in physical pursuits. She had ridden a motorcycle, hiked wilderness forests, gone white-water rafting, hitchhiked between destinations. She made a face in the darkness. She mentally chastised herself for her inability to be a *totally* adventurous single woman. She had not taken another man as a lover. She thought she *should*, but each time it might have happened, she found herself pulling back, unable to go through with it.

Her search for "meaning" had been less than fruitful, also. At least organized religion is *organized*, she mused, and solace can be found in the structure. God, in the lessons of the people she lived and worked with now, was some kind of undefined power, basically good and knowing, who intended for us, His children, to learn from our life here. It was simple, she had been taught, just *become*,

become one with the world, with nature, with her fellow human beings, and God would be there. She closed her eyes. She did not want to be there.

She opened her eyes, saw the far linear glow from his headlights, and stood. Her backpack, stuffed with her possessions, lay beside the chair. She bent to pick it up, then left it. Walking out to him with it in her hands would tell him too much, too soon.

+   +   +

Road travel in the States had become less hazardous than it was during the first couple of weeks after the disappearances, but it was still an uncertain adventure. He had found fuel more readily available, or at least more gas stations open in the larger cities and towns. Food and supplies could be had, also. The whole societal structure of the country was apparently strong enough to rebound from one or two cataclysmic and unsettling events, but there were still elements within the framework that were not completely on-line. Rogue bandits worked the less populated areas and far stretches of lonely roads and as the police agency ranks had been depleted by loss of personnel, they had been augmented by the National Guard and Military Reserves, per presidential order. Even with this framework of security in place, some areas had the feel of the Wild West.

Church, a quick learner, had become a savvy road warrior in the last few weeks. Following the disappearances, he had set out to find his son, Tommy, who was last known to be working a cattle ranch in western Texas. He had, by a miracle, located Tommy, wounded and distraught over the chaos that had cost the life of his first real love, and together they had traveled to Selma, Alabama, to hear a sermon by the Reverend Henderson Smith. There they had met Ivy Sloan and Shannon Carpenter. Thinking about it now, Church again felt the inexplicable but undeniable *bond* he sensed between Ivy, Shannon, and him. The number seven figured into it somehow, also. None of it was clear to him, or really made much sense, but he recognized it as real, and set it aside.

He and Tommy went from Alabama up to Virginia and stayed a couple of days with Tommy's sister, Sissy, and her husband, Mitch. Sissy had told him where her mother was. Church's wife had not communicated with anyone from the family except Sissy since the by-the-book divorce, which had seemed so predictable, simple, and painless when he had signed the papers. He and Tommy had parted after their visit with Sissy and Mitch. Tommy wanted to head back to Alabama, the Reverend, and perhaps the Word. He, Thomas Church, was gratified he had in fact *found* the Word, and he glanced over at the Bible laying on the seat beside him. Sissy had asked him if he was "born again," and he had answered he was not sure, which he acknowledged probably meant no. He was okay with that, because coming to terms with God and Jesus Christ had not been something he had ever expected to happen. He had spent his life apathetic about spiritual matters. Organized religion left him cold. He was a pragmatic businessman, a computer whiz and gadgetry aficionado. He had no time for Jesus.

That was Thomas Church before the disappearances, he mused, before the whole world was turned on its ear, before the loss of so many millions—all the children— and the rise of the crazed mujahideen under the dark and reckless Izbek Noir. It was also before he found his son, he reflected. He found his son and, during that journey, he had found the Scripture, his heart had opened, and now he drank the words like a man with a thirsty soul. His personality would not allow him to flippantly embrace the Word just because he was excited about it though—he needed time, research, study. He knew Jesus was okay with his reticence. Jesus was patient, and knew the inside of his heart better than *he* did, he figured.

But now he was in western Idaho, less than one hundred feet from the woman he had met when they were both college kids, the woman he had married, fathered two children with, and loved for almost twenty years. He had heard the term "confused seas" once to describe the clash and rip of storm tides, currents, wind, and temperature, when waves charged first in one direction, then another, crashing together into cascades of stinging foam. He had those seas in his heart now, and his entire being felt in turmoil. There she was, standing there, waiting. He knew beyond a doubt he had changed through the past weeks, and he understood she would have changed, too. He was scared, scared of being turned away by her, scared of being welcomed.

She began to walk toward him. She wore faded jeans, dusty boots, a work shirt, and an old, tattered jacket. Her hands were jammed deep into the jacket pockets. As she got closer he could see she had lost weight. She still had long, shapely legs, and long, copper-colored hair that hung to her shoulders. It was parted in the middle and fell without adornment, soft and full. Now there were a few thick streaks of silver-gray on both sides of the center part, and he found them immediately fascinating and attractive. Her face was oval, with a long nose and wide mouth; her eyes were green and shone brightly on this morning. She looked healthy and alive, and lovely, and he felt his mouth go dry. He knew he had not really studied her like this in quite a while. If she was aware of it, she gave no sign. She wore a quiet, pensive expression and gazed at him with an easy and bemused confidence. He got out of the Bronco and walked around the hood the meet her.

"I'm afraid I don't know your name," he said shyly. "I'm still Thomas, in some ways."

"I'm Rebecca," she said. Not, I'm Rebecca *now*, or I *used* to be Mrs. Church, or I've *changed* into Rebecca. Just, "I'm Rebecca."

"Rebecca," he repeated. "It's lovely."

"Thanks."

"And you are lovely, too . . . Rebecca."

She studied him with a small smile. She liked what she saw. This was not the man who had retreated from their marriage into the high-tech computer office he had built into their home in an affluent neighborhood in New York. That man had grown soft in the middle, wheezed when he got up from the table, and grunted when he bent to tie his shoes. That man pretty much ignored her, the person that was her, and sort of flowed through the years of their marriage without ever really putting any effort into it. That man had ceased to be her lover, her friend, her confidant. He went through the social motions, was around for all the holidays, and complimented her on her cooking. That man had accepted the divorce with as much energy as he invested in any part of their years together. She had tried to tell that man what they were becoming. Then she'd left, searching for who she was, and what this whole thing was *about*. But this man, this new Thomas Church, she mused, he was fit and craggy, hardened by time, loss, and trial. He had trimmed down, his back was straight, and his beard had a piratical flair, gray flecks and all. His jeans were frayed, like hers, and his leather jacket creased and battered. He wore expensive hiking boots, but they had some miles on them, too.

"Why are you here, Thomas?" she asked.

He hesitated. She knew he was not sure why he was there. Perhaps it was a challenge, a sign to him that she might or might *not* have time for him. Or perhaps she had the same wistful longings he did. "I'm here to see about a second chance," he said.

"Second chance at what?"

"At everything," he replied.

She studied him, their eyes locked. He felt drawn into her heart, into her thoughts. He did not feel threatened.

"That's an awful lot to ask, don't you think? A second chance at everything?" She shoved her hands into the back pockets of her jeans and rocked on her heels. She looked skyward and saw a hawk gliding on the thermals. "That seems effortless, doesn't it?" She pointed toward the bird. "But down here, things aren't quite that easy. I'm not sure that second chances exist, Thomas."

Thomas drew in a deep breath and expelled it past pursed lips. He scratched his nose and nodded thoughtfully. He'd anticipated her resistance. After all, he was smart enough to realize that a few minutes couldn't undo the years that had passed between them.

"All I know, Rebecca, is that some monumental things have taken place. Things that can make the issues that arose between two people like you and me seem pretty small and insignificant. I mean, we weren't taken. We're still alive, still breathing, still able to appreciate the beauty of a hawk's flight, the cool morning air, the sound of a beautiful woman's voice."

He watched as Rebecca's face flushed. Rather than wait to see if her response was embarrassment at his flattery or anger at his insinuations that he could win her over so easily, he plunged ahead. "But all those things, appreciating all those things, seems a cold comfort. I can't believe that we've gone through all of this—you and me, the world, everybody—just so that things could go on as they did before. I know that the usual reaction to these kinds of events is to not take things for granted, to seize the day and all that, but I really believe that there's something more to all of this. It's not just about appreciating what we have in this life, it's about doing something to make sure that we have a next life."

"Thomas, that all sounds pretty as a greeting card, and your bumper sticker wisdom is impressive in some ways, but I don't know. I just don't know."

"That's the beauty of it, Rebecca. You don't have to *know*, you just have to *believe*. It's a question of faith, not facts. Believing in me, yeah, I can understand how that might be difficult, and I'm not asking you to blindly place your faith in me. But I am asking you to put your faith in what your soul says to you, what your quiet center says when you manage to silence all those other voices in your head competing for attention."

Thomas let his voice trail off. In his heart, he knew that words could never convince her, that it would take action, a demonstration of his commitment to her, to his new life, but somehow he had to get her to take that first step, that first leap of faith.

He looked over his shoulder and jutted his chin at the distant farmhouse. "What do you do there? What kind of life do you have? What are the others like? Do you have one, uh . . . you know. I mean, uh, are you, like, *involved* with a uh . . . man?"

"Would you like some coffee, Thomas?" she answered, "I would. I would like a cup of coffee and a powdered donut, and I would like you to tell me about Sissy and Tommy, about you, and about what you've been doing since the disappearances."

She directed him to a truck stop a few miles down the road and waited in the Bronco while he went in. They parked near a two-lane wooden bridge.

She sipped her coffee, took the Bible down from the dash where she had placed it when she first climbed into the passenger seat, and thumbed through it. "Find anything useful in here, Thomas?"

"Yes, actually," he replied, surprised at his defensive tone.

She said nothing for a few minutes. Then she closed the Bible and nodded. "It is a sweet book, in many ways. Lots of different truths in it."

He did not want to get into an in-depth discussion on the validity of Scripture right then. His feelings about his new discoveries within its pages and within his own heart were precious and fragile, and he did not want to bruise them in acrimonious discussion. "I have found it helpful," he said. "Lately it has become important to me." He sipped from his cup of coffee and asked, "Where have you been searching for the truth, Rebecca?"

She stared out the window a long time. Then she shrugged and said, "In the morning sun and evening shadows. In the glow of the moon, the singing of the wind, the pulsing of my heart in concert with the earth. I have been studying varied works, I suppose they would be considered New Age. Some spiritualists might label them the work of cults, I don't know. I *do* know I am cleansing my mind and body, living simply, sharing whatever positive energy I can with others who have hearts that hear." She looked at him and smiled. "Remember that little neighborhood church we got married in and attended all those years? Such a simple little song they sang, and it either went over our heads or beneath us."

He took the last bite of his second donut and wiped the powder from his beard. He nodded cautiously. After a moment he asked, "Rebecca. Are you okay with the concept of God?"

"Of course," she responded. "The source of everything, the center, the prime and initiating power that formed us and set us free."

"That's Him," he said.

She pointed to the Bible laying on the seat beside her and said, "Thomas . . . the story of Jesus? It's lovely, very sweet and uplifting, really. But you know from your own studies the concept of rebirth, renewal, resurrection can be traced thousands of years before Jesus was born. Man could not understand or face death, so he watched the rhythm of the earth, the seasons, the planting of seeds and gathering of fruit, the renewal of spring after winter, and he formed the concept into the something he could be comfortable with." Her eyes were bright, her facial expression animated. "But that is so *simple*, Thomas, don't you see? We are part of a great, cosmic energy, a tiny facet of the universe, each one connected within our own hearts."

He nodded again, respectful of her sincerity, of her lack of guile. She was sharing her beliefs, and he knew already there would be nothing he could say right then that would influence or change them. Besides, he knew from firsthand experience how one-dimensional and unfulfilling the understanding of Christian beliefs can seem to someone who has not experienced Christ.

They were quiet for a moment, sitting together like old friends.

"I want you to come with me, Rebecca," he said.

"What?"

"Come with me," he repeated.

She turned in her seat, took his hands in hers, and said, "Tell me about the kids. Tell me about your life after I left, about the day of the disappearances, about finding Tommy. Tell me about our world, what you've seen, what you've heard. Tell me what it's like out there, where we as a race are headed. Tell me, Thomas."

She listened to him for over two hours. They broke once, both ducking under the bridge embankment to answer a call of nature, laughing like schoolkids as they raced back to the Bronco in a deluge of unexpected rain. She listened as he spoke of his search for their son, of finding him, of tending to his wounds. Of the girl he had lost to the lawlessness that erupted after the disappearances. He told her of a highway terrorist incident, of how their son had risked his life to pull others from the flames. About their visit to the New Christian Cathedral, the Reverend Smith, about meeting Ivy Sloan and Shannon Carpenter.

He told her of the number seven, how it came to him, how he understood it was important, how he believed it was some sort of connective tissue to others, perhaps for some specific purpose.

She listened, and cried softly, as he told her of Sissy and Mitch, of how despondent and angry Sissy was to have a life forming in her womb only to have it taken in the disappearance, about her desire to have a child and her fears that it might never happen. He told her of how he felt he had wasted much of his life, how he had not appreciated the wondrous gifts he had been given, how he had not known how to be a man, a husband, a father.

"Did you see the burning hail, Rebecca?" he finally asked. "Many believe these are the end times, the tribulations. There are many questions, of course, and everyone seems to be searching." He took her left hand in his. "I'll tell you this. I'm alive, our children are alive, and the world is still our world, the place we exist. I intend to *live* here and go about the business of trying to get some answers. I don't know what is going to happen tonight, tomorrow, or next week. Perhaps it is the end of mankind, a great looming battle between good and evil . . . between this Azul Dante and Izbek Noir. I want to be part of it." He turned to face her and looked into her eyes. "Rebecca," he said evenly, "I think you are beautiful. You are new to me, and perhaps I can be new to you. New, and *worth it*. Come with me. We'll check on Sissy and see if we can find Tommy again . . ."

She stared at him for a long time. He was *passionate*. He had an inner *force* and energy she had not seen in him before. She wanted him, but could not shake the deep inner feelings of betrayal. He had betrayed *them* by not being passionate, forceful, and energetic throughout their marriage. Now he wanted to be *worth* it. She gave him a careful smile and said, "And will we find Jesus along the way?"

He shrugged. "Maybe."

She turned her head and stared at the rain for a long, quiet moment. He is the only man you have ever loved, she told herself, and life is a mystery.

He held his breath.

Finally she nodded. "Okay."

He started up the Bronco. "I'll take you back to the farmhouse. I'll wait by the road while you pack, and uh, say your good-byes."

She looked down at her hands and said almost to herself, "I just have to grab my backpack. It's all ready to go. And I said my good-byes last night."

CHAPTER EIGHT

It was the sweet and overpowering bouquet of death, and he gratefully filled his lungs with it. He stood amid a fresh landscape of war, strewn with wrecked and burned tanks, armored transports, and trucks, littered with the broken and burst forms of human dead. His eyes hungrily devoured the scene, relishing it, wanting to capture it in his heart, in his memory forever. Small fires burned here and there, and some of the scorched tanks were still warm to the touch. He never traveled very far behind the actual front lines. He feared nothing and lusted for the carnage that lay fresh and colorful for his taking. He was General Izbek Noir, commander-in-chief of the Muslim mujahideen forces, leader of a cruel and rapacious army unlike any seen in the time of man. For him, man, with his puny, stupid, grasping soul, with his plaintive cries for riches and power, his begging for salvation when it came time to pay the price—man as a whole was a feckless bore. But man made war with gusto and imagination, horror incarnate, and he was a gourmand when it came to war and all it spawned.

He saw movement to his left and walked toward it. His officers and men hung back, fearful and respectful of his unpredictable acts of brutality. He stood before an obsolete Russian-built tank, one of the T-54 series of tracked vehicles. This one came from an Iraqi unit but had faded Syrian markings on the turret. The left track of the tank had been blown off, crumpled into the drive wheels like twisted tinfoil blocks. The tank had exploded and burned, the turret was cocked to the right, the long barrel of its gun pointed impotently at the blackened earth. The men inside had surely died terrible deaths.

But the movement that drew him to the hulk proved that not all inside died. The driver's hatch forward of the turret had been flung open by the blast, and struggling up into the open air was the young Iraqi driver, helmetless, his black curly hair singed, blood smeared down the left side of his head, ear, and cheek. The driver managed to get first one arm, then the other, out of the hatch, and had lifted his head and shoulders. He turned as General Noir approached, saw the general's uniform, saw the others behind him, and slowly raised his hands into the air. His right hand and arm were blackened and burned. He mumbled something in Farsi and attempted a grin. General Noir walked within a few feet, grinned back, pulled out his .45 automatic pistol, and pointed it at the young man's face. When he was sure the Iraqi tanker was focused on the weapon, he used his other hand to lob a thermite grenade. The spoon on the grenade pinged as it separated, and the cylindrical can hit the tanker in the chest, then fell into the open hatch at the man's feet. The Iraqi's eyes widened in terror as he first looked down, then raised his eyes to meet Noir's. The grenade went off with a white flash and explosion of searing tendrils that billowed up and out of the hatch, swirling around the tanker while he writhed and danced in a fiery, agonizing death.

The shrieking screams of the burning man were matched in volume and intensity by General Izbek Noir's demonic laughter as he watched another foul death.

"Soldiers of the mujahideen!" stated the communication he had sent out to all of his units that morning. It would also be broadcast at regular intervals on various radio stations and Arab television networks. "Muslim faithful, Muslim fighters! Brothers-in-arms and followers of Islam! A new phase of this righteous war to rid the world of infidels has begun! No longer must we fight our brothers in this hurtful interfamily struggle! Now come the infidels, the Christians, the nonbelievers! They have seen us make war on ourselves, thinking we were destroying our very core, but they know nothing of Arab manhood! Now mighty Iran has agreed to join us, and Muslims still flock to our ranks from all corners of the earth to fight by our sides in this important struggle! Behind us burn the wastelands of inner and northern

Africa, of Egypt, of Saudi Arabia! Millions have died, millions have joined us, and now we turn our weapons and our faith toward the real enemy, the enemy who would wipe us from the face of Allah's Earth! They are Christians, infidels who know nothing of the Prophet's True Word! Christians who would defile our women and enslave our men! Christians who have perverted their own truth to justify their actions against the one, true God, the glorious and all-powerful Allah! Soldiers! Brothers! Are we not Arab MEN? Now, soldiers, prepare, prepare, turn your faces and your weapons toward this new enemy! Every infidel you kill is a blessing upon Allah! If you fight and die like a true Arab MAN, Allah will greet you in paradise with gifts and riches beyond imagination!"

General Izbek Noir rather liked the communiqué. It was boisterous, bombastic, and justified making war on the basis of faith. Yes, he thought, let's run to battle so we can go out and kill for Allah. A religious war, he mused, the best kind. He was a known and self-acknowledged deceiver, of course, and enjoyed the fact that his message to the troops made no mention of Israel, packed full of those bothersome Jews. Besides, even with their blind fanaticism, their huge and growing numbers, and their reckless combat bloodlust, he doubted if the crazed mujahideen forces were ready to take on the Israelis. The Jews would fight with their usual courage and tenacity, and there was no doubt in anyone's mind they would deploy everything in their arsenal—including nukes—and nukes just weren't part of the equation now. No, better to just aim his forces at the Christians.

He sat in his command and headquarters truck, in his office, staring at a huge wall map tacked to one bulkhead. He looked at Saudi Arabia, at Yemen, Oman, Bahrain, and Qatar. He let his eyes sweep north, across Iran, whose latest fanatical Islamic leader had recently pledged support for his forces, then to Afghanistan, Pakistan, and India. Mixed bag, there, he mused. Afghans were moderates without their stupid Taliban, and Pakistan didn't know *what* it wanted to be. He sighed when he looked at India, such unrealized potential in that vast and sprawling land. Many, many sects and factions, many false prophets and misguided teachers, much hate. Beyond India was China, of course. They were sitting back and watching, and that suited him for now. Japan would side with the bumptious Americans and would be dealt with when he was ready, tough as they were.

He swept his gaze the other way, to Turkey. Muslim and Christian, but would go Muslim given the chance. That's where Azul Dante's European Coalition would come from first, he thought. Down through northern Iraq, picking up those not-to-be-trifled-with Kurdish forces along the way. Finally, he thought, we can get to the real war. Azul Dante's grand bid, his heroic stand against faithless anarchy. He laughed, his head back. Dante will act out the moves of his predestination . . . as will we all. Of course, he wasn't sure Azul Dante was ready to *accept* his destiny, and his duplicitous machinations to take control of his fate would be *very* entertaining to watch.

He paused in his thoughts about the global picture and cleared his mind. Johann Rommel was out there, ordered to make his way to Azul Dante. The combat photographer was with Rommel, or *Jameson*, but meant nothing, so was discounted. This Rommel, a tiny mortal, was given the task of assassinating Dante. I wonder how he'll go about it? I wonder how the wondrous and rather *unknown* Dante will respond?

He felt a disturbance in his thoughts, leaned forward, and rubbed his temples with his long fingers. There came, again, the number *seven*. "Arrrgh!" he shouted. He didn't like it, not one bit. He had no control over it, and that frustrated him the most. He was a *prince*, by all that was unholy, the *first*, the one who had existed here through the ages, boiling with hate and humiliation, venting with petty acts of cruelty, blasphemy, and the erosion of faith among the children of the Carpenter. All things will not be revealed, it is written. *And some things that are written are misconception wrapped in hope and driven by ego and vanity.* He looked down at his man's body, dressed in his simple uniform as a Muslim general. In the mirror of his mind he saw what he really was, the dark, fiery, twisted essence of his being, and it pleased him. "I am beautiful," he said quietly. "Beautiful, supreme, and invulnerable. There are no words, no prophecies, no predestinations, no *sevens*, that can remove me from my divine existence."

He focused on the map again. Let the Christians come from the north. It is time for Azul Dante and his Coalition to act. His mujahideen forces will meet them like the dogs of war, howling on the leash. He looked at the tiny Arab country of Qatar. So moderate, so progressive, so intertwined with, and subjugated by, the Americans. The United States still had a small military presence there. He rubbed his chin and pondered it. That woman president leading America now was already infatuated and aligned with the Prodigal Project, the European Coalition, and Azul Dante himself. The United States will act in concert with the Coalition, especially now that Great Britain and Israel are in support of it. So, if Qatar is attacked, and Americans are killed, it will make no difference. Besides, it would be a learning experience for his troops to fight the vaunted U.S. soldier. It was time to turn the heat up on this whole conflict, and he had already given the orders on several actions that would herald this.

He stood and stretched, grinding his teeth and grunting. He felt a universal dark power pulsing through his toxic blood, felt it surge against the confines of his present limited manifestation, and a low sadistic growl escaped from his bloodless lips. "I am beautiful," he hissed, "and fear not the number seven, or seven hundred, or seven *thousand*. I fear not."

+   +   +

Sophia Ghent stood in the bathroom of her hotel room, one floor below the suite occupied by Azul Dante, near the Old City, in Bern. She held the hotel telephone to her left ear with her shoulder while she finished her makeup. She had eaten a small croissant with butter and marmalade with her coffee, and felt rested and ready for what would be another hectic and intense day in the life of assistant to the man who might possibly save the world. She changed the phone to the other ear. She was on hold. She felt the disquiet deep in her heart, returned the reflected gaze of her eyes in the mirror, and was startled when the young American's voice came back on the line.

"Listen, Sophia," said the American, "you know I think you are good people, and I've tried to help in the past, but I don't know how far I can go with this. I did some asking around about James Devane, and boy, am *I* getting the cold shoulder. I mean, it's like his name has been flagged, you know? If you ask about him, you get these hard looks, and silence. He's an embassy guy, you know that, and you've been around this whole diplomatic society long enough to know there is also a chance he might be working in, uh, duel and parallel, uh, *roles*."

"I understand," said Sophia quietly. "But surely someone there must know if he's been sent home, if he's on some assignment, something, no?"

"Yep," said her source, "you'd think so. All I know is, nobody knows nothin', and if you ask, they get all cross-eyed. Wish I could tell you more."

"Thank you for trying," she said, frustrated. "You are very sweet."

"I'll keep my ear to the ground," he said. "If I hear anything at all about Devane, I'll get word to you, okay?"

"Thank you so much."

"So," he asked, "another fun-filled day with Azul Dante, the man of the hour?"

"That's my life these days," she replied.

"Lucky you." He disconnected.

+   +   +

"Excuse me! Excuse me, please . . . everyone!" cried the young man to the crowd of people seated and standing in the Number Six subway car rocking along under the streets of the East Side of Manhattan. He was tall and thin, with a wispy black beard, his thick curly hair partially covered by a rakish beret. He wore a long trench coat over new blue jeans and clean white running shoes. His hawkish nose curved and twisted, and to those who glanced up and looked closely at him a weird gleam fired in his eyes. The subway car was packed with commuters all trying to leave thousands of offices in time to get out of the city and home for dinner. Special security operations on the bridges and tunnels in and out of Manhattan, and the subway system, had slowed things down, and everyone felt rushed.

When the young man saw several of the people lift their heads from their newspapers or magazines, or turn their faces in his direction, he bent down, picked up what appeared to be a large accordion case, and shouted loudly, "Allahu Akbar!" A click was followed a moment later by an intense explosion, and in that instant every living thing in the subway car was obliterated. The car was the second in line, midtown headed south, and at the moment of detonation was abreast of a Bronx-bound train, also crowded. The effect in the tunnel was devastating. Both trains collapsed into themselves, cars rammed into one another, broke apart, slewed off the tracks and into the walls. Flash fires erupted, skittering and dancing from one combustible to the next, torching all in their path. Billowing clouds of toxic smoke, ash, and fumes wafted out of sidewalk entrances like the foul, hot breath of a dying monster, and after the screeching of tortured steel came the shrieking of panicked and stampeding people. They were blown out with the smoke, blackened, bloody, and burning, tumbling to the harsh sidewalk and into veering traffic as they gasped for air and help. It was a man-made firestorm, and it turned the streets above and below Manhattan—streets that have known their share of catastrophe and disaster—into a place of unrestrained horror.

Death in the city, finite acts of warfare against unarmed and unprepared civilians ripped from their daily lives by carefully planned violent attack, looks the same in any city, in any country in the world. The panicked and injured survivors might speak Japanese, French, English, or Russian; they might pull themselves from the tangled wreckage of a bullet train, a subway, a metro-rail, or a posh trans-European like the Orient Express. The tears of a German housewife glisten with the same opaque silvery wetness as the tears of a Spanish traffic cop or an Australian lifeguard. The tears, if closely examined, are of a similar composition whether from the eyes of an old man on the outskirts of Moscow, a fruit vendor in downtown Toronto, a homeless woman in Los Angeles, or a wailing blind girl blown from her wheelchair in Warsaw.

In this purposely diverse and divided world, oddly enough, blood possesses an identical *sameness* as tears. Televised news coverage broadcast from all the places acts of urban warfare occurred showed scenes depressingly similar. Smoke, fire, rescue workers, wrecked buildings, trains, vehicles, and blood. Spanish blood, Russian blood, American, Canadian, Australian, Japanese. French, British, German, Polish blood. It all looked the same.

Even while the first emergency sirens were being heard, another sound came from the skies above Europe, the whistling growl of rocket propellant. Thirty feet of metal tube, a finned, cylindrical gyro-computer–guided delivery system for a high-explosive warhead, followed its assigned flight path to its apogee. It would be inaccurate to label the device "mindless," as it had been programmed by the mind of man for the express purpose of killing. Once at altitude, it nosed over into a dive, its airspeed increased dramatically and its dreadful parabola described with inexorable certainty. Here, the guiding hand of man sat back and relaxed. There was no need to set the point of impact with exact satellite coordinates, no need to aim the huge flaming arrow at a specific doorway, air-conditioning shaft, or underground bunker. No, this killer needed only to be casually directed toward the heart of any big city. Pinpoint accuracy did not matter.

There were those who paused, turned, looked skyward upon hearing a strange hissing noise. There were those who saw a spot of yellow flame, falling, and they stood, or turned, or took a step even as the world turned to roaring fire. Others heard nothing, saw nothing. They lived, then they did not. Perhaps there was a moment of hot pain, perhaps a moment when their mind had time to rebel . . . No, no, this can't happen now, I have a dinner date, I must meet someone, I am due home they'll wonder where I am what about my cat I have a meeting tomorrow I am traveling tomorrow I must tell my husband I just met a great guy I am going to the soccer match I am going to night class I am going to ask her to . . .

In addition to the urban transit terror bombers, the mujahideen forces under the command of General Izbek Noir launched a spread of ground-to-ground ballistic missiles from sites in North Africa and various countries in the Middle East. These had enough range to hit targets in nine different cities. Where air defenses such as the Patriot-style antimissile missile were in place, some of the incoming ordinance was blown from the sky, but many flew unhindered. Their targets were downtown metropolitan centers in the largest or most important cities in the various countries, places full of nonmilitary, noncombatant people totally unprepared for the consuming fireballs that obliterated their lives in a pain-wracked, hellish, fearful instant. Once again, fire rained from the sky.

+   +   +

What was left of the American military presence in the tiny country of Qatar, squeezed between Bahrain, Saudi Arabia, and the United Arab Emirates, was small. A battalion of soldiers from the First Infantry Division had been assigned to security around the airbase outside Doha. The battalion commander, a hardened combat veteran with a crewcut and jutting nose, who held a doctorate in history, had been squawking to his boss for several days about what he saw as an increased threat level to his mission. The mujahideen forces held all three of the countries surrounding Qatar. That they had allowed the airport to continue to function, had allowed the affluent leading families of the small nation to fly away, had allowed the U.S. troops to remain unmolested was figured to be another example of Izbek Noir's reluctance to antagonize the United States.

But the battalion commander's jutting nose (he preferred "proud proboscis") smelled trouble, and reported it. His boss reported it, and the smell made its way all the way to the Pentagon, and finally to the desk of Clara Reese, president of the United States. She questioned why we still had *any* troops left on the ground there, and said, "Get them out." As a result, the USS *Kennedy*, one of the American aircraft carriers on station in the Arabian Sea, had launched a multi-chopper lift covered by attack aircraft. The orders came almost too late.

"Incoming!" shouted a sergeant as he heard the distant "ploop" of a mortar round being dropped into its tube, and he and his men crouched in their fighting holes, dug in around the perimeter of the airport. As the series of punching explosions erupted around their positions, they began to receive a scything wave of machine-gun, automatic weapon, and self-propelled grenade fire. Across their front, appearing disjointed and wraithlike in the undulating heat waves, came the shouting and screaming Muslim attackers at a dead run. The sergeant yelled "Fire!" even as his young soldiers opened up with every weapon they had. They were a "light company," with no heavy support weapons, designed to shoot and move fast, not to stand against masses of fanatical armed men backed by tanks and artillery. But they were fighters, these young Americans, and they came from a long line of fighters. They fired into the massed wave of men coming at them, inflicting terrible casualties among them, slowing them, stopping them, only to see more run up to fill the gaps in the line.

The battalion commander gritted his teeth and ran from the side of a concrete hanger to the position of his last company of men. The choppers had lifted out over two hundred of his men, and these were his last. He had to punch his sergeant major in the teeth to get him on the last chopper, and watched helplessly as another chopper blew up in a huge fireball after clawing its way a few feet into the air. The attack aircraft were screaming overhead now, wreaking havoc on the mujahideen massed all around them, expending all of their ordinance in run after run. The old A-10, the ungainly tank buster that had been operational for years, wolfed through the lower altitudes, chewing up the enemy armor on every pass.

The battalion commander watched his men fight and die. The numbers told the story of this battle before the first shot was fired. He was grateful they had enough time to lift most of his unit out, and he was grimly pleased to see the carnage his men and the air support wreaked on the enemy, but when he quickly surveyed the tactical situation he knew this was to be their last stand. Being taken prisoner was not an option when fighting Muslim fanatics, and his men knew it. For a moment he fingered the crude handmade wooden cross that hung around his throat next to his dog tags. It had been made and given to him by one of his teenage daughters, lost in the disappearances. As he touched it he was swept with a feeling of calm acceptance, and his fear and anxiety fell away. He threw himself alongside a destroyed bunker, falling heavily beside the large, black first sergeant who manned an M-60 machine gun.

"The lieutenant's been killed, sir!" shouted the sergeant into the battalion commander's right ear. "We're killin' them big time, but we've lost about a platoon so far! Any more choppers comin'?"

He was going to say no, but he and the sergeant both

heard it at the same time. He looked over his shoulder to see another wave of choppers, low on the eastern horizon, inbound. Above then, swarming, were attack helicopters and aircraft. He hit the sergeant on the shoulder and noticed a gold cross on a chain laying against the shiny black skin of the man's neck. "Pull 'em back in squads! Pull back and regroup as you do, pull back!"

The sergeant nodded, turned, and using hand signals, began moving his men back. The wounded who could not walk were dragged, the dead also, and those who brought them were often wounded or killed as they labored in the stinging hail of fire from the enemy. They moved through explosions and fire, smoke, dust, and the savage cries of soldiers in battle.

The struggling remnants of a platoon fell back through the damaged and destroyed buildings on the west side of the airport. The chopper pilots came in low and fast, using the buildings as cover while they barely hovered over the concrete ramp areas to let the soldiers throw on their dead and wounded comrades, then jump on with them. Another chopper was hit, and slewed to a grinding, skidding stop against a burning tank. The crew of the downed helicopter was picked up by another in a hurricane of lead and explosions. The cacophony of battle reached its zenith, and the entire scene was consumed by an unrelenting ferocious roar.

The battalion commander, already wounded in his arm and right leg, watched as the last of the men clamored onto the last helicopter of the last lift. He saw the black first sergeant, streaks of red blood stark against the skin of his face, firing the machine gun with one arm while waving to him with the other. The sergeant had one foot on the deck of the chopper cabin and was calling to the battalion commander, who ran toward him. They had both seen the mujahideen tanks that had managed to survive the air strikes, surrounded by hundreds of Muslim soldiers, firing wildly and charging across the expanse of empty runway at them. The battalion commander felt something slam into his side, and he was spun to the ground.

He heard the roar of battle, the firing, the explosions, from far away. He tried to sit up but had to use his hands to do so. He saw he still held the automatic rifle he had picked up, and he turned toward the Muslim solders rushing at him, firing. He emptied the magazine into their ranks and saw many of them fall. Then he pulled his .45-caliber automatic pistol out and began firing that. As he did, he began to pray. A cloud of smoke wafted over the scene, and he could not see anything in the stinging darkness. Suddenly, he was jerked up by powerful hands, and he felt himself being dragged roughly across the tarmac. He turned his head, saw the bloody, grinning face of the first sergeant, heard the beating of the helicopter blades over his head, and lost consciousness as he prayed, Save my men, Lord, please Jesus, save my men.

+   +   +'

General Izbek Noir had a satellite television hookup in his command and headquarters truck. Being in charge of the television system was a thankless and dangerous job, the men in his headquarters knew. He had demonstrated just how dangerous on several occasions when he had taken out his pistol and, without preamble, warning, or fuss, simply shot the hapless technician when there was a problem with the signal.

It seemed to be working fine on this occasion, however, and the general sat with his feet up on a desk, the TV screen on the front wall of his office. A thin, reptilian smile spread across Izbek Noir's face as he watched the CNN report. On-screen, the streets were a chaotic, choking mass of wide-eyed and shocked commuters. Now his war would proceed on all fronts. The distinction between civilian and soldier was now obliterated. As he had hoped, the world was now divided between casualties and survivors. Noir played a numbers game, a war of attrition, and he would wait with the patience of a spider before attacking with the speed of a viper.

He watched for a few minutes, then said to the perky, blonde woman sitting behind the huge glass desk on-screen, "You want me to kick this game into high gear? You want me to give Azul Dante all the justification he needs to get this war *really* hot? Well . . . there ya go, sweetie."

CHAPTER NINE

Mike Tsakis sat in his office in the operations center of CIA headquarters, Langley, Virginia, hunched over a sheaf of aerial photographs just handed to him by an assistant. They were hot from a satellite feed and showed a stretch of road in Iraq, south of Baghdad. On one side of the road could be seen the burned-out skeleton of a two-and-a-half-ton truck, and on the other, two small trucks, both damaged. Over a dozen bodies could be seen clearly, and there appeared to be more but they were difficult to make out in the charred wreckage.

First the comm center called down to let him know they had a "dead" signal from the BUT dedicated to John Jameson, last known enroute from Kuwait to Baghdad. With this type of equipment, they could determine if the unit was simply turned off or was in fact rendered inoperative. They received the last-known grid coordinates of the unit and recorded them. Within an hour they learned of a deadly ambush or firefight on the road in that area, and on the orders of Tsakis, had arranged for a flyover. While they waited for the photos, Tsakis ordered a site inspection of the area by a nearby team. He had finished off three cups of coffee, a bagel with cream cheese, and a large bag of M&M's while he waited for the photos and report from the ground team. John Jameson had that Sleeping Beauty transmitter, and now it was dead. Was he dead, too?

He got the buzz from the comm center again, picked up his phone, and said, "Go." He listened for three minutes without saying a word. Finally he said, "Good job, now get out and let the locals clean it up." He hung up, leaned back in his chair as he locked his hands behind his head. He swept the photos strewn across his desk and grinned. The guys on the ground could only identify one of the dead on the scene. Good old Omar, a known free-lancer and tricky player whom several intelligence agencies paid for little dirty deeds here and there. Omar had been used to put Jameson in with the mujahideen when he first went in to try and get close to Izbek Noir. Now Omar was dead and rotting in the sun in lovely Iraq. His grinned widened, and he nodded. If John Jameson was on that truck, and Omar hit it with an ambush, and Omar was dead, you could bet the farm Jameson was *not* dead. It meant Jameson was running in the dark, Tsakis understood immediately. His grin faded as he thought of Omar being there to hit Jameson. That could mean only one thing.

The sound of a muted bell interrupted his thoughts, and he glanced at his computer screen. He was being prompted for an in-house chat. It was from the head of the agency, Benjamin Carter.

I've been following your incoming comm due to my concerns regarding Noir mission, read the message on Tsakis's screen. *Looks like Jameson won't get another shot at his target now. Almost certain he was lost in that apparent rogue or highway bandit action. Maybe another approach will be better in the long run. My regrets to you on the loss of an agent so close to his retirement. Carter.*

Mike Tsakis closed his eyes a moment, leaned toward the keyboard, and responded, *Thank you, sir. Looks like your appraisal might be accurate. He was a credit to our gang. I will continue the mission with alternate initiatives. Will keep you informed. Tsakis.*

There was no more.

Mike Tsakis opened up the right-hand drawer of his desk, dug into a plastic bag, and pulled out a root-beer barrel. He unwrapped the candy, put one foot up on the desk, sighed, and said, "Regrets, my *tuches* . . ."

An hour later his phone buzzed again. The voice was the raspy, smoky growl of an old retired police sergeant he had known for years. The man ran a lunch counter in Langley and many of the older players knew him.

"Got a whistle from a friend of yours, Mike," said the old sergeant. "Can you copy?"

"Go."

"Three on the tree," said the gravelly voice, then followed with a series of numbers.

"Got it."

The line disconnected.

Tsakis worked in his office for another hour, then signed off, cleared, and headed home. As he unlocked his car, he thought, Jameson is not retired, and he is not dead. Three on the tree was a crude but effective handmade code he, Jameson, and two other agents had come up with years ago. The other two were now dead. With the code, you added or subtracted three digits to the phone number that would follow, wait three hours, then try the number. If it did not pan out, you waited three more, then moved on. He did the math in his head, and knew the country code was in Europe. Switzerland, maybe?

+   +   +

"Is that you, Mikey?" said John Jameson into the telephone.

"Is that you, Don Quixote?" responded Mike Tsakis.

"How many toes does a three-toed sloth have?" asked Jameson.

"Twelve," answered Tsakis.

"Will this string sing?" asked Jameson, referring to the security of the phone line.

"I think not," replied Tsakis. "I'm on my daughter's cell. She got it on her own." All personal phones, including those of an agent's family, were listed with the agency and supposedly checked occasionally by the electronic eavesdroppers. "What about on your end?"

"I'm in a small room behind an old bar. You were here with me years ago. Owner of the place still thinks we're heroes, and still thinks we're fighting communism."

"Oh, yeah," said Tsakis, and grinned. He sat on a wobbly wooden bench in a small park a mile or so from his home in Virginia. The park was deserted except for him, a few squirrels, and two local police officers sitting in their patrol car in the parking lot under a tree, fast asleep. His mind pictured the small, cluttered office, stacks of cardboard boxes filled with liquor bottles, cigars, and jars of pickles. A four-bladed ceiling fan with three blades, one high window dusty enough to give everything in the room a sepia tone, and an old wooden secretary almost covered over with faded ledgers, files, and magazines. The bar was in the central part of downtown Bern.

"I thought it best for now to speak only with you," said Jameson, "because I think I was supposed to be taken out of the game on that road to Baghdad. Thought I'd continue to fly, but below the radar, if you concur."

"Oh, absolutely," agreed Tsakis. "Omar being there with his friends smells and feels crummy." He paused, looked around, then added, "Still with the photo fellow?"

"Yeah. Nice kid. I think we'll probably go our separate ways here, though."

"Think he's hooked in with any of the agencies?"

asked Tsakis, his whole life woven with suspicion by circumstance and design.

"Nope," replied Jameson. "He is what he is, but he's been good company, and he'd help me if I asked. Hold on a minute." Tsakis could hear boxes or something being moved, then Jameson came back on the line, "I can't believe it, there's a case of Mountain Dew in here, in bottles. Still good, too."

"Go slow," laughed Tsakis. "It'll make your head spin."

After a moment, Jameson asked, "Did you copy my feelings regarding the target, Mikey?"

"Sort of."

"I know it's weird," said Jameson, "but Slim showed me photos where the target is just a blur, except when he *wants* to be in the picture. That, and the fact that his ability to survive direct hits borders on the supernatural. I mean, I've seen him wounded, but the next day he's all new. The guy is spooky."

"You report it as you see it, John," responded Tsakis. "With what's going on around the world nowadays, I'm ready to believe anything." He paused and suddenly felt old and vulnerable. He could not shake the feeling he had not spent enough time considering the important questions through the years. He cleared his throat and said, "Uh, John, you know I'm a reader, a researcher, a guy who has spent his lifetime following, and occasionally participating in world affairs."

"Yeah, Mike?"

"Ah, I don't know. The disappearances, the earth-quakes, the burning hail, and now this spooky Izbek Noir who seems in some ways *otherworldly*. It's like maybe I've been studying the wrong stuff."

John Jameson felt a rush of emotion as he thought of the Bible, about what he had learned, and about his relationship with Jesus Christ. "The book is there, Mike. We've never talked about these things, but I'll tell you right now the answers are in the Bible, plain and simple. What you suspect is happening is exactly that, and Scripture will lay it out for you. Is it still scary? You bet. Believe in right and wrong, Mikey," he said. "Do what you know is right, and we'll keep charging on."

"I hear you," replied Tsakis. He felt curiously excited and knew he was going to go home, go right to the small bookshelf in his bedroom, and get his hands on the rarely opened copy of the Bible waiting there.

"You know my target gave me a *new* target, right?" said Jameson after a moment, "That's why I'm here. I'm surprised he let me go, but he did, and if I am to return to him to resume my original mission, I must at least make an attempt."

"Roger that."

"Any suggestions?"

"It's gonna have to be a near-miss kind of action, as real as you can make it," suggested Tsakis. "Then you gotta get out." He paused, his stomach in knots. "Look, John," he said, "just take it to that point, then lay low and we'll figure your next move from there."

Jameson sat holding the phone, sipping the lukewarm but delicious soft drink, and thinking of his boss, and friend, miles away. "Mikey," he said, "I know I don't have to say this, but someone has me in their sights, someone *close*, *capisce*?"

"I *capisce* big time, John," responded Tsakis. "I'm sniffin' like an old hound, and if I get a whiff, I'll let you know. You play this like you're all alone out there, John, because you pretty much *are*."

"Right now, I like it this way."

"Call me."

"Call you what?"

"Call me your baby, and I'll kiss you maybe."

"Ciao."

+   +   +

The lights shined brightly on Azul Dante's graying hair and silky, blood-red tie. His tailored charcoal suit and crisp white shirt complemented his tall, athletic body, and his handsome face was given a boyish air by the shock of hair that fell over his left eye, causing him to constantly brush it away from his forehead with one hand. Gushy puff pieces in various newspapers and magazines had unashamedly compared him with a popular young president, long ago killed on a bright Texas morning. His attractiveness was increased by his humble and self-deprecating bearing and his refusal to be compared to such a great and loved world leader. He stood at the podium in the lecture hall of the old court, backed by several dignitaries and representatives from many of the world powers, and addressed an audience of politicians, diplomats, military brass, and media people.

"War is the failure of diplomacy, the failure of civil communication, the failure of rational beings to diffuse a problem and create a solution," he said, his shoulders hunched as his hands squeezed the edges of the dais. His eyes were cast down as he went on. "Thus it can rightly be said I have failed, because I stand here today calling for war. I will not attempt to justify war, or sanctify war, only call for war." He looked up at the faces in the crowd seated in the large room, and at the television cameras. "If a mitigating factor could be identified to take the onus from me in these matters, then I suppose it would be the one that states *it takes work from both sides to ensure and guarantee peace.* By that I mean, of course, that I, that we, the civilized nations of this troubled world, have extended the olive branch at every opportunity and regarding every disputed point, only to have it repeatedly slapped out of our hands."

The people in attendance, many of whom already knew the main points of Dante's address, hung on every word, mesmerized by the controlled power and eloquence of his delivery. "It is difficult, nearly *impossible*, to create rational, meaningful dialogue with Izbek Noir and his mujahideen forces, his Muslim forces. I identify General Noir's forces as Muslim with a heavy heart, because I have studied their Koran, and firmly believe the words of the Prophet are being perverted by the Muslim leaders to incite their followers. My heart is saddened also because history might erroneously record this war as a religious war, Christian versus Muslim, and that would be a gross simplification. That, of course, is the central problem. I did not choose Izbek Noir and his Muslims as my enemy. Nor did you. They chose *us*. All of our efforts have been brutally and callously rebuffed. Remember also, as we have tried to remind the free world's moderate Islamic leaders, that the mujahideen have waged brutal war against fellow Muslims more than anyone else so far. Izbek Noir's dark legions have ravaged central Africa while we tried to talk. They gutted North Africa while we tried to exchange ideas. They chewed up the Middle Eastern states as we tried to reason with them. Talk, ideas, reason . . . they have turned their backs on these humble tools of peace while they trampled the bones of nations, of peoples, and governments.

"One cannot successfully reason with a maddened great white shark swimming in a sea of blood. One will have the same lack of success dog-paddling in a river boiling with feeding-frenzied piranha." He lifted his face to the lights, shrugged those athletic shoulders, and in a lowered voice added, "And I actually believe I may be understating the level of viciousness in our enemy by these clumsy comparisons. Izbek Noir apparently sees anyone who tries to reason with him as a foolish irritant. He has clearly demonstrated his desire, and perhaps capabilities, to become sole ruler of the world by systematically and cruelly destroying each of the varied civilizations that have lifted man from the mud."

Azul Dante paused, and millions who watched the telecast around the globe paused with him. He sighed, pinched his nose, straightened, and said, "Clearly, we cannot allow him to do that. Anyone watching or hearing me today, anywhere on Earth, knows there have been some worrying events taking a toll on the peoples of the world recently. Whether it is simply Mother Nature run amok, something caused by unknown hostile life-forms outside of our galaxies, or acts of God as prophesized in Scripture, I do not know. Again, I am hesitant to connect our worldly machinations and convolutions to the workings of God, Father of all things." He lifted his eyes again, scanned the faces before him, then looked directly into the bank of cameras as he spoke. "I am a simple human being, a crude and wondering entity trying to make sense out of my life, and *life*. I have not only read the Koran, of course, but also, and more importantly, the Bible. I seized, even as a young scholar, as a young believer, on the concept of *free will*—the gift of it, the burden of it. We have free will, and with it we must now come to the reluctant conclusion that the only way to bring peace to our struggling world is through the abomination of war."

His eyes shined and his jaw jutted. "And make war we *will*!" He let those words hang for a moment, his eyes fierce. Then he continued, "Life is precious, and meaningful, and we intend to keep life with those qualities. We cannot stand mute, or stand passive, while a twisted force, with complete disregard for the laws of man or the *future* of man, amputates whole civilizations from our ranks. We cannot wait in hope for the moment when reason prevails. We must act." He took a deep breath, looked down at his hands, then back into the faces watching him, and said, "And we *will* act. It is an honor for me to tell you the European Coalition I have been able to form with the help of so many willing to take risks in the interest of world peace has declared war against General Izbek Noir, his mujahideen forces, and any country or people who support him. The Coalition Force will have at the command level experienced warriors from the United States, Germany, Japan, France, and Canada, and the overall military commander will be General Reginald Urquhart of Britain."

He turned to his left and nodded at a rugged, red-faced older warrior wearing dress greens and a scowl. The man nodded back. "Ground, air, and naval units from over thirty countries have been melded into the Coalition Force, and they stand ready. I will not, of course, discuss strategy with you today, and when the time comes I will leave that to the able professionals who will conduct this war."

He nodded, as if accepting a mantle. "It is with great pride, however, that I announce today that my own Prodigal Project staff will work in concert with the military authorities, to ensure a peaceful and effective transition of power and control in those ravaged areas freed from the deadly grip of the mujahideen. I will continue to head the Prodigal Project initiative, of course, and with the help of Providence and the good peoples in the world, will work hard to restore stability and comfort in those regions torn asunder by the plunderers."

Azul Dante let a tentative smile transform his countenance and told his listeners, "War is the last thing we want, the first thing we hate, but as it has been written, there is a season for all things. Let us resolve here and now to make war with commitment and determination, to *get it done*, so we can get back to the business of living in peace. Thank you."

The strong applause continued as Azul Dante smiled into the cameras, then turned from the podium to shake hands with the military and diplomatic figures behind him. Then he simply stepped off the low stage and into the sea of faces waiting to be seen, hands hoping to be shaken, and hearts longing to join with him as part of the righteous team, the just team, the winning team.

+   +   +

Cat Early leaned against a wall near the main entrance doors to the wood-paneled lecture hall and watched the throng as it milled around Dante. She was there at the behest of her boss in Paris and was glad she had the assignment. Azul Dante clearly was the most powerful, charismatic, and just plain *likable* leader to appear on the world stage in years. He projected hope, even when he spoke of war. She looked around at the assembled dignitaries and wondered if they really comprehended the magnitude of what Dante had told them. She had seen how the mujahideen made war. She had seen, and spoken with, Izbek Noir. She felt a chill trip down her spine. Noir was evil, cruelly brilliant, and driven to destroy civilization. Coalition forces massed against him would meet a fanatical enemy who knew no restraint, as the recent wave of terror bombings against mass transit and the indiscriminate missile attacks on civilians demonstrated. The story of the last American battalion in Qatar had already been told. They had, along with air support, destroyed almost fifty tanks or other armored vehicles, and the number of mujahideen dead was estimated in the thousands. The battle had shown once again Izbek Noir's disdain for his own troops and disregard for his losses. The Americans had fought with skill and bravery and had managed to extricate the shot-up unit, all of its wounded, and most of its dead. But the waves of mujahideen stood on the bloody ground, even as the helicopters carried the battalion out of there. Fire and rain will fall upon this world, she thought, and there would indeed be rivers and lakes of blood.

A movement caught her eye and she saw Dante's attractive assistant, Sophia Ghent, giving her a cautious wave. The woman pointed at a door near the podium. Cat waved back and took a deep breath. She felt uneasy about sitting face-to-face with Azul Dante again. As a professional she knew she should be jumping at the chance, but there was something about him, some undefined feeling of *hesitation* that coursed through her veins when she thought about him. She smiled. She chided herself for being almost *disloyal* with less than admiring thoughts about him. He was the man of the hour, and he had been gracious and accommodating with her. She shook off these disquieting feelings and made for the door.

Sophia waited for her in the hallway and lifted her wrist to glance at her watch. Cat got the point.

"Miss Early," said Sophia with a smile. "So good to see you again. Minister Dante mentioned you arrived last night from Israel. How exciting."

How did he know that? Cat wondered. "Call me Cat, please, Sophia," she said, "And it's good to see you, too. That was some announcement from the minister."

"These are frightening times, Cat," replied Sophia, "and I am so thankful we have Minister Dante here to guide us." They walked together, stride for stride, down an ornate hallway toward a set of double doors. "I'm afraid Minister Dante can only spare a few minutes for you this time, Cat," Sophia added. "He's booked solid all day, and we'll be on the move again tomorrow."

"I'm grateful for any time he can give me," said Cat.

As they reached the doors, Sophia hesitated. Then she touched Cat lightly on the left arm and almost whispered, "When you are finished in here, would you spare a moment for me, Cat?"

"Of course," Cat managed to respond before she was ushered into the officelike chamber. Sophia closed the door behind her, and Cat saw Azul Dante. She was disappointed to see they were not alone. Drazic, Dante's personal aide, stood a few feet from where Dante sat. The tall, thin, stoop-shouldered Drazic looked as dour as always, she thought, as his obsidian eyes inspected her with snakelike intensity. Sitting with Dante were two men, and on the small table between them what looked like official papers were scattered and stacked.

Azul Dante stood as Cat walked across the room, his hand outstretched. She shook it and he motioned her to a small sofa near a window. They sat, knees almost touching.

"Cat Early," said Dante. "I'm glad you were here today, a historic day indeed."

"Yes," replied Cat. "Great speech. Scary, but straightforward."

"Thank you," said Dante. "It is a daunting task, being placed in my position, but I feel like I'm surrounded by competent and dedicated people." He leaned forward. "Sophia would have told you I'm pressed for time today, Cat, and I apologize. I wanted to squeeze you in, however, so why don't you fire away with a couple of questions and make old Simon Blake, your boss, happy."

"Yes," said Cat. She did not need to look at her notebook. "Minister Dante," she asked, "is Prodigal Project, which was formed as a church-affiliated organization—faith based, if you will—is it really now a shadow government, waiting in the wings for the hopeful moment hostilities end with the defeat of Noir and his mujahideen?"

Dante stared at her for a long moment, and the skin at the corners of his eyes tightened. "No," he said.

She waited, but there was no more. "But, sir, as you

explained today, the framework of Prodigal Project, with its network of New Christian Cathedrals all over the world, is actually the planned organization for recovery and stabilization, is it not? And you are the head of the Prodigal Project, yes? It could be postulated you are, accidentally or by design, poised to be *the* world leader after—if—peace comes."

"Postulated?" he almost, but not quite, sneered. "No, Miss Early, you are reading way too much into my role. I am here to serve. I am a coordinator, my skills lie in bringing diverse groups together for the common purpose. *When*, let me stress, not *if*, peace comes, I will be one of those helping to restructure governing bodies where needed, and Prodigal Project has a structure already capable of implementing these. We are here to prevent peoples from being subjugated, we believe it essential that all peoples be given the opportunity to experience life in a free and just society mandated by their own interests. Not ours. Not Izbek Noir's. But their own enlightened self-interest. A self-interest we all share. Peace and prosperity. Someone must show the way, be a shining beacon." Cat noticed that his hands were balled into fists. "I must remind you of something you already know from school. There have been many times in the history of man when a single entity, the right man at the right place at the right time, a benevolent, *compassionate* leader, filled a void left by turmoil and unrest."

"But what about the New Christian Cathedrals?"

asked Cat. "What about religion? Are you planning to form a one-world government backed by a one-world *faith*? I mean . . ."

"Ah, yes," interrupted Dante, "I see my man Drazic is signaling me." He looked at her, his smile fierce. "Bother. Well, Cat, perhaps we can explore this further at another time. Will you be at the reception tonight? The *Americans* are going to attend, isn't that exciting?" He stood, and so did she. They shook hands, briefly, and she felt the pressure of his hand on the small of her back as he guided her to the door. Without knowing why, she counted the number of steps from the sofa to the door. There were seven. "Anyway," he said, "until next time."

"Yes, thank you, Minister." And the door was closed behind her.

She found Sophia Ghent waiting in the richly carpeted hallway, but not close to the door. She could see the young woman was nervous and worried.

"There you are," she said to Sophia.

"Yes," replied Dante's assistant. "How was your interview? Brief, but okay?"

Brief, but evasive and not okay, thought Cat, but she said, "Good."

"Could you, um, would you like a cup of coffee, Cat?" asked Sophia, then turned without waiting for a response and walked a few doors down the hallway to a small open salon where coffee urns, juice, soft drinks, and pastries were placed for those wishing to take a break.

They both got coffee and sat at a small table by a tall, draperied window filled with the soft, white light of the day. Cat waited.

Sophia created a small vortex in her coffee cup with her spoon, and after a moment looked at Cat and said quietly, "I, um, I am in the awkward position of having to beg a favor from you, a *confidential* favor, when we have not really established a friendship yet."

Cat sipped from her cup, smiled, and said, "Maybe that's how friendships are made."

"Maybe," said Sophia as she looked around the room even though they were the only ones there. She stirred her coffee again, then wiped the spoon off with a napkin. After a moment she looked up and said, "I know you probably know people in various positions, within different organizations. I mean, as a journalist, you have established contacts, right?"

Cat nodded.

"Americans?" said Sophia. She made a face, "Of course you *are* American, but I mean American agencies, not news agencies, like, well, like embassy staff types. You know."

Cat looked at the lovely, oval-faced girl sitting across from her. She had heard male reporters talk of her, of how she seemed unreachable and aloof even if she was a looker. She had such a fine complexion, thought Cat. She was troubled though, no doubt. "Who are we looking for?" she asked with a small smile.

Sophia stared at her coffee cup, then looked around

the room again, leaned closer, and said, "James . . . James Devane." A panicked look crossed her face momentarily. "Did I mention this must be very confidential?"

Cat nodded again, reached across the table, and patted Sophia's hand.

"James Devane," said Sophia. "He works in some capacity with the American embassy in Paris, I think. I mean, that's where I met him. I met him and we talked, and we danced once, and we stood out on the balcony and there were a million stars, and we talked and he made me laugh and . . ." Her cheeks reddened and she turned her face away. Then she looked up and went on. "And I liked him. And he liked me, and this sounds very high-school-girl, I know. So. Then, I don't know, Azul—Minister Dante—became very agitated because I guess he could tell I was, we were, attracted, me and James. Azul was angry, and he and James exchanged words." She held Cat's eyes as she lowered her voice and said, "James told me Azul was 'crazy.' He, James, did not like Azul one bit, which I thought odd. No matter. What matters is, shortly after their confrontation, James told me he was ordered not to 'harass' me any longer. We were not to communicate." She sat up straight in her chair. "I am a grown woman. Educated, my professional skills and references are impeccable. I serve Minister Dante well and faithfully. It should be all right for me to have a special . . . friend, or perhaps some small romance, no?"

"Yes," agreed Cat quietly, afraid to break the spell.

"So," continued Sophia, "after Paris we travel, then

arrive here in Bern. It is very busy, lots of developments, all big meetings and important people." She shrugged. "Okay, that's what I do. But . . . but I cannot get James off my mind. I want to talk with him, maybe even see him again, but no. Azul is adamant. I tried to bring it up once, but as soon as I mentioned the name, Azul shut me off." She looked at Cat and pleaded, "Will you help me find out where he is, or who he is, what he does, something? I cannot find him. I have a contact in the embassy in Paris who told me James may be more than he seems, but that was all. Even asking about him is not permitted, apparently."

"Of course," said Cat.

"Excuse me?"

"Let me check around like the nosy little journalist I am," said Cat as she squeezed Sophia's hand. "If there is a James Devane out there somewhere, maybe I can find him for you. If so, the message would be . . . ?"

"Oh," said Sophia. "The message would be—it would be Sophia, call Sophia, Sophia wants to talk with you. Sophia wants to be with you. Sophia misses you." The young woman tugged at the hem of her skirt and sat bolt upright, her face flushed. "What? Why are you shaking your head and laughing at me?"

"Sophia," answered Cat, "slow down, girl. Let me find him, then we'll send him a message, but you don't want it to seem too easy for him, do you? You don't want him to think he's got it made in the shade, do you?"

"I don't know," said Sophia with a sheepish smile. "I

am shameless, I suppose." She looked into Cat's eyes. "I *like* him."

Cat stared back. "Let's find him, then," she said.

Two women and a man entered the small room. One of the women nodded at Sophia, who nodded back. Then she leaned across the table and said quietly, "Thank you Cat, even for trying. What can I do for you in return?"

"Be my friend," answered Cat.

CHAPTER TEN

Cat Early walked the few blocks from the court building to her hotel. It was a mid-range place, small and neat, close to everything and priced within a journalist's expense allowance. The only thing Cat didn't like about the hotel was that it was filled with reporters as a result. She really preferred working alone, actually preferred *being* alone most of the time, and all the contrived bonhomie and "pooled" sources left her cold. She entered the small lobby and walked to the desk to check messages. There was one, given verbally by the clerk. Go to the bar. She almost ignored it. She wanted to take a bath, maybe stretch out on the bed for a half hour, collect herself for the evening. She suspected there would be one or two, maybe more, international reporters bellied up for drinks. First they would try to pump her for the results of her private interview with Azul Dante, which they knew about. Then a couple of them would put the moves on her . . . how about a few drinks? See you after the reception tonight, my room, or yours? The usual.

But she turned from the desk and walked into the bar to see who was in attendance. Maybe she could wheedle some interesting tidbit from someone else for a change. She entered the crowded bar, stopped, and scanned the faces. Some she recognized, but no one seemed to notice her. Then she heard a voice behind her, close.

"You are one very pretty lady, Cat Early," said Slim, "but I'm really attracted to your manly work ethic."

She turned, looked at him, and threw herself into his arms. He lifted her off the floor and spun her around while she held him tightly. "Slim!" she said, her face buried in the side of his neck, "Oh, Slim! This is, this is . . . Slim! Look at you!" They stood holding on, leaning back, looking at each other and laughing.

"Hey, hold it down you two," said someone at the bar. "I'm trying to concentrate on my drink here."

"Must be prom night," said another.

"They are entirely too happy to be journalists," opined one more.

Cat stepped back from Slim, still holding his hands. He wore clothes that were surprisingly presentable, pressed khakis, deck shoes, and a white polo shirt. He had a lightweight sport coat thrown over one arm. His rust-colored mop of hair looked as if a comb had passed reasonably close to it, his skin was reddened by the sun. She thought he looked great. She wiped a tear from one eye and said again, "Oh, Slim, thank goodness you're alive. How did you escape from Noir's camp? How did you get out of there? How did you manage to get here?"

"Whoa, girl," laughed Slim. "We've got a lot to catch up on, and we will, but first I want to buy you a drink and sit and stare at you while you bring me up to speed on what's been happenin' in the world while I was at summer camp." He pulled her by the hand to a small table tucked into a corner, caught the bartender's eye, and in a moment two cold drinks were placed in front of them. They leaned close and talked. They exchanged short versions of their experiences since they had last seen each other, both genuinely pleased to see the other healthy and whole.

Almost an hour later the beers remained untouched, and Slim looked at his watch and said, "Cat, listen, can you skip the reception tonight? Or just make an appearance. Then duck out of there?"

"Why?"

He looked around, then replied, "I want you to meet the guy I've been traveling with, the one I told you about."

"He's *here*?" said Cat, intrigued.

"Yep. And he wants to meet you."

"Why would he want to meet me?" asked Cat.

"He wants to hear your take on Azul Dante."

She hesitated a moment. She liked Slim and trusted him, but she did not know this one Slim called "Johann."

"Who does he work for, Slim? I mean, he's . . ." She

looked around the room, and lowered her voice, ". . . an agent of some kind, right?"

Slim nodded, not surprised by or uncomfortable with Cat's suspicions. "American. But listen, Cat. This is one of the *good guys*. I can't explain it. He's older than what you'd expect for the mission he's on, but he is an eagle scout and I don't mean maybe. He's tough, and smart, and . . . heck, I don't know . . . I've seen him in battle, and he is *somethin'*. He's a good one, Cat, and I feel like the two of you meeting is, like, inevitable."

"I've got to at least be seen there," said Cat, almost to herself, "but I don't think there will be anything new or earth-shaking happening." She took both of Slim's hands in hers across the small table, squeezed them, and said, "Okay, I'll slip away after I see who is there tonight. Then we'll get together."

+   +   +

They both felt it as soon as their hands touched and their eyes met.

Slim had seen Cat enter the small Italian restaurant and escorted her to the corner table in the back of the place. It was almost ten, the night clear, cool, and wet, the streets of Bern subdued. Cat had sensed it earlier, when she made her way to the reception. It was as if the Swiss, ever neutral, were holding their collective breath until Azul Dante and his meetings left town. The tall, black-haired, rugged man with a strong jaw, serious dark eyes, and down-turned mouth stood as Slim walked Cat to the table. His face changed as he smiled and put his hand out for her to shake.

"Cat Early," he said.

"Johann?" she replied.

They sat. She saw he had selected the seat that put his back to the wall and gave him clear vision of the front door and the kitchen door that lead to the back. He was sunburned, angular, and solid, with big hands and wide shoulders. He wore black—slacks, with a gold-buckled belt, shoes, and a long-sleeved turtleneck shirt under a black leather jacket. She wanted to ask if he shopped at the Secret Agent Haberdashery, but concluded he looked . . . nice.

"Please," he said easily, "call me John. Will you have wine? We ordered three glasses of the house red. Slim still calls me Johann because he thinks the mujahideen have spies following us everywhere."

"Did you take a look at that cabdriver?" said Slim as he buttered a breadstick. "And put an eyeball on our waiter when you get a chance."

Cat and John Jameson sat very still, looking into each other's eyes. For them, for one moment, no one else existed. Cat felt herself drawn, as if the intangible essence deep inside her heart was being gently pulled out. It was like a warm, very gentle, puff of air, and she knew immediately he felt the same thing. He had a slightly startled look, as if he had been caught off-balance. She did not want the moment to end, and held her breath. His eyes captured her, held her in respectful appraisal, and she should have been uncomfortable in his gaze, but was not. She did not know how long the moment lasted, but she felt a very subtle ripple in the flow of emotion, and then it came.

SEVEN.

John Jameson felt blindsided, completely unprepared for what happened to him as he sat looking at Cat. She was at least ten or twelve years younger than he, trim, fit, and lovely, with stylishly short hair, big brown eyes, nice skin, and a soft mouth. There was a vibrancy, an energy about her, and he understood at once that she was a female entirely comfortable within her skin. She wore some kind of dressy pantsuit, silky, in iridescent royal blue. Her hair shone, and a thin gold chain hung on the tanned skin of her neck He was not a man who had known, really known, many women in his life. He and his wife had met in school, and theirs had been a good marriage. He had adored her and always secretly thought he did not deserve her. Then he lost her to the disappearances and was swept up in the fast-moving, dangerous game this assignment had become. Not once in the months since the disappearances had he consciously desired a woman. He looked across the table, let his eyes drink in the woman sitting there, and felt immediately unsettled. Then it came.

SEVEN.

Cat forced herself to focus. She saw John lean back in his chair, a frown on his face.

"So then," said Slim as he looked at Cat, then at Jameson. He took a long drink from his wineglass. "Don't mind me, you two. No . . . just pretend I'm not even here. It's okay, really, I'll sit quietly, mumbling to myself, maybe humming a bit to keep myself occupied."

Jameson put one big hand on Slim's left forearm, squeezed, and said quietly, "Hold it a minute, Slim, hold on a minute." He continued to stare at Cat, who nodded as he said, "Did you, was there a number . . . ?"

"Seven," answered Cat, suddenly swept with an odd sense of relief, as if she had been holding something in and now she could share it.

"Seven," said Jameson.

"Seven," repeated Slim. He looked at his menu and said, "Seven. That would be, whoa, number seven is linguini with clam sauce, Johann, and garlic rolls. Hope you brought some breath mints with . . ."

Still looking at Cat, Jameson said again, "Slim, hold it. Stop." He turned to the young man, grinned, and said, "Something important is happening between us, uh, me and Cat. Give us a minute to figure it . . ."

"Hormones," said Slim, as he gulped another drink of his wine. Then he leaned back in his chair and folded his arms across his chest. He put his chin down, glanced at Cat, and added, "That's what happening here, hormones. Both of you have been steering clear of the opposite sex for so long you don't know how to act . . ."

It was Cat's turn to say, "Slim, stop." She reached out,

took his right hand, brought it to her face, and softly kissed it. He stopped.

"John," said Cat after Slim quieted, "the number seven has been, I don't know how else to say this, with me for some time now. It is palpable, very real. It means something, and I had the feeling, I can't explain it, I had the feeling I would meet someone else who knew of it, or sensed it. Perhaps it means we, um, you and I, we are part of seven, perhaps there are five more out there who sense it too . . ."

"And we as seven have some purpose," agreed Jameson. "Seven of us will be joined, or work together somehow, toward an unknown goal, we have some . . . mission." He shook his head and grinned, "I don't know, but I'm glad I'm not the only one with this idea bumping around in my head."

"No," she said, troubled as she thought of Azul Dante's first question of her, *his* interest in the number seven, "you're not the only one, and neither am I." She lay Slim's hand on the tablecloth and smiled at him. She turned her gaze back to Jameson and wondered if *all* the emotion they had both felt flowing between them was because of *seven*, or if there was more. She decided she hoped it was more.

Slim emptied his wineglass. He stared at Cat. He knew at that moment he loved her, had loved her from the first moment he saw her, just as he had loved her sister, Carolyn, before she was killed. He knew they were very close, very special friends, he treasured that, and had not allowed himself to think about Cat in any other way.

"Somebody at this table want to take a moment and explain to poor dim-witted Slim here what this number thing is all about?" he said.

Jameson looked at Slim. He saw how the young guy looked at Cat, he remembered Slim talking about her as they traveled out of Iraq on the cargo plane he had bribed space on. It figures, he thought. "Hey," he said, "what do you say we order some food, Slim? I bet this place does it right. We need some real food after what we've been existing on, right?"

"Oh, man," protested Slim. "Who drank my wine? Stupid wineglass must have a hole in it."

+   +   +

"He'll be all right," said Jameson as he came downstairs to the small living room. "A few glasses of wine can hit you hard if you don't drink."

Cat smiled. She sat on a small sofa, one arm propped on a cushion, the extended fingers of her hand pressed against her temple. "Or even if you do."

"I got his shoes off," said Jameson, "and he was already snoring." They were in the small, safe house that Jameson and Slim had first gone to when they arrived in Bern. Jameson explained this one usually sat empty and unused, because what intrigue happened in Switzerland? It was a tidy two-story, the furniture basic but comfortable. Slim was once again impressed with government planning when Jameson showed him the selection of clothing hanging in the closets. From it they had both been able to find something presentable.

Jameson and Cat had been able to give each other a brief sketch of their lives up to, and since, the disappearances, during the awkward dinner. Slim had downed another glass of wine and was working on his third when Jameson stopped him and paid the bill. The young man needed a little help navigating as they headed for the house, and had agreed it was best to hit the sack when they got there. He had shyly kissed Cat on the cheek when he said good night, and she had hugged him tightly and told him, "It's okay, Slim. It's okay, *we're* okay, and I'm so glad you are here."

She watched Jameson as he took a chair on the other side of the coffee table, rubbed his forehead with one big hand, and sighed. She wished he would have sat beside her, and resisted the urge to pat the sofa with one hand while beckoning to him with the other. She cleared her throat and said, "Slim is my closest friend. He has been super to work with, and I'd travel with him anywhere."

"He's a good kid," agreed Jameson.

They looked at each other.

"Do you think these are the end times, John?" asked Cat. Her emotions were in a jumble and she was hungry for answers. John Jameson, her heart told her, might have some.

"For me," he began, "It makes the most sense. Saying that, of course, means I have accepted Scripture, the

Word of the Bible, as, well . . . the gospel. You told me earlier your feelings of faith were almost overwhelmed by your cynicism throughout the most recent years of your life, and believe me, I can identify with that. But you also told me when Slim gave you your sister's backpack, and you found her Bible inside, it impacted you, that you've been reading it and finding some solace there." He stopped, took a deep breath, held it, then let it out. "I am not a preacher. I mean, I don't preach to people about *anything*, let alone religion and the Bible. I've always kept my counsel, tried to be respectful of others and their opinions, and basically minded my own business." He grinned. "But I guess I'm gonna preach to you, Cat. It's like I can't help it." He leaned forward in his chair. "I told you a bit during dinner, about going home to my house in Indiana right after the disappearances, everyone I loved in this world gone. You experienced it in your world, too. It flat ripped my heart out, and I didn't know what to do. Until I found my wife's Bible, and like I said earlier, I believe she left it for me. She had marked it, places for me to read and study, and it was like she walked me through my survival. That Bible *saved* me, and there came a moment when everything kind of made sense, and what didn't make sense I accepted as part of a *plan*." He shook his head, his eyes staring at something far away. "I accepted Jesus into my heart and found peace. Then I joined the Muslim mujahideen so I could go to war."

"I want to learn more," said Cat, "about the Bible, about God, about Jesus Christ, because I think there *is* more. But at the same time, it's scary, because Revelation, if taken literally, is *bad* . . . or so it seems bad to me, a mere human who happens to like this world God gave us." She shrugged, "Being scared of the unknown, it's hard. What's *known* is hard, too, John. I mean, if I accept Scripture as you have, and we've already had plenty of signs, occurrences, that can't be ignored—not the least of which were the disappearances—then we can expect the Antichrist, right?"

"Scripture makes it clear," he replied. "He will exist, and he will try to dominate the world."

They were quiet a moment, looking at each other. "What is your take on Azul Dante?" asked Jameson finally. "You've watched him, listened to him, interviewed him. Is he for real, Cat?"

"He's for real, yes," answered Cat. "And he is a very, very impressive person. Very strong, capable, smart. He has vision, he has courage. He is a diplomat and organizer without peer. He is smooth, charming, and beguiling. His confidence has made him arrogant to a degree, and I've found he can be difficult and defensive. If anyone can bring the forces together that might destroy Izbek Noir, who I can tell you from personal experience is pure evil, Azul Dante can."

"So he'll save the world, Cat?"

It was her turn to gaze far off into the inner distance. The room was quiet for a long moment. He waited. Finally she shuddered, took a sharp breath, and said, "He asked me about the number *seven*, John. He asked me about it, but it was like he was on the other side of it somehow. It was like he knew of it, and was, *concerned?* I don't know. It worried him. It doesn't worry us, does it?"

He remained quiet. Neither one wanted to take that next step.

"Slim told me Izbek Noir sent you away from the mujahideen, on a mission, John," Cat said very quietly. "A secret mission." She held his eyes with hers. "Can you tell me what it is?"

"Izbek Noir wants me to assassinate Azul Dante," he replied with no hesitation, even though he understood the moral dilemma he created for her by doing so.

"Oh, my," whispered Cat, the fingers of one hand touching her throat. "But of course you *can't*, right? I mean, I have seen Izbek Noir up close and personal, and I believe him to be raw evil, up and walking around on its hind legs. I have no doubt he would give you such an order. Azul Dante is really the one single force that has the power and capability to stop his mujahideen hordes. But certainly it is an order you must ignore, right?"

"You understand I have made my way into the ranks of the mujahideen for the express purpose of getting close to Izbek Noir," he said carefully, "and . . . stopping him. Yes?"

"Yes."

"Noir has proven to be a difficult target," Jameson said, hearing again things he said to Mike Tsakis. "You can ask your friend, Slim. Noir may be more than . . . man."

Cat nodded, her eyes went far away, then focused on

Jameson again, "Yes. Yes . . . but he is Noir, and Azul Dante is something *else*, John. I mean, Dante might be this world's last best hope. You know this. I mean, his Prodigal Project, his ability to form such a strong coalition quickly, to stand against the evil we *know* is Izbek Noir. Assassinating him would work for the dark forces, right, and not for *us?*" She looked at her hands, then at him, and continued. "What kind of man are you, John Jameson? One who simply follows orders, or one who does what is *right?*"

John Jameson was not surprised by her question. It was one he had asked himself often through the years. Could it be he was just a triggerman? Another Omar, with better connections? A man who had accepted Jesus Christ into his heart, but went from one mission of death to another? He looked at her face and drank in what he saw, the depth and passion in her eyes, the intelligence, the strength. He wanted her to know who he was, but he was not sure he himself knew. "What did you tell me about Dante a few minutes ago, Cat?" he asked gently. "About the number seven, our feeling, as opposed to *his?* You have a doubt, it's not clearly focused yet, but it is there."

She took a deep breath and let it out. "Yes."

He kept his eyes locked on hers and said evenly, "I pray for guidance every single day, Cat, and my heart tells me I have some small part in God's plan. I have to rely on that. The fact that I believe there is *reason* behind all of this craziness makes me able to play this game, frightening and distasteful as it is." He reached out for her hands, and she leaned forward until their fingers were entwined. "I've just gone against all of my years of training and experience, telling you what I'm supposed to do here. This puts you in a bad spot, I know. Do you warn him? Do you report it as raw intelligence? Do you do a *story?* It is not my intention to put you in this spot, Cat, but you are . . . you are *special,* and I trust you. I trust you because I trust God, and I do not believe for one minute our coming together now is an accident. We, you and me . . . and maybe five more, I don't know. We have a common purpose, and we must *trust.* Do you trust me?"

"Will you kill him?" she asked, her mouth dry. "Will you kill Azul Dante?" I cannot allow this, she thought as she looked at him. I cannot allow him to destroy Dante, himself, *us.* He is a good man, a *good* man. How can I allow this?

"I don't know if he *can* be killed, Cat. Or if a mortal man can kill him." He hesitated, knowing he had already told her too much, not knowing how much more. "I am in this . . . game, and I must continue to make the moves that will *validate* me." His eyes seemed to deepen as she watched, and he said, "Trust?"

She felt his strong warm hands on her skin, felt the intensity of his gaze, felt the beating of her own heart. She looked deep into that heart now. She thought of Carolyn, her sister, and of Carolyn's Bible, of the truth she knew was there. She thought of the number seven, the simple reality of it, and she thought of what she felt when she met this man, John Jameson. Still, she thought, *Will he kill Azul Dante?*

They walked together through the night streets, back to her hotel. They walked with their arms locked, hands in jacket pockets. They did not talk much, both swept with swirling emotions. She stopped him on the wet sidewalk half a block from the hotel lobby entrance and stood looking up at his face. He leaned down and gave her a quick kiss on her cheek. She put her hands on his elbows, stood on tiptoe, and kissed him back. A real kiss. She turned and walked to the hotel entrance, stopped, and smiled at him. He smiled back.

She climbed into the bed in her room a little later, her cheeks wet from unexplainable tears. She fell fast asleep, hugging one of the pillows tightly to her chest.

CHAPTER ELEVEN

"Take my hand, Reverend Smith," said Ivy Sloan-Underwood gently, "don't be afraid. Take my hand and walk with me through those doors, down the aisle, and to that pulpit." She put her right hand against his cheek and brought his face around until his eyes met hers. "I need you, Reverend Henderson Smith, my *soul* needs you. Walk with me to that pulpit, and there we'll kneel together and pray to Jesus Christ for His strength, for *strength*."

"But, you see them, don't you?" said Henderson Smith, his eyes big, his nostrils flared. "You see them just like I do, standin' out there under that bottlebrush tree, just starin' at me, laughin'."

"But they won't come into the cathedral, will they, Reverend?" responded Ivy, "They won't because they can't, and you and I need to ask Jesus for the strength to make our hearts into cathedrals."

Nateesha Folks, Shannon Carpenter, and Ted Glenn stood on the front steps of the New Christian Cathedral, a few yards from Ivy and the Reverend Smith. They had all arrived at Ivy's room in Selma General Hospital to find Ivy dressed and waiting for them. She had been released, the abbreviated formalities already finished. She was bandaged and a bit unsteady on her feet, but the drain had been removed from her side, her scar was healing nicely, and she was eager to leave. Henderson Smith had remained in the hallway, Lakeesha behind him, when Shannon and Ted went into Ivy's room, but he went to her when Ivy stood and called his name. They embraced, both crying, and then all of them were crying. Every time Henderson Smith tried to apologize for what had happened, or thank Ivy for what she had done, she put one finger against his lips, smiled, and shook her head. "I could not let my Ron shoot you, Reverend Smith," Ivy told him. "I just could not let that happen. Perhaps God has a plan, or some work for both of us, Reverend, I don't know. I *do* know I felt guided that day, and was ready to accept . . . embrace . . . my death." She looked at each of them, reached out and took Nateesha's hands, squeezed them, and added. "Maybe our death is a gift from God also, given to us only when it is time."

"That's right, Henderson," said Nateesha, as she wiped the tears from her cheeks, "It was not your time, Ivy's either. She's right about the work you still have to do, too. You got a whole lot of hungry and frightened souls just waitin' for the Good Word, and you're the one that's gonna give it to them."

Henderson Smith looked at the lovely woman who had been his protector and nurturer since *that day* and nodded, his face sad. He turned back to Ivy and said firmly, "Don't shush me now, Ivy. The words I want to say are stitched into my heart, and I've got to say them to you."

"All right, Reverend," said Ivy.

Henderson Smith took a deep breath and said, "I want you to know I am sorry for what happened." He put up one hand to stop any protestations and went on. "I don't understand why, or how, but I know in my heart I was in some way responsible for it, I was somehow responsible for that man's anger, his blind desire to kill me." Even as the words fell, he heard an inner voice say, Maybe you *do* know, Reverend, maybe ol' Ron Underwood had already figured what you're all about. He straightened and added, "I'm sorry, and I'm grateful for what you did. So thank you, Ivy, for giving me another chance at whatever this life holds for me."

She watched him closely and saw he was still troubled. Nateesha saw it, too.

"You are welcome," said Ivy.

Shannon and Ivy hugged, looked at each other and laughed, and hugged again. Then they all turned and looked at Ted Glenn. He had a paper grocery bag, and into it he put almost everything not nailed down in the room: toilet articles, wipes, magazines, tissue boxes, soap, shampoo, hospital slippers, a small pillow, and two or three containers of Jell-O. He saw them all staring at him, smiled sheepishly, and said, "What? Did you know they *bill* you for all this stuff? Ivy might be able to use it. I mean, this shampoo hasn't even been *opened*."

"We'd better leave," said Shannon as she took Ted's arm, "before he figures out how to get the TV off the wall."

On the drive from the hospital to the New Christian Cathedral, Ivy told the others about her last visit from the police. The detective had been a nice young man, she said, very serious. He told her it didn't matter if the world was coming to an end, as it had been going to you-know-where in a handbasket anyway. What did matter to him was the law, and Ron Underwood, her husband, had broken it by shooting her. The fact that Ron was actually trying to shoot the Reverend Henderson Smith, whom the detective had heard speak several times, was a separate crime, but still a crime. He explained to her that Ron was in the county jail, and because of the "confused state of things," he would stay there until the case was sorted out. The prosecutor's office was apathetic about the case, the detective admitted, but it *was* a case and he was going to work it. She had listened politely and then reminded the detective that she had no intention of pressing charges against her husband. This meant the case would have no victim. She said she had been touched by the sincerity of the detective, aware of his frustration and his fear for her safety. He had left her with his card and a few pamphlets about spousal abuse from the Victim Advocate's Office.

It wasn't until they parked their car in the church lot, and Henderson Smith was assisting Ivy from the backseat, that they became aware of the two figures watching them from under a nearby tree. One was tall, dark, and rakishly handsome, the other ginger-blond, overweight, jowly, and sweaty. The tall one wore a tailored suit, black; the porcine one had on a wrinkled linen suit, which appeared to be blackened in places with ash. They did not approach the car or say anything. They just stood there, staring at Ivy and Henderson, twisted grins on their faces, a weird gleam in their eyes.

"Oh, Lord," said Henderson Smith as he gripped Ivy's arm.

"What is it, Henderson?" asked Nateesha. Then she followed the reverend's gaze, saw the heavyset figure with the other, and said quietly, "Oh, my sweet Jesus, it's that Andrew Nuit thing, isn't it, Henderson? The one who burned your old church down, the one who came to your room to torment you?"

Shannon and Ted saw how rigid and pale Ivy had become as she stared at the two, and moved protectively closer. "What is it, Ivy?" asked Shannon.

Ivy tried to speak, but her mouth was totally dry. She swallowed a couple of times and licked her lips. She was as angry as she was frightened, and when she could speak she spit the words out like pieces of something bitter. "It's that demon I told you about," she said, "Thad

Night." She shuddered. "Do you really see him, too, Shannon?"

Shannon was transfixed and could not even nod her head.

Ted Glenn stared at the two figures under the tree and said hoarsely, "Did you say, *demon?* Like . . . *demon?*" He took a deep breath and began walking toward the two, waving his arms. "Get outta here!" he yelled, "You! Yeah, you two. Get off this property now!" The two under the tree did not move, but the tall, dark one made a small motion with his hand, and when he did Ted Glenn doubled over as if kicked in the groin, and fell to the pavement, ashen. He curled into the fetal position with his hands between his legs, his face red with anger and pain. The others heard him say, "Well I'll be a . . ." He rolled to his knees, coughed, and stood up slowly. He took another step toward Andrew Nuit and Thad Night, and shouted huskily, "Don't matter, boys. You still gotta go."

Shannon came out of her spell and shouted, "No, Ted! Stop! Don't go near them!"

Ted stopped, swayed, and glared at the two tempters, who laughed.

Now Ivy Sloan and Henderson Smith held tightly to one another and entered the cool, quiet, and spacious interior of the cathedral. Nateesha Folks watched Shannon go to Ted Glenn, take his hands, and pull him gently toward the doors. The two figures under the tree stood and watched, but did not follow. Nateesha waited for Shannon and Ted, and the three of them entered behind Ivy and Henderson. They stood just inside the doors and watched the reverend and Ivy slowly walk down the long, carpeted aisle, which stepped down until it reached the front stage with the choir lofts on either side. There the two stopped, and Ivy sensed the reverend could go no further. He looked up at the soaring pulpit, which reached above their heads, the rich, polished wood gleaming. His eyes widened. She held his arm and felt him tremble.

"Reverend," she said gently, "let's climb that pulpit . . . your pulpit. Let's climb it together and pray. Look around, now, look at this beautiful church." She made a sweeping motion with one arm. "This is where you are going to help us, all of us, Reverend. You are going to tell us about the Word, *explain* it to us, help us find God." She sobbed quietly. "Oh, Reverend Smith, I want to find Him, I need Him and want Him, but I don't know Him, *I don't know Him.*"

He turned and looked into her eyes, and in them he saw the longing of a child. "Please, Reverend Smith . . . please."

He took her hand, and together they took the curving steps to the top.

At that moment the Cadillac Seville driven carefully by Stan Sariel rolled into the large front lot of the church. They had been looking for a parking space at Selma General when Stan stopped the car, looked skyward with a puzzled expression, and said, "Oh, my. Your wife, Ivy, has already been released from here, Ron. She has gone back to the New Christian Cathedral with her friends."

Ron did not care how Stan, his former cellmate-turned-lawyer, knew this. He was simply impatient to see Ivy again, excited, and nervous. "Well, head that way then, and how about trying to drive a bit faster while you're at it."

Stan would have none of that. He held his hands at the ten-and-two position on the steering wheel and moved through the traffic with calm majesty. He seemed amused by the radio, and had found a local station that played tunes like "Earth Angel" and "Pretty Little Angel Eyes." When they were a block or so from the cathedral, Charlie Daniels began fiddling and singing about how "The Devil Went Down to Georgia," and Stan kept time on the steering wheel, humming along, and saying under his breath, "Go Johnny, go . . . show that loser how it's done . . ."

He stopped humming when he pulled the Seville into the church lot and saw the two shimmering figures under the funny-looking tree. "Will you look at that," he said.

"What?" asked Ron.

"Those two, over there," replied Stan, his face set. "Why, the unmitigated gall and audacity. What cheek. Can you believe how *bold* they are? I was told I might meet some of their kind while here, but *this* . . ."

"Those two guys under the tree?" asked Ron. He looked again and said, "Wait a minute. They were here the day I, the last time I, *on that day*."

"Hang on," said Stan tightly. He turned the wheel and the big car headed across the lot, right toward the tree and the two under it. He accelerated and said loudly, "Now hear this! Prepare to *ram!*"

Thad Night and Andrew Nuit saw the shiny automobile turn and head toward them. They both immediately recognized the driver—if not the personality, the *type*. They said nothing, but contemptuous sneers twisted their faces, and they stood rock still.

Ron hung on to the passenger door handle, wide-eyed. When it became clear Stan had no intention of stopping, he yelled, "You're gonna hit the tree!"

They *did* hit the tree. The front tires hit the median curb, bounced on the sparse grass, and impacted the tree dead center. The front bumper and hood of the car hit exactly where the two shimmering figures stood under the drooping branches, and there was a loud crash. The car stopped. The tree shook, then slowly fell over onto the parking lot. Ron looked through the windshield but could not see the two figures. *Oh well*, he thought, *back to jail*.

But Stan jumped out of the car, ran to the broken tree trunk, and grinned. His grin turned to a frown when he saw Thad Night and Andrew Nuit appear, standing side-by-side in the reaching, tangled, branches. They smiled at him.

Ron saw them. They were not there, then they *were*, and a chill ran down his backbone when he saw their caterpillar-like smiles.

Stan, his eyes bright, waved one hand imperiously at the two and said loudly, "Be gone!" Nuit and Night bowed low, smirked, and were immediately . . . *gone*.

Stan slid behind the wheel again and backed the car off the tree. As he did, the tree stood up once more, just as it was, apparently undamaged. "Well," said Stan, his face red. "Well!" Then he took a deep breath, turned to Ron, and added sheepishly, "Sorry about losing my temper, Ron, but seeing those two here really ruffled my feathers."

Ron, bewildered, simply nodded.

Stan parked the car near the front steps of the church, turned off the motor, and said quietly, "I'll wait here, Ron."

Ron nodded, got out, and walked to the big double wooden doors.

Nateesha Folks, Ted Glenn, and Shannon Carpenter stood together in the doorway. All three of them had witnessed what the driver of the Cadillac had done with the two under the bottlebrush tree, and all three of them immediately recognized Ron Underwood. Glenn stepped protectively in front of Shannon and Nateesha, put his big hands up, his face still pale from the pain, and said, "No way, buster. You just get back in that car and . . ."

"Wait," said Shannon, as she put one hand on Ted's forearm to stop him. "It's okay, Ted." As Ron walked toward her she felt a warm rush in her chest, and her mind was filled with *seven*. She saw the startled look in Ron Underwood's eyes at that moment and knew he felt the same thing. "He's okay, Ted. He won't hurt any of us now."

Ron stopped in front of the three of them and said quietly, "I'm sorry . . . about what I did. I'm truly sorry."

Ted still wasn't convinced, but he trusted Shannon's feeling. Besides, he had just witnessed what Ron's partner had done with the car and those two . . . whatever they were.

Nateesha, unable to completely relax either, nodded, her face set. She had carried her Bible with her when they left that morning, and held it tightly to her chest.

Shannon reached out slowly, took one of Ron's hands, and smiled. She tossed her head back and said, "Ivy's in there, Ron, with the reverend." Then she moved out of the doorway so Ron could pass.

Ivy and the Reverend Smith sat on the carpeted steps at the base of the pulpit. They had come down together and sat holding hands and talking quietly. They saw the commotion at the door and stood slowly as Ron came down the aisle toward them.

"Oh, my," said Henderson Smith. "Oh, my."

Ivy Sloan-Underwood looked at her husband as he approached. She saw how he held his head up, how he walked. She saw his clothes, his clean-shaven and neat appearance. She saw the intensity in his eyes, where strength had replaced madness. "It's all right, Reverend

Smith, he is not here to hurt us." At that moment she felt and saw *seven*, and could tell by the reverend's gasp that he had felt it also. Ron was part of it, she realized, and she looked up the aisle at Shannon, saw Shannon's look, and knew.

The Reverend Henderson Smith, loathing his own cowardice, licked his lips, hung onto Shannon, and asked Ron, "Are you going to try to kill me again? Are you?" Deep in his heart he wondered if he wouldn't *welcome* his own death now. Perhaps in death he could be released from his torment, perhaps in death he could throw himself at the feet of the judge, beg forgiveness, and find peace.

Ron hung his head, took off his glasses, and said, "No, Reverend." He turned to Ivy, his eyes vulnerable, sad, and filled with tears, and whispered, "Oh, Ivy . . . I'm . . . I'm . . . oh, Ivy, thank God, thank God."

Ivy let go of the reverend's arm, stepped close to her husband, kissed him on the cheek, and embraced him. They both wept as Henderson Smith stood watching.

"Ivy," said Ron, "I did not mean, I did not know what . . ."

"It's okay, Ron," she replied, her voice muffled, her face buried against his shoulder. "I know, I know." She pulled back so she could look at his face. She took his glasses from his hand, slid them onto the bridge of his nose, smiled, and said, "I know."

"I love you, Ivy," said Ron.

"I love you, Ron," she replied.

They stood close enough to breathe each other's breath, and looked into each other's eyes. "I miss Ronnie," said Ivy. "I miss our son."

"What happened, Ivy?" he asked. "What happened?"

She heard him and knew he meant, What happened to us, what happened when Ronnie was born damaged? *Why* was Ronnie born like that, why did our child have to live like that and be cared for like that? Why did we have to become so hardened because of it? What happened to our marriage? What happened that day Ronnie disappeared, and why? What is happening to the world, what is happening to us, what is happening?

"Love happened, Ron," she said softly. "Love happened, and I could not see it. You tried to show it to me, but I could not see it."

"I want to be with him," whispered Ron. "And you. I want us to be together." He looked at the reverend, and he turned and looked all around the lovely, open church, which was filled with a soft, golden, natural light. "Can we find a way here, Ivy?" he asked. "Can we find God here and go home?"

Ivy thought of *seven* and answered, "Soon, Ron. But not yet."

Stan shook Ted Glenn's hand, hugged Shannon Carpenter and Nateesha Folks, smiled, and said, "Ted, Shannon, Nateesha, isn't this a great day? Can someone give me a 'Yay, God' for this great day?"

He stepped past them and into the church, where he

stopped, looked all around, and took a long, deep, breath. "Ah," he said, his eyes closed. "Fill me up with the breath of saved souls, man is it *sweet*."

They all stared at him. He looked at each one in turn, winked at Ron, smiled at Ivy, and asked, his voice carrying strongly in the church, "Ivy? If there are two across the ocean, and four standing right here, how many is that?"

Ivy looked at the tall, handsome man with the nice suit and thick blond hair, smiled without knowing why, and said, "Six."

"Can't get your kicks with six," said Stan. "And who wants to congregate with eight?" He put his hands on his hips, his fingers pulled his lips, he nodded, and asked, "Shannon, how many do we need?"

Shannon laughed in spite of herself, shook her head, and said, "Seven."

"Right on, sister," said Stan, "as the good Reverend Henderson Smith would say."

Ron took a couple of steps toward his new friend, looked at the others, and said as he shook his head, "Everyone, please. This is Stanley Ayak Sariel. You can call him Stan. He's . . . he's been helping me, and I suspect he's going to help *us* now."

Stan turned to Ted Glenn and said, "Um, Ted. That bag you left in your car. Do you want those little containers of the substance Jell-O you recovered from Ivy's hospital room?"

+   +   +

Later they sat together in the Cathedral dining room, talking quietly. Many people who worked in the church or were visiting politely interrupted to shake the Reverend Smith's hand, to pat him on the shoulder, to tell him they missed having him around. Everyone seemed bolstered by his return, and there was a renewed energy pulsing through the building. Smith greeted each one with a handshake, kiss on the cheek, or pat on the shoulder. He seemed to be back in good form, animated, strong, reassuring. Stan, who had been very respectful of the reverend, introduced himself to each person who stopped by the table until finally Ron asked him if was running for office. Stan just grinned at him.

Their talk became serious when the discussion turned to the number seven and its meaning. Nateesha and Ted admitted they had not "sensed" the number, but agreed it could not be coincidence that the others had felt it so strongly. They also agreed it was Biblical, but could not add more than that. Shannon suggested they had been picked to form a team for some common purpose, and wondered who the others might be.

Ivy looked at Ron and said, "Church. Thomas Church. We met him and his son, Tommy, here, then they left." She turned to Shannon, "Remember, the young guy was like a real cowboy? He had been burned and cut up a bit pulling people out of their cars after one of those terror attacks against fuel-tanker trucks out on the interstate. You and I both felt something when we first met his dad, Thomas, like we had known him before. We commented on it later. Where is Tommy, anyway? He returned here, I remember seeing him, I think, in that burning hail . . ."

"He was here," agreed Ron, "He tackled me as I ran across the parking lot like an idiot after I, after I . . ." He stopped when Ivy took one of his hands, squeezed it, and shrugged.

"He was here for a few days," said Shannon, "Then he got restless. The Reverend Smith wasn't giving the sermons, and it . . . wasn't the same. He's young and said he wanted to 'do some exploring.' Took off in that white pickup truck of his. He told me he felt he might try to find a way to travel to Europe, or the war zones. He was very interested in Azul Dante, the Coalition, that weird Izbek Noir, all that."

Henderson Smith ducked his head for a second at the mention of those names, but no one noticed but Nateesha, and Stan.

"Wait a minute," said Ron suddenly. He pulled his jacket off a nearby chair where he had thrown it, dug into the inside pocket, and pulled out the sheet of legal pad paper from his jail cell. He passed it around to the others, and they inspected it with amazement.

"But how did you know this, Ron?" asked Ivy. "How did you know these names?"

"Ask Stan," replied Ron, shaking his head.

"Don't look at me," said Stan, with an innocent expression. He saw they *were* looking at him and added, "Well, all right, look at me. But don't ask me that which I cannot answer."

"Who are these other two, then?" asked Ted. "This John Jameson, and uh, Cat Early?"

Everyone sat staring at the list. Finally Nateesha said, "I don't know for sure, but that girl's name there, that *Cat*. I think I've seen her name in the paper, and maybe the TV, too, on one of the news channels. She might be a reporter."

"And Jameson?" asked Ted.

No one said anything. Stan waited.

Ivy cleared her throat. Everyone turned to her. She seemed reluctant to say what was in her thoughts, then took a deep breath, looked at her hands, and asked in a small voice, "Um, isn't there something about the Prodigal Project, and um, Azul Dante, that is the connector here? I mean, in speaking with each of you, at different times, I know every one of us has . . . questions . . . about it. It's like, the message from Dante kind of skirts the issue regarding God's plan for our world or, more specifically, anything having to do with Jesus Christ. I know in your sermons you have supported Dante and the Project, Reverend Smith, and I understand this church was actually formed to support it."

Smith frowned.

"But there is a difference," continued Ivy. "Your sermons take us to the Bible, Reverend, to Jesus. You are strong, and focused, and right." She sat back and ran the fingers of her left hand through her hair. She winced, her surgery scar still sensitive, quickly covered her ribs with her right hand, and shrugged. "That's all."

"Well," said Ron tentatively, "we know who the seven are, now we have to figure out what it is we're supposed to *do*." He turned to Stan and again they all looked at him.

"*Well*," responded Stan, folding his hands in front of his chin, "why don't you pray about it?"

CHAPTER TWELVE

"Stand up!" shouted and signaled the jumpmaster on the huge C-141 as it leveled off in the night sky over the reaches of the border area between Morocco and Algeria. Four lines of paratroopers stood, their camouflaged faces like miniature abstract paintings, their eyes bright. Helmet chin straps gave the young faces a determined look, even if butterflies fluttered inside many a soul.

"Hook up!" shouted the jumpmaster. "Count off!" The voices of the troopers barked out in sequence. "Check your equipment!" The plane veered suddenly, then straightened, and the jumpmaster, all of his signals exaggerated for clarity, pointed at the threshold of the two side doors and called, "Stand at the door!" The first troopers took their positions, staring into the howling gale that blew alongside the fuselage of the aircraft, staring into the night below, staring into their own destiny.

There was a pause, a collective holding of breath, a moment of suspended animation while the miles and seconds ticked away. The order filled the jumpmaster's headphones even as the traditional green light flashed.

"GO!"

Like a giant metal sky creature, a roaring dragon with wings of fire, the huge aircraft began disgorging its young, who fell away and downward as the beast plunged through the darkness. Beside the aircraft was another, and another, lines of them in flight, and great reaches of Earth passed beneath their aloof and condescending wings as they spawned the children of Mars. At that moment the night was cut and torn by anti-aircraft fire, which burned tendrils of scar tissue through the darkness as it passed. Missiles clawed the air, and exploding bursts of fire opened like instant tears in the violent tapestry. Here and there a giant, metal sky creature was holed by the tracers, troopers still strapped in mangled and burst by their impact, falling in agony against their comrades as the others watched in horror. Here and there one of the roaring dragons was hit by a missile, to explode into an expanding fireball and become a tumbling mass of charred junk, falling toward Earth in a molten, blistering moment. Others veered away, one wing folding with graceful certainty, troopers tumbling out of the wreckage even as it collided with another to take it down in a long, terrible fall. As the roar faded, the night became a fluttering thing, a whispering place, where warriors drifted and turned on silk while their hands gripped the steel implements of death. For everything there is a season, and this was a season of swords, not plowshares.

The first paratroopers touched the ground, and those who had not already had the life punched out of them by the hungry, searing bullets of the enemy began their grisly work. They went about it with a vengeance, having seen the carnage visited upon them as they fell, witnessing still the burning aircraft, the tumbling bodies overhead. The mujahideen forces of General Izbek Noir were dug in, well provisioned and armed, and prepared. They had been alerted to the coming attack by their leaders, and when the skies were fat with the enemy, they had cried out to Allah and opened fire.

The Coalition Forces, who wore the flag patch of their own country and one made from the design of the Prodigal Project insignia, were prepared also. Where Muslim fire reached out, Coalition fire was returned. Attack aircraft and helicopters swarmed the edges of the drop zone, hurling missiles, cannon, and automatic weapon fire at targets too many to count. Ships on either side of the Strait of Gibraltar, miles away, launched their smaller missiles in support. As feared, the mujahideen had held their own attack and fighter aircraft out of battle, until now. They came, rocketing through the night, seeking the electronic "lock" that would send their air-to-air missiles screaming out in search of Coalition aircraft. These elements, too, were met with fire, and the skies became a place of shrieking death. Their attack helicopters whirled in, and the air became a six-axis jungle where awkward and ferocious metallic insects fought and died, their fiery ends a fall of clattering wreckage and writhing bodies.

On the north coast, again in the Moroccan-Algerian border area, war came as Coalition ships disgorged wallowing, bellowing chariots of steel, which formed up in waves and growled toward the beaches wreathed in tracer fire. Geysers erupted throughout their formation as the mujahideen shore defenses threw everything they had at their attackers. They had listened as their leaders told them that the more Coalition infidels destroyed before they reached the beaches, the less would have to be hunted down later. They were dug in, and in many places had constructed hardened concrete bunkers to house their guns. They had ground and air radar, too, of course, and even a limited smart weapon capability, secured by their supreme commander from their vanquished foes, and from foolish Muslim arms traders who thought to indebt General Izbek Noir. Some of these flashed and ripped into the support ships standing offshore, turning hulls into red-hot charnel houses, decks into twisted and canted fields of blood.

The Coalition ships of the line took the mujahideen shore battery sites under fire immediately upon them being spotted and identified. Old-style battleships reared back as flights of sixteen-inch shells left their guns in a billowing shroud of smoke and fire. Describing their path with the sound of freight trains waffling through the air, they fell on their targets with unimaginable fury, destroying Muslim defenses in powerful, repeated, accurate firestorms. Under this umbrella of steel waddled the amphibious armored personnel carriers, behind them the battle tanks, and rocking and jolting inside came the soldiers and marines, armed with their assault rifles and their faith.

No politician or diplomat, no world leader, not even the rising superstar Azul Dante wanted to use the word *crusade*. That word carried with it the connotation of religious war, and the modern world at peace had assimilated many varied religions into many cultures and societies. The Muslim religion had been rapidly growing worldwide at the time of the disappearances, and no national leader wanted to lose the trust of a sizable part of the population by insulting or angering it. America, especially, had problems with this because of its very formation and belief in religious freedom. No one of any faith, Muslim, Jew, Christian, any variation or sects within those larger groups, or any other faith, was to be harassed, excluded, or discriminated against in any way. Strains were put on this with the aggressive terrorist activities of fanatical fringe Muslim groups, and leaders struggled to control it. With the worldwide ascension of Izbek Noir and his Muslim mujahideen, things had changed. Muslim fanatics warred against other Muslims, the center of the African continent had been eaten out, South America scarred, parts of the Far East ripped apart, and the Middle Eastern states trampled. The line had been drawn, and when Izbek Noir ran out of other

Muslim societies and countries to dominate, he turned toward the rest of the free world. The internecine battles had destroyed many Muslims, yes, but they had also swollen his ranks and strengthened his soldiers through battlefield experience and the martial spoils of war. When Azul Dante formed the European Coalition, supported by his worldwide Prodigal Project, a Christian faith-based group, and stood against the mujahideen, this conflict became a crusade . . . a crusade to stop the destruction of the world.

Soldiers have always carried their faith into battle with them, of course, or they join the ranks of the foxhole faithful the first time they experience the hot, foul breath of death, close and personal. The extremely finite moment between life and death, living and *not* living, is exacerbated in combat. A soldier turns to his friend to say something, turns back a second later, and his friend is a broken, burst, and bleeding thing with staring eyes, mouth stretched in a silent scream. Gone. The soldier reaches out sometimes, in the darkest hours before dawn, to lightly touch the thin, diaphanous membrane stretched so finely between life's potential and death's cessation. Faith in God lets him look on the other side of that delicate curtain, tells him to fight for life, but not fear death, tells him there *is* no ending of potential, only a continuation of life.

On the huge battlefield, convulsed with fire, explosion, and death, all the machines of war were actively engaged or standing by in reserve. Tanks and other armored tracked units rumbled across the terrain, helicopters and jet aircraft roared overhead, and huge ships stood offshore, their guns blasting. It finally came down, like all war on Earth, to the individual warriors. Men and women, protected by basic body armor, armed with light weapons and resolve, had to get up from the ground, lean into the storm of fire and lead that tore at them, and close with the men who were their enemy. The defining battle in war pits flesh and blood against flesh and blood; the eyes of the enemy, his voice, his smell, his strength, weaknesses, and heart, are *right there*. His face is stretched as he rises to throw a grenade at you, his eyes wide as he fires his assault rifle on full automatic into your ranks. When your fire reaches him, you hear him scream or call out for his mother in a strange tongue. Perhaps you hear him laughing as he machine-guns your wounded brothers, or you hear him beg for mercy as you offhandedly shoot him and move on. War up close is personal. You smell the food of the enemy, his waste, his rotting body. The human being that is the enemy has a face, and only the infantry warrior sees it.

"Hey, lieutenant," called the Coalition Force sergeant, "we got one that speaks English." The sergeant was nineteen years old, from Atlanta, Georgia. He and the men in his squad had moved against a line of bunkers near the center of the front lines, which faced west. It was an area of sand and rock, where most buildings and dwellings had been reduced to rubble. They had fired rocket-propelled grenades at the gunports in the bunkers, had thrown white phosphorous grenades, and advanced under the cover of machine-gun fire. They had lost three killed, three wounded in the assault, and had routed the mujahideen fighters, who fell back across exposed ground to another position. Their ranks had been decimated in that move. Three had come out of the dirt, their empty hands raised high, pleading for mercy. The Coalition Force soldiers had been told to take prisoners for their intelligence value as much as for the conduct and code of war.

The lieutenant, who was twenty-two, a member of the German infantry who was raised by his grandparents in Hamburg, looked out of the open ramp of the armored personnel carrier with curiosity. "You have searched them?" he asked the sergeant. "We patted 'em down, but we haven't strip-searched them yet, sir." He jerked a thumb over his shoulder at the three forlorn, dirty and bloody mujahideen fighters, and added, "Brought them over here pronto because this one speaks the English, and seems to know the disposition of forces to our front."

"Very good," said the lieutenant. He motioned to the three prisoners, and they stepped forward awkwardly, their eyes downcast, their beards matted and filthy. As they got closer, the taller one in the middle mumbled something. The lieutenant and the sergeant leaned close to try to understand. The mujahideen straightened, grinned, and exploded with a punching, squeezing blast that ripped outward in volcanic expansion, tearing and burning everything within a thirty-foot circle. The lieutenant, sergeant, six other Coalition Force soldiers, and the three mujahideen died instantly. Many nearby were wounded, and more were burned as they moved in to treat their comrades.

+   +   +

Izbek Noir had gone to ground. The mujahideen supreme commander had let his generals on the Morocco-Algeria front control the battles there without interference. They had their clear instructions. He knew he could not maintain a two-front war for long and understood the Coalition Forces were using Spain as a willing springboard to put large numbers of troops on the ground in North Africa. The other front was the one in northern Iraq. The Coalition Force battalions were massing in Turkey, prepared to launch at any time. Noir saw the North Africa campaign as one of delay and attrition. Every kilometer of worthless ground the Coalition Forces took on their long march east toward Egypt, then across the Red Sea into Saudi Arabia, would be soaked with the blood of the fallen. It didn't matter whether they were fallen mujahideen or Coalition troops, death was death, and delay on one side meant more forces or logistical reinforcements on the other. A war of attrition, he liked the sound of that. Attrition was the wearing down, the constant erosion of men and materials, the constant assault on the senses, the never-ending battering of the heart. Thousands of body bags stuffed with what used to be sons and daughters, what used to be hopes, dreams, what used to be the future. It would be like that delightful "Great War," he mused, when there were so many dead the government simply printed long lists and posted them, and the sad mothers had to line up, necks craning while they whispered impotent prayers, their frightened eyes finding the names of their sons but reading up and down the list anyway, in the vain hope the name would not be there the next time they looked.

His strategy of delay and attrition meant the mujahideen fighters were prepared to fight fanatically for every inch, falling back only to the next line of defense, there to stand again. While the mujahideen infantry held the Coalition Forces in the deadly, grinding bear hug, he would use his limited air power, including his arsenal of obsolete tactical missiles, to hit anyplace the armies of Azul Dante and his Prodigal Project–backed Coalition massed. His desire was to inflict casualties. It would come down to a test of will, like most wars. Which side could continue the fight? Which side would be worn down, its desire and confidence weakened, its resolve washed away in the flood of mothers' tears?

Again, in his center, Izbek Noir did not care. What he wanted was to prolong the horror of war, to make the killing go on. What he wanted was death, death again and again, the death of men by the thousands. The very population of the earth had already been diminished by the disappearances, the chaos and government breakdowns that followed, the earthquakes, the burning hail, the global famine on the heels of the loss of crops. He was almost jubilant when Azul Dante had finally stopped preening and declared war. To him, it seemed Dante took his own sweet time forming his Coalition, and he wondered if the real fighting was ever going to start. Now, finally, it was on, and a gut-busting *religious* war at that. The best kind, in *his* view.

He had sent out another pep-talk communiqué, reminding his mujahideen hordes that their common enemy was the Christian infidels, backed by the hated Jews. It was the pure Muslim manhood against the mobs who turned away from the one true faith, and only the mujahideen believers could stop them. He included the little cachet about the paradise rewards that awaited brave Muslims who died fighting for Allah as a sweetener. Man, whom he considered a primitive beast at best, was so easily manipulated, actually *motivated* by this nonsense, it became entertaining for him. The slaughter would be immense, he knew, and his greedy bloodlust fired his imagination and coursed through him like electricity.

Then, after seeing his plans set in motion, he fell from the radar screen. The Coalition Forces had those irritating smart weapons, like the old cruise missile, and every time his headquarters group was located the missiles and attack aircraft came thundering down. He could shake it off, and did, but it cost him staff personnel, Muslim career military men of different nations who understood

men and materials, weapons, logistics . . . bullets, beans,
and the means to get them to the front lines. These attacks on his headquarters also played havoc with his communications capabilities, and these he needed. So he had
prepared an elaborate game board of hide-and-seek,
using body doubles, false headquarters units, and radio-
electronic and computer-enhanced counterfeit signals.
The Coalition listeners might think they had pinpointed
the location of Noir's headquarters, only to send a flight
of missiles at a three-quarter-ton truck squatting in the
sand, one hapless believer sitting under the hot metal
cover, sending out a barrage of false signals that left the
headquarters' footprint. His favorite ruses were the ones
he set up, secretly, within the walls of hospitals, large
markets, and mosques in the many countries already
under mujahideen control. He would watch CNN and,
even better, the Al-Jazeera telecasts, highly indignant
correspondents almost apoplectic over the wanton destruction of Islamic holy or noncombatant places. These
reports would make their way to the Muslim soldiers, of
course, and they would be like gasoline thrown onto the
flames of hatred. Yes, he mused, these were fruitful times.

He had literally gone to ground, finding the dark and
dank spaces within ancient and forgotten tombs of those
whose souls he already possessed. It was an accidental
catacomb, a place of massacres followed years later by
new massacres, the dead thrown haphazardly on top of
one another in natural caves and folds in the earth. The
dead lay tangled in intimate repose in a mass grave, all

dignity stripped from them. This was such a place of
bones, still echoing, to his ear, with the screams of the
damned. It was his place, within the putrid stench of
decay, the grinning proof that man's time always runs
out. His staff continued the propaganda war in his absence, the news agencies of the world still very interested
in him, his views, his desires, his plans. They seemed to
like his sound bites, and his photo ops were guaranteed to
include plenty of gore. He thought then of that American combat photographer, who had come to him with the
journalist, Cat Early.

Seven, he thought, hunched in the darkness, his hands
rubbing the smooth contours of a dusty skull. Then he
thought of the one called Johann Rommel, or Jameson.
Seven, again. Came to him as a Westerner, a Muslim warrior . . . and a fighter he was, no doubt. But he wasn't
Dutch, passport or no, and he did not act like the mujahideen rabble he fought beside. He closed his eyes,
kissed the top of the skull, breathed deep the smell of
bone, and thought, Now I have sent him to kill the one
who has chosen to be called Azul Dante. I believe he will
try. He rubbed his wicked lips across the zippered fissures
in the bone. He wondered how Dante would react. Certainly he knows I have sent him, and he will understand
why. He will be amused and pleased. His eyes suddenly
widened, glowing red orbs with piercing gold centers,
and his tongue slithered serpentlike around his lips before withdrawing as he growled, low and edgy, But I

wonder how Monsieur Dante feels about seven . . . and I wonder what he will do about it.

+   +   +

Armored units led the charge across the border from Turkey into Iraq. A massive artillery and aerial barrage fell with a thunderous roar, and before the smoke and dust cleared the tanks came rumbling and clanking, their main guns blazing. Above them came the air support helicopters and attack aircraft, looking for trouble. The old battlefields around Mosul and Erbil once again became places of carnage and death, and in many places the wrecked and rusted hulks of dead tanks from previous conflicts received high explosive rounds through their hulls. Again the mujahideen fighters had their orders, again the plan was delay and attrition. Bitter fighting took place between the free Kurds and the mujahideen, and General Reginald Urquhart, the Coalition Forces' supreme commander, unashamedly took advantage of it to bring his first units up. In a war without rules, a war already marked by cruel and merciless actions by both sides, this conflict between the Kurds and the mujahideen was particularly foul. No quarter was expected or given, and lucky was the soldier who simply died in battle.

On the northern Iraq front, as it was along the battlefields of North Africa, the noncombatants suffered horribly. There were no children, of course, but there were women and elderly. They were caught up in the fire. The mujahideen forces viewed the women as theirs for the taking, and they were taken. The elderly were simply in the way, except when used as "human shields." The Coalition Forces did their best to protect the noncombatants but were often powerless to prevent the wholesale slaughter.

War, unleashed and encouraged, ravaged across half the earth.

CHAPTER THIRTEEN

Cat Early filed a lengthy story about Azul Dante, his Prodigal Project, and his apparent vision for the world. It was a positive piece, overall, the only doubts discussed had to do with the state of the world, the difficulties in managing a diverse collection of cultures and government, and the unpredictable nature of war. In the story Cat described Dante's wish to be "in the background." He would let the military professionals make battlefield decisions. He would stand behind them with the resources of the Prodigal Project, a vast and growing network of people from around the globe who desired peace, stability, and prosperity. Dante did not doubt the outcome of this war, she wrote, and kept his eyes on the future, a future where the world would need an organization, and a leader, who could make it whole again. In the article, she had carefully mentioned her observation that Azul Dante, through the Prodigal Project, was poised to become *the* leader of the postwar world, the positives and negatives of this, the ramifications and complexities of a single-faith world power.

The article that appeared in major newspapers, excerpted in one or two news magazines, and quoted on CNN, did not contain these observations or ramifications. They had been edited out.

"Nice is nice," said Slim, "Been there twice." He and Cat stood on the sidewalk outside her hotel in Bern, waiting for a hired car. They were traveling together to the lovely vacation beach town in the south of France where Azul Dante was next scheduled to appear. Dante would host an international gathering of Prodigal Project leaders, there to discuss world needs, growth issues, finances, and other matters concerning the organization. They would lay the groundwork for a proposed upcoming international convention of actual church leaders from New Christian Cathedrals worldwide. One matter to be settled was the choice of location for the upcoming convention. Israel had been considered, as had Spain and Italy. Many felt these countries were simply too close to the crazed mujahideen armies, and perhaps Izbek Noir had weapons that could reach such a gathering. Paris, again, was discussed, but the French had lost so much credibility over the last decade some felt it would be inappropriate to gather there. London was a maybe, and Azul Dante himself had hinted a city in America be considered. It was still relatively safe there, and American Prodigal Project organizations provided a disproportionate share of collected revenues, personnel, and resources. The planned convention of church leaders was, as Dante was quoted as saying, "a meeting to look beyond war, to look to the future, to a world at peace under a central, strong, leadership."

Slim was so pleased to be working with Cat again he let other worries slip away. He tried to put aside his thoughts of her and Jameson, his heartache that came with the realization that he and Cat were the "best of friends" and always would be. He tried to discipline himself to be grateful for their relationship, to be glad for their friendship, to accept it and enjoy it, and forget about being more to her. Besides, he *liked* John Jameson. Other than the fact that Jameson was a hard guy, a spook, and probably wouldn't survive much longer in the dangerous game he played, Slim thought he was a good man who would be good for Cat. He wasn't sure, but he had the feeling Cat thought so, too.

"I know why you like Nice," replied Cat with a grin.

"Great hotels, fine restaurants," said Slim, "international airport, close to Italy, good wine, sunshine, long beaches facing the pristine waters of the Mediterranean . . ."

"French girls who wear only half a bathing suit."

"Well," admitted Slim, "yeah."

Cat rolled her eyes. She, too, enjoyed their being together again. She knew Slim would do anything for her, and had shown this more than once. She loved him dearly, as a friend and companion, and respected him as a fellow combat journalist. Slim was easy to travel with, a veteran who kept his gear light, his focus on work, and his professional enthusiasm undiminished.

Their car, arranged by Simon Blake, her editor in Paris, arrived. They had a full day on the road ahead of them, out of Bern, through Geneva, then south on those high-speed French highways to Nice. Blake would also be there, and had reserved a room for Cat in the same small hotel. The Prodigal Project meetings were to take place in the Hilton Nice, not far away. The driver was an older Italian man, portly, polite, and quiet. Slim sat in front with him—she knew he was prone to motion sickness if he sat in back too long—and talked about food. Cat spread out in the backseat with her laptop, writing, watching the scenery flow past, and thinking of John Jameson and the secret she still held like a hot ember against the skin of her heart. Every fiber of her professional and personal self reverberated with the knowledge of his confessed mission. She had told no one. Could she let it happen? She wondered again. Would he *make it* happen? She bit her lower lip and let her memory play over their last moments together.

+   +   +

It had been in the Bern safe house. They were alone, the house quiet, Slim out to "take the air."

They knelt together, holding hands, and prayed. After the prayer they sat on the carpet, still holding hands.

"I think it's great that you and Slim will travel together

down to Nice, Cat," he said. "I know you can handle yourself, but Slim is a good guy, and he's dedicated to keeping you out of trouble, if that's possible." He had not said anything further regarding his mission in Nice, or if they would even see each other there. "I'll make contact with you, when I can, Cat," he said. "And maybe we can share a bit more time."

"Maybe," she replied with a small smile. She liked to watch his eyes watch her as she spoke to him. He was a powerful man, and he looked at her as if she was a *woman*. There was sadness in his eyes, too, loss, and concern. The moments they shared were rich for her. She found comfort in being near him, his strength, his warmth. She had not been in the arms of a man in quite a while and already knew she would be comfortable in his.

"*Seven* is real, Cat." he said. "And I can't tell you why, exactly, but it brings me comfort . . . knowing you are a part of it, with me. It is a simple thing to say seven is a classically *Biblical* number, but it has become immediately more to me, because of you, and because I truly believe not one thing happens in our world without some reason, purpose, or plan. God's plan."

"Will you tell me about your relationship with . . . God?" asked Cat, "With . . . Jesus?"

He fidgeted a moment, then asked, "Do you think they would have tea bags in a safe house?"

She followed him into the kitchen. Together they found cups and tea and fired up a pot of water on a battered stove top with a forty-five-degree list. They leaned against opposite counters as they waited for the water to boil.

"My wife's name was Sylvia," Jameson said shyly. She guessed he felt suddenly awkward talking about the woman he had loved for so long . . . to her. "She was . . ." he said, "I loved her and we had a good marriage and raised two good kids until they all were . . . until the disappearances." He looked at her evenly. "I always felt I didn't deserve her." He crossed his arms and looked down at his boots.

She waited.

"I've already told you she was into her church, with the kids, and tried to get me into it, Cat," he said. "But, you know, I traveled, had my work, no time. After the disappearances, though, her Bible was there, and I *seized* it, and she was there, her voice, helping me." He looked up at her and grinned. "Cat, it was all just *right there*. God, I already believed in; Jesus was more abstract. But as I read, even as I went to my headquarters, watched the world convulse, got my assignment from my boss, went for a submarine ride, for crying out loud. I don't know . . . Jesus became real. He became *alive* for me, and when He did, I simply *accepted* Him." He stopped, shook his head, and said quietly, "It's hard to explain."

The water steamed and she poured the tea.

"God is real?" she asked. "Scripture is real? Jesus was born to Mary, died on the cross, and rose again . . . for us?"

"Yes," he said simply.

His sincerity, his wondrous, quietly joyful certainty hugged her soul and made her long for the same faith. She knew the Bible was alive for him, Christ was as real as the earth he stood upon, and this life was a gift from God no matter what kind of life it was. She bathed in his strength and felt empowered by him.

She squeezed the tea bags, found some pretend sugar in little bags in the cupboard, and handed him a cup of the tea. She took a chance, her heart thumping, and asked, "What about us, John? You and me. We both have our work, the world is rocking and rolling around our ears, you are on the move, and so am I. Do you think we'll see each other again, after we leave Bern?"

"I hope so, Cat," he said as he watched her face. "I really do." He paused, sipped his tea, and added, "If these are the end times, as described in Revelation, it doesn't mean we . . . people . . . men, and women, should stop, uh . . . living. If we accept that God has a plan, and I do, then we must continue on with life, the *living* of life." He cleared his throat, grinned at her sheepishly, and said, "Like man and woman. You know, living life as God's children." He hesitated.

She watched the conflicting emotions ripple across his face and waited.

"Ah," he said. "I'm not saying it right. Look, Cat, if there are two days left in this world, two months, two minutes, or a thousand years, it doesn't matter to me. I am going to *work*, to do my job as whatever part of the plan God has for me. I am going to thank God every day for each breath, and for meeting you. I want to see you again, be with you, spend time with you. I don't know what our world will be like, I never thought about being with a woman until I met you, and all I'm telling you is if there *is* a future, I want to be in it with you."

She did not know what to say and reached out for his hands. She smiled at him, swept with emotion, and said quietly, "John. Say a prayer for us, for our future, for . . . us."

They stood close, holding hands, their heads bowed together, touching. He prayed for strength, and clarity of vision, for guidance, direction, and help in doing whatever big or small thing they could to further God's plan. He prayed for her safekeeping, for a guardian angel to watch over her through the upcoming struggles, who might, if God willed it, keep her from harm's way. After he said "Amen," overwhelming emotion flooded her heart—a mixture of joy, sadness, longing, and hope. He put his arms around her and they hugged tightly, their bodies warm, their hearts beating in concert. Before they parted, he had tenderly kissed away her tears. She had backed away slightly, just enough to look deeply into his eyes for a long time.

+   +   +

John Jameson was on his way to Nice from Marseille, just down a bit along the coast. The two towns could not be more different, he thought. Nice was *nice* . . . touristy, crowded sometimes, but a vacation place, a place where people went to relax. Marseille, on the other hand, was brawny, noisy, tricky, and driven. Marseille had a long history of waterfront intrigue, of organized crime, narcotics in and out, fast money, false identities, instantly rich arms dealers, and unidentified bodies floating to the surface next to the docks.

He had taken up lodging in a seedy motel he knew of that had a back room for private business. From there he was able to contact Mike Tsakis at CIA headquarters in Langley, Virginia, once more. Through their own form of doublespeak, he was able to tell Tsakis where he was headed, and that had made a decision regarding the action he would take. He discussed escape and evasion tactics he would need after the action. He was believed dead, or if alive, a rogue agent acting illegally. He could not use any of the resources the Agency had in place in the area; he had to go it alone. But, like many old hands, he had constructed an informal network of sources through the years, and told Tsakis he had two possible methods he might use in this case. Italy was nice this time of year, he had hinted, and close. Tsakis agreed, told him to play the whole thing for real. Tsakis had learned his boss, Benjamin Carter, had gleaned volunteers from various U.S. intelligence agencies for a top-secret assignment. They were to protect Azul Dante now that war had begun. The volunteers, Tsakis learned, were all "believers," as he described them to Jameson. They were hard guys, former Special Operations types, and they believed in America's covenant with Azul Dante and the Prodigal Project.

Jameson had thanked him for the heads-up, and they disconnected.

Jameson did not tell Tsakis how he came to make his decision. He had prayed with Cat Early before they said good-bye, and after he was on his way to Marseille, when he was quiet and deep within his thoughts, he prayed—just he and Jesus Christ. He simply gave himself over to his Lord, asking for help, for guidance. He had learned prayer worked best for him when he could really focus. He would make himself relax and give himself over to the *communing* with God, with Christ. He asked for nothing for himself; rather, he asked for the Lord's blessing and care on Cat and Slim, and for strength and surety of purpose that would allow him to carry out an act that went against the laws of man and God. As always, after he finished, he felt refreshed and rejuvenated. He did not expect an answer immediately, but believed his prayers were heard, and an answer, or direction, would be forthcoming.

After he left the small hotel, he had made his way to an area on the edges of the waterfront. There he pulled the bell-ring on a large wooden door in a stucco wall that opened into a tiled courtyard filled with flowers and hanging baskets. Behind the wall sat a small villa half covered with vines. In the basement of the villa was the heart of the place. A specialist lived and worked in the walled villa, an old one-legged South African who had made a good living for years selling specialized firearms to spooks of all stripe, good guys or bad guys, didn't matter. Money was all the credential they needed. He worked only with professionals, however, and considered the modern terrorist, any terrorist, a loser amateur, and he would not deal with them. He had been genuinely pleased to see John Jameson again. He did not know Jameson's real name, of course, and would have considered it bad form to ask. He was surprised by Jameson's request, because it was a weapon for a special type of killer, and he had not known Jameson to do that kind of operation in the past. The weapon did not have to be an "exotic," that is, it didn't have to be of a custom caliber, or handcrafted to pass as some innocent piece of equipment. It could use standard ammunition and did not have to be cut down or modified.

The old South African listened. "Would the piece need a silencer?" he asked. Jameson told him no, noise would be helpful for this scenario. The man pulled on one ear, shrugged, and said, "Wait." He went into an adjoining room and in a few minutes came out with two he thought might work. He and Jameson discussed the pros and cons of each piece. Jameson hefted them, worked with them, and finally they agreed on one. The old man's eye lit up when he saw the diamonds Jameson offered as currency, and spit as he spoke of the Eurodollar. They shook hands and the South African bid Jameson adieu as he held a heavy steel door open and stood aside. Jameson nodded, passed through the door, and walked almost half a block under the streets of Marseille through a lighted tunnel that finally exited in the storage room of a bakery owned by the South African's son-in-law. Jameson walked another block farther away from there to his nondescript rental car, carrying a soft-sided cello case on a strap over his shoulder. He threw the case into the backseat of the car and headed out of Marseille for Nice. In the case sat a bolt-action German Mauser, .308 caliber, with a powerful scope, and one box of copper-jacketed bullets. It was a basic, industrial-strength sniper rifle. It was nothing fancy, but in the hands of a marksman, a professional, it would be most effective. John Jameson was both.

+   +   +

Sophia Ghent, well aware that Azul Dante was in conversation only a few feet away, shook hands with Cat Early rather stiffly, smiled, and said, "So glad to see you again, Miss Early." She looked at the rugged, rather careworn young man who stood beside Cat, cameras dangling, eyes taking in everything in the open room, and asked, "And who is with you? A photojournalist, of course, but have we met?"

"Slim Piedmont," said Cat, "meet Sophia Ghent, Minister Dante's personal assistant."

"Miss Ghent," said Slim as he shook Sophia's soft hand. He wanted to ask, *How personal?* But Cat had warned him to be on his best behavior or they'd be tossed out of the room in the blink of an eye.

Sophia looked at the cameras hanging on the rangy young man and added, "As I'm sure you know, Mr. Piedmont, Minister Dante finds too many cameras focusing on him rather tiresome, so he always arranges for what you journalists call a 'pool' photographer to record the event. Then all the major news organizations tap into that one source for their photographs."

"Of course," replied Slim politely. I know another big shot who is also pretty weird about having his photograph taken, he thought. Who wants to shoot this boring stuff, anyway? He liked the way Sophia Ghent looked, though, and wondered if she'd like to hear some fun war stories someday.

Sophia stared at Cat intently, and Cat said quietly, "I managed to check around a bit. See you in the loo?"

A few minutes later Sophia rushed into the ladies' room, grabbed some paper towels, wet them, and dabbed her eyes carefully. She hugged Cat impulsively, then stood with her arms folded, waiting.

"James Devane is alive, well, and apparently still with the U.S. State Department, but working the diplomatic end of things. He is known, but what he really does is not so clear. He is here, now."

"He's *here*?" said Sophia, her eyes widening. "In *Nice*?"

"That's the word I got," said Cat. She hesitated, then added, "I passed on your message, Sophia, and I'm pretty sure my contact can get it to him." Sophia reached out and took Cat's hands in hers, and Cat squeezed them and went on. "But you must remember he's *working*, and you are working, and your boss, arguably the most important man in the world right now, has put the hex on James Devane somehow. I mean, Dante doesn't want you two communicating. Things are going to be busy here, so it might not be possible . . ."

"You are telling me he might not call me, yes?" said Sophia. "You are concerned about my feelings?"

"Yes."

"You are very nice, Cat Early."

Cat grinned. "Just another hopeless romantic, that's me. Let's get out of here."

The function, a glorified cocktail party and reception for Dante, was uneventful. Dante knew Cat Early was there, had Sophia pass word to her that he saw her last article on him and thought it was "quite good," then ignored her. That was okay with Cat. She and Slim made note of who was there, and she spoke with a few of the Prodigal Project people, whom she thought were very sincere, informative, and nice. She sensed nothing outwardly sinister about them and came away with the feeling they really believed they could make positive changes in a world gone mad. She also managed to introduce Slim to her boss, Simon Blake, who had used some of Slim's work in the past. They all went back to their rooms fairly early, to get rested for the long day tomorrow.

Cat wanted to access an e-mail that had been forwarded to her from the Paris office that afternoon. She wondered where John Jameson was.

+   +   +

Azul Dante, along with French politicians and members of the Prodigal Project staff, were to motorcade to the principality of Monaco the next morning, there to embrace the young heir, attend a dinner in Dante's honor, and glad-hand members of the very rich, who held the citizenship awarded to them by the rulers of the tiny domain. They were to leave the Hilton in Nice after breakfast, and, as was usual wherever Azul Dante was, a crowd of onlookers was expected. The local French gendarmes were already being pushed around by their condescending comrades from the National Security Forces in Paris. Security specialists provided by other countries, including the United States, competed with one another zealously. Their very number, and the crisscrossed chain of command, made for an awkward, almost Keystone Cop–like situation, with often the left hand not knowing what the right was doing. Azul Dante, for his part, never seemed to worry much about his own security, though, content to let his hosts take care of it.

CHAPTER FOURTEEN

They gathered in the nave, in the shadow of the reaching pulpit. The New Christian Cathedral in Selma, Alabama, had finally emptied, the group of worshipers larger than it had been the past few weeks because word went out that the Reverend Henderson Smith was back. He had conducted a low-key service, almost sweet in its introspection, his prayers for them all textured to show his pain, his desire for forgiveness, his need for direction. "Keep the faith," he had said, after closing his Bible and looking out at the upturned faces. "Such a simple phrase, but *loaded*. Faith? Faith in what? Faith in tomorrow, or justice, or reason? Faith in redemption, faith in salvation? Keep it, *keep* it? Keep it where? Tucked into your Bible, to bring it out now and then, dusty words from dusty pages falling impotently against your dusty heart? Keep it in an ornate gold cross like the one I have at my throat? Keep it in fancy words and grand oration? No, brothers and sisters. You keep the faith even as you would keep the flame. You keep the flame of light, heat, warmth, promise. You keep the flame of covenant with Jesus Christ, the one true way to salvation. All of us here in this beautiful church know sometimes there are troublesome, or even evil, winds that blow against our faith. The flames flicker, clinging to the thin wick of hope, the smoke of lost dreams spinning away like the woven threads of heartache."

He had closed his eyes and turned his face heavenward. Nateesha Folks, standing with the choir behind and below him, heard his words and knew he was speaking to himself as much as anyone in that church. "Oh, God," he pleaded, "please help me to keep the sweet and pure faith in Your Son, my Lord, Jesus Christ, my *Savior,* in my heart. Help me keep the flame burning, help me protect my flame from insidious evil, from misdirection, from false promise, and yes, from my own ego and greed. Let the flame that is my faith cast a bright and knowing light across the darkness of my poor soul, so that I might see *clearly* the promises of my covenant with you. I am just a man, Lord, a tiny, clumsy creature who is nothing without Your flame, without faith. I want to stand tall when it comes the day for me to stand before You . . . I want to stand tall. Let me keep my faith undiminished, let me keep my flame forever bright. Amen."

After the congregation filed out, after the many handshakes, kisses, pats on the shoulder, smiles, and encouraging words exchanged with the reverend, the New

Christian Cathedral became empty and quiet. Henderson Smith, Nateesha Folks, Ted Glenn, Shannon Carpenter, Ivy Sloan-Underwood, Ron Underwood, and Stan stood in a loose circle under the aspiring, ascending pulpit. Stan, who wore a linen suit with a matching tie adorned with tiny cherubs, seemed relaxed but subdued. It was as if he understood he was to be more observer than participant on this day. His eyes burned with a new intensity, and he leaned forward as if to hang on every spoken word.

"Let's join hands," said Smith. They did, Stan between Nateesha and Ted, who both felt an energy ripple through their skin when they touched his fingers. They bowed their heads and Smith began, "Lord Jesus Christ, please hear us now as we pray to You for direction and strength. Hear the words of our sister, Shannon, as she speaks for us."

Stan raised his eyes momentarily and glanced at the reverend.

Shannon did not lift her head, but was momentarily caught off-balance. Then she cleared her throat and said, "Lord, we are here, apparently called here for a purpose not made clear to us at first. We have found strength here, through our faith in You, and through the friendships we have formed. We are as brothers and sisters here, Your children. We have grown, through our pain, loss, anger, temptations, and confusion, we have grown through Your promise." She took a breath and lifted her head to look at the faces around her. "Now, Lord," she continued, "we have determined we are a part of seven, and that seven of us are to work on Your behalf. We, through perhaps a special messenger," she glanced at Stan, who seemed to be studying his fine-grained, sand-colored loafers, "have learned the names of the seven, but we are not all joined yet, as You know." She stopped again, thought about it, and went on. "Now we pray to You, Lord. We ask if You will reveal to us our mission, our purpose. We believe, based on what we have seen and what we have learned from Your sacred Word, that these are the end times. We believe You have a purpose for us that extends beyond our small circle, that it somehow involves the Prodigal Project. But we cannot see our mission clearly. Please, Lord, help us to see what it is we must do. We stand here together, and we stand willing. Only tell us what You will have us do, and we will do it." She squeezed the hands of Glenn and Ron, and ended with, "We ask these things in the name of Jesus Christ. Amen."

They stood silently, holding hands, each wrapped in his or her own thoughts. Shannon hoped her prayer was okay. She sensed the importance of it to the others and wanted it to be right. She had not told the others that she and Ivy had *already* acted on strong feelings that had come on them. Ivy had called her to the office early that morning to show her a Web site she had found on the Net. It listed various news organizations and gave e-mail addresses for some locations and journalists. The name Cat Early was listed, with a forwarding capability through her Paris-based editor, Simon Blake. As they saw this information glowing on the screen, they both knew *right then* what they must do. They talked over the wording for a moment, then Ivy's fingers flew over the keys. She hit the "send" icon and they looked at each other and grinned.

"Excuse me, then, brothers and sisters," said Henderson Smith, breaking into Shannon's thoughts. "I'm a little tired. I think I'll lie down for a while. Perhaps I'll join you for coffee later." He let go of Ivy's hand but still held Nateesha's as he added, "Thank you, Shannon, for that perfect prayer. Let's keep our hearts open, now, and be ready." He and Nateesha walked out of the nave.

"My friends," said Stan. They turned to him. "I must leave you now. Thank you for welcoming me as you have."

"What do you mean?" asked Ron. "Where do you have to go? You're my *lawyer*, remember?"

"Don't go, Stan," said Glenn. "We kinda like havin' you around. You bring a touch of class to our humble little group."

"Why don't you stay?" asked Ivy.

"I'll bet there's more Jell-O in the fridge," added Shannon.

Stan smiled at her and wagged one finger. "Don't be a temptress, Shannon Carpenter. That's not fair." He shook his head at Ron. "You don't need a lawyer, Ron, and I'm not sure I'm cut out for that role." He looked at their faces for a moment, then said, "Thank you, for . . .

your love. But I must do what I must do, and for now I cannot be here." He hesitated, then said quietly, "Perhaps I'm overstepping my bounds, but I am compelled to tell you one more of you, of *seven*, will join you within two days. That, and you, each one of you, will be tested. Stay the course. Remember what Henderson Smith said about keeping the flame. I promise you this—we will meet again." He shook hands with and hugged each of them, then he and Ron walked out of the church. He punched Ron on the shoulder, climbed into the Cadillac, started it up, and drove slowly out of the lot, onto the street, and out of sight. Ron could hear the music from the car radio hanging in the breeze. It sounded like Paul Simon's "Bridge over Troubled Water."

+   +   +

Shannon read the e-mail again. "We are the Prodigal Orphans. You and another there know of a special number. We, together, are that number. Please contact us." It had been sent via the Paris office by Ivy@SelmaNCC.com. "We, together, are that number," she read once more, her eyes wide. Prodigal Orphans. Why *Orphans*? She wanted to be outside the hotel when Azul Dante left this morning, so she shut down the laptop. She would think about responding later. Right now she did not know how she would word her reply to whomever "Ivy" was. Great, we're all a part of seven . . . do you have a clue as to what it *means*?

+   +   +

Thomas Church headed down the highway, south-bound from the University of Virginia campus. He glanced over to see Rebecca in the passenger seat of the battered Bronco, quietly reading his Bible. He wanted to point things out, passages he particularly liked or found informative or challenging, but he held himself in check. He understood that this was *her* journey, and she would make it at her own pace. She was relaxed, gently turning the pages, jumping from the Old Testament to the New, letting her eyes stop at passages that grabbed her atten-tion. He knew from his own experience how rich it was. He kept his eyes on the long stretch of road ahead and thought about their visit with their daughter, Sissy, and her husband, Mitch.

Sissy had opened the door to their small apartment, looked at the two of them standing there, and broken into sobs. She put her arms out, grabbed her mother, and they hugged, both crying. She had a slight build, fine skin, and hair and eyes the color of her mother's. Her hair was cut in a short shag. She pulled back from her mom, looked at her father, reached out one hand and put it on his chest, and began crying again. Mitch stood in-side, watching and nodding, a crooked grin on his bearded face as he watched Sissy.

"Well, Sissy," said Mitch, "back up, girl, and let them come inside." He stepped forward, gave Rebecca a quick hug, and shook hands with Thomas in his awkward and gangly way. He was tall and solid, known for wearing overalls and hiking boots when he taught classes at the university. "How was the trip?" he asked them both. "You guys okay? Want somethin' to drink? Can I help get your bags from the truck?"

"Mitch," said Thomas easily, "we're fine. We've got two bags, we can get them later, and I guess some ice water would be great."

Sissy and Rebecca stood holding on to each other, and Sissy, still crying, said, "I can't believe it. I can't believe it."

"That we're here?" asked her mother.

"That you are *together* again." Something in her voice made Thomas look at her closely. Before he could say anything, Rebecca responded.

"Sissy," she said gently, "your father came looking for me, found me, and asked me to travel with him." She looked over at Thomas, shrugged, and went on. "Truth is, I didn't know what I would say to him . . ."

"I can believe that," said Sissy as she stepped back and crossed her arms. "You two *are* divorced, remember?"

"Sissy . . ." said Mitch.

"What?" cried Sissy. "Why is everyone looking at *me*? I'm not the one who had two kids, a home, a life, then got divorced and shot off in different directions, am I?" She looked at each one of them in turn. "It's just a bit of a jolt, you know? Of course I'm happy you two are together again, but, I mean . . ."

"Sissy," said Thomas. Something in his voice made them all look at him. "*I* failed. I let your mother slip away from me after you and Tommy left the house. It was *me*, not you, not Tommy, and not your mom. It was me." He looked at Rebecca. "Now I feel like I have a second chance, another shot at getting it right. Does it make the pain of what I did go away? No, and I didn't expect to come waltzing in here like, 'Look Sissy, Daddy made everyone good again.' These are crazy times, perhaps the *end* times, and I feel like God is giving me a last chance to be . . . I don't know . . . to be a husband, and a father."

"Sissy," said Rebecca, "when your dad showed up out at that farmhouse where I've been living, I was *ready*. He came all that way for *me*, Sissy, even in these times. That should tell you something, no? And after we visited for a while I knew I wanted to be with him." She looked at her husband and went on. "I want to be with him, but I don't know what we'll be, or *who* we'll be. Like him, I have to say if this world is ending, then I want to be with him when it does."

"I wish we had something stronger than ice water," said Mitch.

Sissy and her mother hugged again, and both cried softly. Mitch and Thomas stood nearby, watching them. Finally Sissy wiped her eyes, smiled at them, and said, "Like you said, crazy times, huh?" She looked at her husband a moment, then back to her mother, and said quietly, "You know I . . . I lost a baby, during the um, disappearances. She was just beginning inside me, but we knew she was there, didn't we Mitch?"

Mitch nodded briskly, his glasses fogged, and he turned away.

"How do you know it was a girl?" asked Thomas quietly.

Sissy shrugged. Then she went on, "Anyway. After your visit, Dad, and our talk, I decided what you said about life going on made sense. If we are part of God's plan, and we *live*, then life goes on. I lost my first baby, but no one knows if there might be *more* babies during these times."

No one said anything. Mitch looked down at his big hands.

"So I guess Mitch and I are doing what you and Dad are doing, Mom," she said with a shy smile. "Accepting another chance from God, and living as man and wife, and praying for a child." She wiped her nose on the back of her arm, rubbed her eyes with the palms of her hands, looked at Thomas and Rebecca, and shrugged. "I love you both, and I'm glad you are here . . . together."

"Good," Rebecca said. "Now. Tell us *everything*."

Sissy told Thomas and Rebecca she had heard from her brother, Tommy. He told her there had been a shooting at that church in Selma, and that he had managed to grab the gunmen. The woman they met named Ivy had been shot, but not killed, he said, and the last he heard she was in the hospital but expected to recover. The crazy man that shot her was in jail and, as far as Tommy was concerned, could stay there. Church had been saddened to hear that, but not surprised his son had put himself in danger again. Sissy told them Tommy's pickup was still running great, that he had traveled all the way down to

Miami Beach and was headed for Ocala, Florida, which was a place he called "horse country." From there he planned to return to Selma, to the Cathedral, to decide whether to make a trip to Europe in search of whatever truths the Prodigal Project had to offer. Sissy had reminded him there was a bit of a war going on, and Tommy just laughed. He told her to tell his father he was pleased old Dad had finally "found the right girl" and was hoping to see them soon. Their parting was bittersweet, but okay, each of them filled with the sense they would not be apart for long.

Church had found that the task of trying to turn his wife, now Rebecca, to the Bible, to the truth found in Scripture, and to Jesus Christ, had in fact become a gift to him. He learned as he taught, gently, at first, patient with her almost defensive New Age responses and explanations. He heard his words to her and felt them impact his own heart. He told her of what Jesus Christ meant, who He was, and discovered him filling his own heart with strength. During the long hours on the road east from Idaho they had talked of their life, their children, what had happened to the world, and finally of what it all meant, the big picture, life, love, and spiritual survival. It came back to the Bible, and when she began to read it, first in argument, then with more sincere interest, he felt a kind of joy, as if he held a fragile bird cupped in the palms of his hands, and felt the tiny, fluttering wings of faith.

He also, to his great delight, fell in love, again, with his wife.

Everything that had attracted him to her so many years ago was still there, actually enhanced by the years of struggle, children, business failure and success, and misunderstanding that led to his losing her. She was beautiful, in his eyes, female, healthy, alive, teasing, serious, sweet, tough and, most importantly, *his*. She was in her forties, with two grown children, many lost dreams and what-ifs behind her. And he loved her totally.

They headed south as friends, young again in their newness, with their recent and shared discoveries. He had told her all about the New Christian Cathedral, of course, about the Reverend Henderson Smith, about him and Tommy meeting the two women he was sure he had known somehow. He had told her about the Prodigal Project, and Azul Dante, confessing to her that in his mind, at least, the jury was still out on it. He also told her, tentatively, about *seven*. It hadn't even phased her. She figured it to be real, and have meaning, and agreed without hesitation that he had no choice but to investigate it fully, to act on it.

He drove while Rebecca sat beside him reading their Bible, and glanced out through the starred windshield at the strange pewter skies.

CHAPTER FIFTEEN

Blurred shapes, colors, objects jumped into sudden focus as John Jameson adjusted the powerful scope mounted on the Mauser sniper rifle. He put the crosshairs on a small potted palm at the side of the main doors to the Hilton Hotel. There were three large, flat steps that descended to the curved drive, and from there Azul Dante would come out of the lobby, wave to the adoring, jostling crowd, and climb into his limousine for the pleasant ride to Monaco. In reality, the distance from where Jameson lay on an old apartment building rooftop to the front entrance to the Hilton was a little over 120 meters, but the magnifying power of the scope made everything close. With it he could see the gold thread on the doorman's sleeve and a small gold cross on the lapel of the dress worn by a woman who walked out carrying a purse and a cup of coffee.

He saw the coffee, grunted, and reached for the small

thermos in the backpack beside him. He lay on his side
under an old cardboard box and pieces of discarded aluminum duct. The apartment building was being partially
renovated, and construction trash had been scattered
across the flat roof. If he was in charge of Azul Dante's
security, he would have helicopters overhead beginning at
first light. He had been there since before the sun came
up. That had been over an hour ago, and so far the skies
were empty of aircraft. They were an odd color, a muted
light, and he wondered if it had to do with the proximity
of the sea. The nearness of the Mediterranean Sea was an
important part of his escape plan, so he had to keep the
weather in mind. He was considered "neutralized" by
someone pulling strings back at Langley, but that didn't
mean he didn't have access to the field agent's potpourri
of sources, safe houses, transportation, and equipment.
In this case it was a small boat, and he laughed quietly as
he thought of it. He had checked around, learned there
was one that could be had for charter from a local with a
checkered past. It was an old fishing boat, shabby but
sound. It lay not far away, tied to a disreputable dock, far
from the shiny and pretentious mega-yachts, nestled
among rough fishing boats and other painted ladies of
the night. He thought of her name and chuckled.

He stopped chuckling when he thought of what he
had to do. He took a deep breath, let it out, and sighted
through the scope. With it he scanned the area in front
of the hotel. He passed a face, stopped, searched for it,
and found it. He looked at a ruggedly handsome young

man in a business suit, over it a light trench coat. It was the man's eyes that drew his inspection. They were the eyes of a watcher, a professional, a cop or a security type. The man came out of the lobby, talking and gesturing to another, older man. Jameson studied the man's face closely. So many faces through the years, the faces of enemies, friends, and the friends that might be enemies. This face was one he had seen before. He focused on it while he wracked his brain. The guy was an American, a security specialist from one of the agencies. If Jameson remembered correctly the guy worked on the diplomatic side of things out of various agencies. *Devane*. Jameson had never met him, but knew who he was. He wondered why Devane would be here, working to protect Azul Dante, for that could be the only reason the guy was out and about with his game face on. Jameson let the rifle lay beside him, sipped his coffee, chewed on a stale bagel, studied the sky, and waited for his prey to show. He wondered how Slim was doing, and he wondered where Cat Early was.

+   +   +

"It is the sky for rain," said the Frenchman with a heavy accent. "See how it lays there, indolent, soggy, lifeless? Not a storm coming, but fat, heavy, how do you say it? *Drizzle*. It will be the rain of drizzle, all day, soaking everybody, and us, too."

Great, thought James Devane as he stood with his local counterpart on the steps near the lobby of the

Hilton Hotel, I get to work with a French Chicken Little. He shrugged at the man, nodded, and said "Maybe it will keep the crazies inside for the day." He was in an accepting mood. He had to be, he felt, or he might just ditch the small radio he wore, earplug and all, the nine-millimeter Mac-10 automatic weapon he carried slung under his trench coat, and walk away from this dumb assignment. He had no clue as to why his bosses at the National Security Agency sent him "on loan" to the stupid CIA. He could give two figs for Benjamin Carter, or his stumbling, bumbling band of has-been agents who still thought Nicaragua was a big deal. And, truth be told, he wasn't all that impressed with Monsieur Azul Dante, either. He was convinced Dante had tried to nix what might have been between him and Sophia out of simple, petty, jealousy. What a control freak, he thought. He didn't think anyone would take a potshot at Dante, either; the guy was universally loved. Maybe some fanatic Muslim, he mused, but he doubted if that rabble could really put anything together.

He turned and scanned the buildings on both sides of the street near the hotel. According to his French counterpart, the local cops had already made a sweep, and a surveillance helicopter was on call. He felt an uneasiness in the air, though, and could not relax. He picked out a couple of building rooftops that would give a shooter the best angle on the front of the hotel, and made a mental note to keep an eyeball on them when Dante and his staff made their appearance. Maybe he'd get a glance at Sophia, too.

+   +   +

"Ah, Drazic," said Azul Dante to his dour aide, "there is something in the air this morning—do you feel it?" Drazic shrugged, his dead eyes revealing nothing. "Of course you don't feel it, Drazic, but it is all right, because *I* do." He put his coffee cup down, stared out the hotel room window, and said, "Something to do with the weather, or the . . . *atmosphere*." He rubbed his chin. "And perhaps there is something from our friend Izbek Noir, as he calls himself. Some part of his little game. About time, I must say."

A soft knock came at the door. It was opened, and Sophia Ghent, looking lovely in a soft skirt, blouse, and jacket combination in violet and white, offset by her hair, which was pulled back in a businesslike bun, looked into the room. "Azul?" she said. "I'm told we have about ten minutes until the car gets here."

Drazic, upon hearing her, turned and walked out as she stepped aside to let him pass.

"Very good, Sophia," said Dante. "Will you have coffee? Pastry?"

"No, thank you, Azul," she replied politely, "I had some in my room."

"Excellent. See you downstairs, then."

Sophia closed the door. As she walked down the hallway toward her room she wondered if James Devane was out there this morning, if she'd see him. For a moment she allowed herself to think about making a road trip from Nice to Monaco, in a hired limousine, with James Devane instead of Azul Dante. She fetched her briefcase, laptop, purse, and cell phone from her room, straightened her shoulders, and headed for the elevators, trying to push the daydreams out of her head.

+   +   +

"What?" said Slim defensively. Cat Early had come beating on his hotel room door, bleating something about coffee downstairs for the working troops. He had come swimming up from deep sleep and was still groggy.

"Did you comb your hair with a lawn mower?" asked Cat.

Slim straightened. "No," he said, "this is my *look* today. We're in France, everyone has a *look*."

"Well, get dressed and get your gear, and come downstairs with your *look*," said Cat with a smile. "This is gonna be a long day of chasing Dante and entourage from here to Monte Carlo and back. You need coffee and some breakfast."

"I'll be down in five, Mom."

A half hour later Cat and Slim waited in the lobby of the Hilton for Azul Dante. Simon Blake was there, as were other newsies, Prodigal Project staffers, French dignitaries, and cops.

Cat saw Sophia and waved. The young woman hurried across the lobby, took Cat's hands, gave her a quick kiss on the cheek, and said, "Good morning, Cat. I'm glad you are here." She turned to Slim and added, "You too, Slim."

"You look too pretty to hang around with a bigwig like Dante," responded Slim. "You might want to think about experiencing life through the eyes of a real combat photographer."

Sophia, not used to such openness, laughed shyly. She glanced at Slim's hair and asked, "Is it windy outside?"

"No," said Cat, laughing too. She turned and glanced out through the lobby doors. "The sky is weird, though, leaden." She made a face. "Maybe it will rain."

There was a small flurry of activity near the main bank of elevators, and Sophia said, "I must go. I'll be looking for you throughout the day, perhaps we can have a cold drink or something between activities." She walked off.

Cat and Slim watched as Drazic walked past them, headed for the entranceway drive.

Without turning his head, Slim said out of the side of his mouth, "I've seen eyes like his before, Cat, but they were on dead guys."

"Let's go outside," said Cat.

+   +   +

"Man," said the young engineer to another sitting at a console nearby at NASA headquarters outside Galveston, Texas. "The satellite and ground telescope reports coming in are not kidding about increased and sudden sunspot activity. Look at it. I'll bet we can kiss half the world's communications capabilities bye-bye for today."

"Yeah," agreed his partner. "Sat images are fried . . . see? It's like a huge magnetic blanket, like a screen almost." He manipulated the keyboard on his desk. "Infrared, radio, spectrum . . . we got *nada*. The window has definitely been closed."

"We can't see anything beyond our own moon," said the first.

They were interrupted by an early-morning-shift co-worker, "Hey, you guys," she said. "You should see take a look outside. The moon looks blood red, there are no stars, and the sky looks all *sooty*. What's going on?"

+   +   +

Ivy was awake when Ron knocked softly on the door to her room. She had given up trying to sleep, her head filled with thoughts of . . . everything. When the knock came, she knew it would be him. She wore a cotton sleep-shirt and pulled a robe over it as she let him in. He wore jeans and a T-shirt, no shoes, his hair was mussed, and his chin was shadowed with beard. His eyes shone behind his glasses.

"Ivy," he said, "I . . . I just wanted to talk."

"Sit down, Ron." She pointed to a chair and sat on the edge of the bed. She yawned, smiled, and said, "It's okay."

"I've told you I'm sorry," said Ron. "Sorry about what

I did, sorry about everything I've done to let you down. But Ivy, the words . . . those words *I'm sorry*, they don't carry enough weight, they don't *say* it."

She watched him, not sure of her feelings. She knew he loved her, always had. And she knew he probably was genuinely sorry for his actions. She used *probably* because she wondered if he really understood what he almost did with that stupid and deadly gun. And what had he expected to solve? What had he expected to accomplish, to make right? She waited.

"Ivy," he tried again, "look at us. We're just two little people in this world, two of millions and millions in a world being turned inside out by a power we cannot begin to comprehend. But we are *part* of it somehow . . . part of it. I loved Ronnie, Ivy, and so did you. I know being Ronnie's parents changed us as a couple, but we were a couple, and his parents, and we did the best we could, and then he was taken. Taken." He stared at her, then looked down at his feet. He made fists with his hands, and they rested on his knees. "And I loved you, Ivy. I love you, and I want you to *understand* why I came here with that gun, understand, and maybe that will help you love me again."

There was an expectant stillness to the early-morning hours, a listening quiet, a hesitation in the beat of the night. They were just two little people, she thought.

"I don't have to love you again, Ron," Ivy said softly. "I love you." She watched as he lifted his head, and their eyes met. "But I don't know who you are, Ron, who you are, who *I* am, who *God* is. I came here because I was *pulled* here, pulled by Henderson Smith's voice. You know what? I've come to realize even *he* isn't really sure what's going on. Doesn't matter. We're here, and it looks like we—you, me, the others—we are part of *something*. Let's say it's God's plan." Her eyes went out of focus, then came back hard and brittle. "I did something terrible just before we lost Ronnie, something terrible and selfish, and maybe irreversible. I love you, Ron, and we are together, and maybe the world is ending around us. I don't know if saying *I'm sorry* means that much anymore."

"Do *we* mean that much, anymore?" he asked.

"I don't know, Ron," she answered. She felt something in the quiet morning, saw by the expression on his face he did also, and said, "We have to meet the others."

One by one, they gathered in the nave. They had been asleep in their dormitory rooms provided by the New Christian Cathedral. Each one had awakened with a start, had hastily dressed, splashed some cold water on his or her face, and headed for the church. They were not surprised to see the others as they came together. Shannon Carpenter was first, with Ivy close behind. Then came Ron Underwood and, after a few minutes, Henderson Smith. Smith seemed reluctant, at first, to enter and join them. His face was hardened with worry, his eyes darted all around, as if trying to see what was outside. They sat in the first pew, quiet. A few minutes later Ted Glenn came in and, behind him, Nateesha Folks.

"What's goin' on?" whispered the black woman as she

took one of Ivy's hands. "I heard Henderson get up in his room next to mine, and when he didn't come back I came lookin'."

Ivy shrugged and glanced at Ron, who returned her gaze. "I don't . . . we don't know, Nateesha," she said. "I just woke up, and when I did I knew we had to be together."

"Sun shouldn't be up for over an hour," said Ted Glenn, "but I looked outside comin' over here, and the whole eastern sky is dark red. The rest of the sky looks like lead, just layin' there."

"Oh, Lord," said Henderson Smith under his breath, and Nateesha went to him and put an arm around his shoulders.

"What more can this poor world take?" said Shannon. No one had the answer.

CHAPTER SIXTEEN

The crosshairs lay dead center on the broad forehead of Minister Azul Dante. The thin black lines quartered Dante's head and face, and John Jameson knew he had the perfect shot. He carefully sighted the sniper rifle and allowed his breathing to settle. By moving the weapon a tiny bit, he was able to scan the scene immediately surrounding his target. He had seen several people pass in front of Dante, including his lovely assistant that Cat had told him about. She was in the scope, then moved out of the picture. Dante's valet, or aide, or whatever he was, the tall, stooped, dour man with pale skin, a pronounced widow's peak high on his forehead, and sort of lifeless eyes, was in the sight, too. The man stood slightly behind and to Dante's left, as the minister stood on the top step of the hotel entrance, waving to the cheering people across the street. Cat had told him about the valet, too.

Jameson looked down onto the street without moving his head. He could see uniformed police officers keeping the crowd on the sidewalk, and plainclothes types, male and female, wearing their dark sunglasses even on this hazy day, their earphones, buzzing with instructions. He had heard and seen one helicopter circling overhead, but for only a few passes. Then it was gone, and the streets of Nice were strangely quiet. He was glad. He did not need any distractions. The smells of spicy food being cooked wafted up from the apartments below him. He concentrated on the crosshairs. There was enough room between Azul Dante and his valet for a safe shot. This was a dangerous game about to be played, with no room for error. He saw the potted palm sitting near the doors, conveniently off Dante's shoulder. Its round, soft trunk would be the perfect place for the spent bullet to be absorbed. He sighted the crosshairs, took another breath, began to let it out, and slowly squeezed the trigger.

On the street below, James Devane watched the crowd, scanned the rooftops, glanced at Azul Dante standing on the steps smiling and waving, and adjusted the weapon under his coat. "Stop soaking up the love, Dante, and get into the limo," he said under his breath. Like all security agents, he was convinced his charge would do anything to expose himself to an assassin for the greatest amount of time possible. He forced himself not to stare at Sophia, who stood a few feet away from Dante and that weird aide, waiting. He thought she looked lovely and wasn't sure if she had seen him or not.

He glanced at the sky. No wonder the chopper left so soon, he thought. The air had an oppressive feel. It wasn't hot, or sultry, just oddly palpable. He shifted his shoulders under his trench coat and let his right hand rest easily on the nine-millimeter hung against his ribs. He scanned the rooftops once more, his eyes never still.

John Jameson squeezed the trigger, the firing pin struck the cap in the center of the shell, the powder exploded, and the copper-jacketed bullet was blown from the end of the barrel at over five thousand feet per second. The round left the barrel spinning, following an unwavering trajectory toward the target. The heavy rifle bucked against Jameson's right shoulder, and there was the punching roar of the heavy-caliber weapon being fired. The sight picture was jolted, then returned briefly to Azul Dante's face, and in time reduced to a microsecond, Jameson found himself staring into Dante's eyes. There was no doubt in Jameson's mind in that instant that Azul Dante looked up, saw him, saw deep into his eyes, and knew a bullet was headed his way. In the intense and unreal moment, Jameson thought he could actually see the round he had fired, running straight and true toward the exact spot where Jameson wanted it to hit. But, still within that strangely compressed time, Jameson saw a twisted smile appear on Dante's face, and he watched as Dante's eyes blinked in slow motion. Incredibly, as Dante blinked, the bullet veered from its path. Jameson watched in horror as he saw death in the crosshairs.

James Devane's world became the punctuated roar of

the sniper's rifle from overhead. His ears told him instantly that a shot had been fired, the path of the bullet, and the probable location of the shooter. He whirled around to see a fine mist of blood explode in the crowd where Dante stood, heard the beginning of the screams, and saw the tall figure spin and fall. He whipped his head back to the opposite side of the street, two buildings down, and saw for a brief second a furtive movement. With the quickness and surety of a pro, he brought the barrel of his nine-millimeter out of his coat, whipped it up, squeezed the trigger, and fired off a burst of six in a tight arc. He saw bursts of plaster erupt at the edge of the roof he aimed for, but could not tell if he hit the shooter.

Sophia heard the sharp report from the gun across the street, flinched, then spun around to look at Dante. She saw someone falling, but then the group of men and women on the front entranceway steps to the hotel panicked. She heard screams, saw people diving down, kneeling, cowering with their hands over their heads, and shoving others in their mindless efforts to get away from the terrible bullets, from the explosion of blood, from death. She was knocked over by someone who crashed into her side, and as she fell backward another person kicked and stepped on her legs. She went down onto the steps, arms flailing behind her in vain. The back of her head hit the step solidly, her eyes were filled with crimson, and she blacked out. Her last thought was, *Why would anyone shoot* him?

Seven, thought Cat Early, and she said, "John."

Slim, beside her, kept firing his camera, moving to the side to get a better angle, focusing on the death and panic blowing up on the streets of Nice.

Cat flinched even as Sophia had, but it was when the agent a few feet from her fired the automatic weapon he had pulled from under his coat. The agent had fired at something up on a nearby rooftop, and when Cat crouched and spun to see, she knew who the agent was firing at. She turned back to the hotel entrance in time to see the tall figure slowly crumple against the glass, a smear of greasy red blood behind his head. She saw Sophia trampled by the panicked crowd. "No!" she shouted.

"C'mon, Cat!" shouted Slim as he lunged forward, running across the street to get closer to the crowd on the steps. Cat took a step, then *seven* filled her mind and she turned away and began running wildly through the crowd of people, running away from the Hilton, toward the buildings where the shot came from.

Jameson knew he must attempt to kill Dante, and the attempt must cause panic, and news, if he was to continue his mission against Izbek Noir. He knew he would not, could not, kill Dante, no matter what Noir wanted, and had carefully sighted the rifle so the bullet would pass within a hair of Dante's left ear, to impact harmlessly in the thick trunk of the potted palm. But Dante had blinked, and the bullet veered ... right into Drazic's skull. A black hole appeared between the sallow man's eyes, in the center of his forehead. Drazic's head snapped back, his mouth opened into a stretched, oblong hole, his eyes widened, and a spray of red blood flowered behind him. His arms jerked upward as he took one step back, then fell heavily against the glass wall of the hotel lobby. He was dead as he fell to a sitting position, leaving a wide swipe of his syrupy blood on the glass. Jameson had killed a man.

He stared for only a moment, but it was one moment too long in the life of a professional. He sensed, more than saw, the agent on the street below whirl around, weapon up. Then the world exploded in John Jameson's face, and his head jerked and spun as several pieces of lead and plaster shrapnel cut and gouged into the left side of his face, his head and ear, and his eye. Jameson grunted, his left hand flew to his eye, and he fell prone beside the rifle. Then, in pain, blinded by the blood and damage to his eye, heartsick at the death he had caused, he reacted. His years of combat experience, as an agent and warrior, kicked in.

He pulled two black bandannas out of his backpack and quickly folded one, placed it against his bleeding eye and ear, and tied the other tightly over his head, holding the first in place. He did this even while he scooted back away from the edge of the roof, came up into a crouch, and duck-walked toward the rooftop access door leading into the building. He left the rifle, extra bullets, and the cello case. He knew they could never be traced to him, or even back to the old South African. They meant nothing to him now. Getting away, however, meant everything, and he lunged down the stairs, jumping from landing to landing, falling once because of a sudden onslaught of dizziness. As he ran he pulled a large, floppy straw hat from his pack and stuck it over the bandanna. He passed closed apartment doors, but saw no one in the stairwell. He finally reached the low-ceilinged basement, stumbled to the small side door he had discovered when he did his initial recon of the building, kicked it open, and fell into a side alley. The alley joined another, then another, finally opening onto a small waterfront street blocks away. From there it was another two or three blocks to where the ugly little fishing boat waited. His head pounded with a blinding pain, he felt weakened by the loss of blood, and muttered under his breath as he gained his feet and stumbled forward, "Oh, Jesus . . . help me now."

"Alors! Alors!" James Devane heard the shouts coming from the apartment building he had fired on. He ran that way even as the first shots rang out, then there were several sustained volleys, and more shouting. He charged into the small lobby of the place, saw two uniformed policemen and a couple of plainclothes guys crouched down with their pistols out, their eyes wide, and headed up the front stairs. He smelled it on the second floor and cautiously looked around the corner into the hallway. There were several French security agents standing around a splintered apartment door, including the man he had been paired with earlier. "It's okay," said the agent when he saw Devane approach. "It is *finis*."

"What?" said Devane. "What's finished?"

The Frenchman pointed into the room, which still hung heavy with smoke. Devane leaned against the broken door frame and looked inside. Four young men, with black hair and shaggy beards, jeans, jogging shoes, and polo shirts, lay sprawled in grotesque postures of violent death. Each one had been shot several times. Scattered around them on the floor were several automatic weapons, and on a nearby bed lay an eight-by-ten glossy photograph of Azul Dante, spattered with blood. A hot plate sat on a table, a pot of something spicy still cooking.

"Some kind of Middle East men," said the Frenchman contemptuously. Then he actually turned his head and spit into the hallway. "Muslim crazies," he said. "We had information on them from before." He stared at James Devane, shrugged, and said, "So, American, it is all *finis*, yes?"

Devane stared at the dead, the weapons, the photo, the blood. "How positively convenient," he said as he turned away.

He ran headlong back outside, through the milling crowds, across the street to the front steps of the Hilton. He saw Azul Dante standing stiffly, staring at the skies, the crumpled, bloody, dead Drazic behind him, ignored. He looked around wildly and finally saw Sophia, sprawled on the cement, her eyes closed, red lips open, pale skin translucent. He knelt beside her, cradled her head with one arm while he used his fingers to check her pulse. It was strong. He kissed her on her forehead, and her eyes opened. He heard Azul Dante laugh wickedly behind him and turned to look at him.

But Dante stared up into the skies, his eyes bright, his lips pulled back from his even white teeth. "Do it!" he shouted, his voice hard and strangely deep. "Yes! Do it!" He laughed again, a demonic, full-throated laugh, his fists raised above his head. Yes, he inwardly exulted, now we begin, now we can take the next step! Because of what the one who calls himself Izbek Noir has done, I will gain only more power, more believers. He still believes he and I act as one, the fool! And now the people of this world will suffer even more! Not at *my* hand now . . . no! They will suffer at my hand to be sure, but *this*, this, it is not my doing. He laughed again, his eyes watering from the heavy, gusty air, and shouted, "Yes . . . yes!"

James Devane stared, too, and did not understand what he was seeing. He knew the wind had begun to howl, ripping around them suddenly in foul gusts of warm air. He turned back to Sophia and saw her smile up at him. "Sophia," he said, "hold on, hold on now." He reached under her, lifted her, stood, and carried her past the staring Azul Dante and into the hotel lobby.

Slim moved from point to point, snapping photos of the panicked crowd, the people knocked down and sprawling, the agents with their weapons out. He photographed the dead Drazic and shuddered as he looked at the man's eyes through his lens. The eyes looked no different than they did an hour ago. Slim stood, turned, and shot three or four of Azul Dante in quick succession. He felt the wind, saw how dark the day had become, and looked around in vain for Cat.

Several blocks away, John Jameson fell to his knees on the sidewalk. The crazy, dark day spun weirdly around him, the side of his head felt numb, and he vomited. He put his hands flat on the ground, got his feet under him, and stood again. He knew he was not far from the boat. He took a deep breath, gagged again, and took a step. He did not fall but went down on one knee, unable to go farther. His floppy straw hat was ripped from his head, and he felt the suddenly strong wind tugging at the edges of the blood-soaked bandanna. He turned his head to look all around. The few people he saw were running or pointing at the leaden skies. He knew he was blind in the left eye, but everything seemed so dark he feared he was losing the right one, too. He took another deep, shuddering breath and tried to stand. *Seven* came to him, and he felt warm hands on his face, then under his arms, pulling him to his feet.

"John," cried Cat. "John! What happened to you? Oh, God, please help us." She pulled his backpack out of his hand, slung it over her shoulder, and said, "C'mon, we've got to get you to a hospital." She pulled on his arm. "C'mon."

"Wait, Cat," he said. "Stop." He forced himself to focus on her face, into her lovely bright eyes filled with concern and fear. "No hospitals, no doctors yet. I must get out of here. Help me."

She felt no hesitation, no doubt. She felt strength in her heart. "Where, John?"

He pointed down the curving street. "Do you see the

cluster of fishing boats? Nets, traps, stuff? Maybe a dozen grungy-looking boats?"

She shielded her eyes from the wind and squinted through the weird darkness of day. "Yes . . . yes, I see them."

"Help me get to them, Cat," he said. "That's how we'll get away from here. I want to get out of the harbor and head east."

She looked at the roiled waters of the small harbor, took a deep breath, and asked as they walked, bumping together, "What boat, John? What boat?"

He had a daunting thought, and asked, "Cat, can you operate a boat?"

Fine time to ask a girl a question like that, she thought. "Yes. No. I've driven small ones around the Florida Keys, back home."

"We can do this, Cat," he said.

"Yes," she replied. They came to the boats, rocking and grinding together in the disturbed waters. "John," she asked, "which boat?"

"*Dulcinea*," he answered. He had managed to come full circle to Omar's old boat, the one the freelancer had used to get Jameson ashore in Tunisia, months ago. "She is called *Dulcinea*."

+   +   +

The heavy pewter skies seemed to draw close around the earth. People all over the planet had the sensation of being able to reach up and touch the blowing clouds of black ash and dust. Then, again everywhere at once, came a thunderous series of great, crashing, bellowing peals of sustained thunder, and the ground shook with the deep reverberations.

The people of the earth, those not cowering in fear, looked into the skies to see wide swaths of color, streaming and screaming across the sooty expanse, leaving trails of fire in their same shades. It did not matter if it was viewed from Japan, India, Norway, England, Zimbabwe, Brazil, New York, Texas, Vancouver, Alaska, or Siberia . . . the colored swathes were there, emboldened and heralded by the peals of thunder. The first streaking swath painted across the skies was white, the next fiery red. Black came then, not clear at first against the dark backdrop of ash and dust, but highlighted when swords of lightning burst forth with the clashing of giant cymbals. All living things shuddered as the next rode across above them . . . it was pale, this one, pale and hideous in hue and design. White came again, not pale, and not the first white, but white, with tendrils of light twisted like filigree around it. The sixth streak came as a blend of the first five, the moon blood red, the sun black. Every continent was shaken by strong earthquakes, which tumbled buildings, fragmented roadways, and destroyed bridges. People died by the thousands, crushed by the structures they hoped would protect them.

Then came silence, as if the broken world, the ravaged skies, and heaven itself waited expectantly for the next catastrophic episode. The skies were filled with the glow of gold, and all was still. Some said it lasted for half an hour, some said for only a moment. No matter. What came as the gold hung there was seen through the eyes of all the peoples of Earth.

It was not there, then it was. None of the world's telescopes, satellites, or radars picked it up, none saw it approach from deep in space, none gave warning. Something like a mountain, huge, fell from the sky. It was a gigantic clump of burning ash, soot, rock, and dust, awash in flame and sparks as it entered the earth's atmosphere, roaring in friction against the wind, tumbling as it fell. High above the earth it broke up, still tumbling, and followed seven different arcs toward the surface. The seven large chunks were thrown into the seven seas, exploding through the surface of the waters in a storm of toxic steam, froth, and boiling foam. Instantly the seawater off the coasts of continents from Australia to South America, from Russia to Canada, from India to China, turned blood red, and millions of fish began to die. The oceans of the world, battered by these falling masses, flailed and convulsed as tons of water were pushed away, then sucked back, and huge tidal waves were formed. These roaring lines of water one hundred feet high, heavy at the base and steep in front, rushed shoreward at speeds over fifty miles per hour. Many ships of the sea, navy warships, merchant vessels, and fishing boats, were swamped and broached by these marching behemoths, lost in the swollen gales, battered and shoved down by the onslaught until they succumbed, and sank beneath the angry, wind-whipped furies.

Many coastlines around the world were flooded in the thundering tides and rush of bloody seawater thickened with the distended bodies of dead sea creatures. Beaches suffered massive erosion, and piers, buildings, and houses collapsed slowly, their foundations awash in the foam. Cities and areas that directly fronted the ocean, like Miami Beach, the North Carolina's Outer Banks, and Hawaii were almost swept clean by the crushing, giant waves that came in ranks to batter them into submission. The north coast of South America, the western bulge of the African continent, and southern Japan were struck with hurricane-force storms, which lay waste to miles of coastline. The Seychelles Islands, in the Indian Ocean, were lost, reduced to spits of clean sand, inhabited by not one living soul. Manhattan was flooded, but stood. In some places, days afterward, dead fish were found rotting in rooms and landings on the second floor of buildings, and several ferryboats and harbor cruisers lay canted awkwardly in the streets. What struck people most, besides the destruction and the dead fish, was the color of the water. As much as a third of the earth's oceans, it was estimated, shimmered with the color of blood.

CHAPTER SEVENTEEN

Thomas Church held his wife, Rebecca, and watched the rain run in torrents off the starred and cracked windshield of his old Bronco. He had his back to the passenger door and window, his legs over the center console. The Bronco lay canted on its side in a ditch, the right front and rear tires sunk into the muddy grass, the left side of the truck a few feet from the southbound lanes of I-95. Rebecca lay snuggled in his arms, her head on his chest, dozing. He smelled her hair, felt the warmth and weight of her, felt the beating of her heart, and drank her in.

They had been driving on the wind-whipped and rain-slicked highway as the storm increased in fury. Church had been fiddling with the truck's radio, trying to get any station giving out information about what was going on. The last report they had heard sounded like the entire world was under siege by a series of hurricanes, or typhoons, ships lost, shores battered. They had seen with their own eyes the streaks of colors that filled the skies, and as they came in sequence, Thomas said to Rebecca, "My word, will you look at that!" Rebecca wanted to stop driving as soon as they came to a rest stop or exit, and he agreed.

When the wind buffeted the truck, forcing him to turn the wheel sharply, then recover, he told her, "I'm going to get off the road, right now." But as he did, the truck was hit broadside by a strong gust, and began to skid. He came off the gas, left the brake pedal alone, and turned into the direction of the skid to no avail. The unrelenting wind shoved the Bronco off the pavement and onto the wet grass. With no small amount of wounded majesty, the truck plowed with a great spray of mud and rainwater into a four-foot drainage ditch and came to rest on its right side.

Church tried four-wheel drive, forward and reverse, low revs, high revs. It was immediately apparent they were going nowhere. "Been there, done this," he said.

"What?" asked Rebecca.

He almost had to shout over the noise of the pounding rain and howling winds, but managed to tell her about getting the Bronco stuck in a deep hole on an old dirt road in western Texas while searching for their son, Tommy. Getting out of there had taken some doing, and as he stared out at the storm flailing them, he knew he could not tackle *this* situation until things calmed down.

He and Rebecca shared some water and some cookies Sissy had packed for them, and made themselves as comfortable as possible in the awkwardly tilted truck. They dozed, talked of life, love, and their kids, and watched the rain. After a while Rebecca said, "Thomas, read me a little bit from the Bible."

He reached across her, took the Bible that had fallen to the floor, let it fall open, and in the storm's flashing light, read the first passage he saw. It was Ecclesiastes 11:1–6.

> Cast your bread upon the waters, for after many days you will find it again.
>
> Give portions to seven, yes to eight, for you do not know what disaster may come upon the land.
>
> If clouds are full of water, they pour rain upon the earth. Whether a tree falls to the south or to the north, in the place where it falls, there will it lie.
>
> Whoever watches the wind will not plant; whoever looks at the clouds will not reap.
>
> As you do not know the path of the wind, or how the body is formed in a mother's womb, so you cannot understand the work of God, the Maker of all things.
>
> Sow your seed in the morning, and at evening let not your hands be idle, for you do not know which will succeed, whether this or that, or whether both will do equally well.

Without doubt, Thomas Church knew he was one of seven, destined to serve. He looked at his wife. She slept, unafraid.

+   +   +

"The heavens declare the glory of God; the skies proclaim the work of His hands," read Shannon as the others sat in a close group on the carpeted floor of the New Christian Cathedral. She held her Bible open in her hands, and like Thomas Church, had begun to read the first passage her eyes fell upon. It was the Nineteenth Psalm. "Day after day they pour forth speech," she read. "Night after night they display knowledge. There is no speech or language where their voice is not heard. Their voice goes out into all the earth, their words to the ends of the world."

Ted Glenn sat beside Shannon, and beside him was Nateesha Folks. She held Henderson Smith's head in her lap, her fingertips lightly brushing his brow as they listened. Next to them sat Ivy and Ron. They held hands, and Ivy's head lay on Ron's shoulder. The fury of the storm had reached its crescendo, buffeting the main building of the church. The electric power had gone down during the first moments of the storm, and the darkness was not chased away by the morning's blackened sun. Some of the high glass windows in the church had been blown out, and sooty rain had blown in, streaking the ceiling, soaking the floor. Ted Glenn had made periodic checks on what was going on outside and reported back to the others the destruction to the neighborhood he saw—trees down, cars tipped sideways, the roofs of several houses damaged. He saw no people out in the streets and figured everyone in the church buildings would be all right if they stayed inside.

When he stood on the front steps of the church and saw the streaking colors appear, he called to the others. They cautiously followed him outside to stare into the ash-darkened skies at the swathes of white, red, black, pale, white again, then a mix, then gold. They were silent, each with his or her own thoughts, until the Reverend Henderson Smith said in a quavering voice, "My Lord. My Lord."

They returned to the nave and sat on the floor in the shadow of the pulpit. Ron pushed his glasses up on the bridge of his nose, cleared his throat, and said, "Reverend Smith, would you read to us?"

Smith looked at him, at the offered Bible, and stared down at his hands in his lap. Then he raised his head, smiled tentatively at Nateesha, and said in a barely audible voice, "I'd rather listen now. I'd rather listen as the sweet words are read." Read by a pure heart, not a doubtful heart, like mine. "I'd rather listen this time, Ron."

"In the heavens He has pitched a tent for the sun," read Shannon, "which is like a bridegroom coming forth from his pavilion, like a champion rejoicing to run his course. It rises at one end of the heavens and makes its circuit to the other; nothing is hidden from its heat."

Ron watched Shannon read and listened to the words. He glanced down occasionally at the Bible given to him by the old black prisoner, following along as she read. Even as the words fell into his heart, he gave thanks to God for this second chance, for this renewed time with his Ivy. He understood she still loved him, and he understood she was still struggling with her own demons, her own doubts, her own failures and pain. It didn't matter. He was resolved to stand with her, to help her in any way he could, in any way she wished. He knew they would never be the same as a couple, as husband and wife, but he accepted that, too. He would stand with her, and pray with her, and learn about God's Word and God's work with her. He thanked God for Ronnie, their son, for the moments of time they shared. He thanked God Ivy had the chance to be a mother, to experience that total commitment and covenant of love, even to feel the unbearable pain and heartache of loss. He knew she was poisoned by guilt and hoped to help her wash it away with the waters of renewed faith. He would be patient, he would be strong. He would let her run when she needed to, and take her back when she was ready. He wished Ronnie could be there, now, during this frightful and wondrous storm, to comfort her, to tell her it was all right . . . it was all right.

"The law of the Lord is perfect, reviving the soul. The statutes of the Lord are trustworthy, making wise the simple. The precepts of the Lord are right," continued Shannon, "giving joy to the heart." She was gratefully lost in the words and the sure knowing in her heart that nothing had happened to her, to those gathered with her, by chance. She was part of seven, and they were part of God's plan during these unbelievable times. She was thankful for the certainty in her heart and knew without question she would act as His servant in the coming days.

Ivy heard the words of God, understood that each one

should be held as precious, and worked hard simply to open her heart and let the strength and clarity make her whole. She, like Shannon, knew she was part of seven and understood there was work to be done regarding the Prodigal Project, Azul Dante, and life on Earth. She was committed to the challenge, to do what she must as part of His plan, but she gave the commitment grudgingly, shaded by skepticism. She felt the warm skin of Ron's hand on hers and glanced at him. She was his wife and had once loved being simply that. He was once a good man, simple, honest, and giving of his love. Who he was now, she was not sure. She took a deep breath, tried to fight it, and could not. From the depths of her heart, from some dark place in the fold, came fine and wrenching *desire*, and *anger*. She wanted her life back, she wanted her son back, but she feared she had thrown any chance of that away when she made a deal with the dark one who sang such a pretty and knowing song. Where were you then, God? It echoed in her mind. Where were you when Ronnie was born, when he was taken? Were you *right there*? She shuddered. Ron felt it and squeezed her hand. Oh, Ron, she thought, we did not deserve this. She wondered if she deserved God, or anything, and remembered hearing something about God simply *being*, with deserving Him not really a part of it. She took another long, deep breath, filled herself with the love she still held for her child, and tried to balance that against the anger she felt over losing him and the way in which it had happened. She listened as Shannon read from Scripture, and the words fell like rose petals against the hardened walls of her heart.

"The commands of the Lord are radiant, giving light to the eyes," she read, and the words seemed to resonate throughout the large church. "The fear of the Lord is pure, enduring forever. The ordinances of the Lord are sure and altogether righteous. They are more precious than gold; they are sweeter than honey, than honey from the comb. By them is Your servant warned; in keeping them there is great reward."

Outside, the storm continued unabated. Across the earth, humanity watched as the wind and waves vented their destructive energies under the blackened skies. In the church called the New Christian Cathedral, in Selma, Alabama, six people huddled together in the strength of Scripture. Four were members of the seven destined to serve.

"Who can discern his errors?" stated the Word. "Forgive my hidden faults. Keep Your servant also from willful sins; may they not rule over me. Then I will be blameless, innocent of great transgression."

"May the words of my mouth and the meditation of my heart be pleasing in Your sight," each of them heard. "O Lord, my Rock and my Redeemer."

+   +   +

Cat Early held tightly to the wooden steering wheel as she stood at the helm of the *Dulcinea*, staring at the crashing seas breaking over the pointed bows of the small, rust-streaked fishing boat. John Jameson stood beside her, occasionally adjusting the throttle, backing off on power, then adding it each time the force of the seas held the small boat in their grasp. They were an hour out of Nice, following the coastline in the howling, tearing wind, rocking and tumbling against the raging waves.

With Cat's help, he had clamored aboard, found the promised hidden key, and managed to get the cranky ancient diesel engine started. He and Cat struggled with the crisscrossed lines that had the *Dulcinea* tied to the dock and other fishing boats, until she floated free of her sisters. He took the helm to guide her out of the small harbor and steered as Cat stood beside him to work on his wounds. He had a survival-style first-aid kit in his backpack, and with it she cleaned the deep cuts in his scalp, across his ear, and carefully around his left eye. The left side of his face was swollen, and his left eye was filled with dark blood. She hung on as the boat tipped and shouted into his ear, her lips close, and told him she could not determine how damaged the eye actually was. He had shrugged. "We'll get a chance to look at it later," he told her. "Just clean it up and bandage it as best you can, Cat." She did.

After they were clear from the breakwater, they rounded the flashing harbor buoy and swung her left. This put them against a stern-quartering sea, and the waves began to batter the starboard side of the old vessel. The bilge pumps were already working overtime, Jameson noted, and the decks were awash each time a wave overtook them, blood-red water rushing in torrents out through the scuppers. The underwater exhaust on the rattle-trap diesel engine bubbled and puttered, and when the stern was lifted out of the water between the towering waves, the single bronze propeller would spin into high revs until digging in again. A ripple of nausea swept over Jameson, and his knees buckled. He told Cat, "You take her! I'll try to watch the throttles!" She stood at the helm, gripping the slippery wooden wheel with white knuckles and using it to help keep her balance as the small boat pitched and tossed. Jameson stood beside her, hanging on to the main hatchway rail, dizzy and weak.

"Look at the water!" shouted Cat as she watched a looming wave approach.

"The color?"

"It's like blood, John," she said. "And those streaks in the skies! The colors . . . the order they appeared!"

Jameson looked into her wide eyes, diamond drops of water scattered across her cheeks. "How can anyone have any doubt as to what this is?" he said.

They were silent a moment. The boat lurched, and the wheel spun out of Cat's hands.

"Hang on, Cat!" shouted Jameson. He began to reach for her, but she managed to stop the wheel, turned it, and swung more to the right.

"I'm afraid of getting pushed too close to shore," she shouted into his right ear. She looked all around, her eyes bright. She leaned to him again and said, "John. Where are we going in this thing?"

"Italy," he answered. "A pretty little place called Portofino."

"Will you know it when you see it?"

"I think so," he said. "We should be able to see the harbor markers, and the town will lay above it."

Cat wiped her wet hair out of eyes, squinted into the pelting rain, and said, "I hope so."

"We'll be all right, Cat," he said. "It will be all right, now."

He watched the night rage around them. He was bloodied and weakened, but unafraid. The action he had taken against Azul Dante weighed on his mind, and he saw an image of the man he had killed. He was struck with a sudden thought, I know my aim was true. I know where that bullet should have hit. Did *Dante* alter its path somehow? And if he did, why use me to kill his own man? To up the ante?" He understood, as he was sure the dark General Izbek Noir did, that an attempted assassination against Azul Dante would only make Dante a stronger world figure. A missed shot would have less impact than the terrible sudden death of Dante's personal valet, that, too, was certain. Death had come for Dante, and the world would point the finger at the enemies of his righteousness, and his Prodigal Project. First it would be the Muslim mujahideen, of course, but then it would expand to include *anyone* opposed to the Prodigal Project.

He felt the soft cloak of unconsciousness falling across his mind, and he shook himself. He knew he must stand with Cat, guide her and their small boat to a safe harbor. He pinched his nose, gingerly felt the bandage over his left eye, and made his tongue look for spit in his mouth. There was none. He bent carefully and pulled a bottle of water from his pack. He let go of the rail long enough to open the top, then passed it to Cat, who smiled and gulped some down. She gave it back and he drank his fill. He looked at her face in the flashes of lightning. She was beautiful and strong, and she had come to him when he needed help. She had not hesitated, accepting his action, giving him of herself. He knew at that moment he would have never made it to the *Dulcinea* and out of Nice by himself.

Cat watched the night, the raging winds and crashing seas, saw the color of blood and the streaks across the skies, and felt tiny in the universe that surrounded her. But she did not feel alone. John stood beside her, wounded but strong, a man who *believed* in something, who *believed*. She knew *they* were not alone, either. Seven was real, and they were both part of it. What had happened back there in front of the hotel, with death and Azul Dante, was destined to be, it was part of a plan. There was *reason*, she exulted, and if there is *reason*, God exists, and if God exists, *it will be all right*. She knew God was real, as was the Word of God. Her sister had known it and had tried, gently, to break through Cat's own cynicism so the truth could be shared. But her sister had left her that Bible, down below in the musty cabin, in her own backpack, and with it she had begun her journey toward the light. I am a child of God, she thought, in this tormented, barren world where there are no children. I am a child of God, and *I believe*.

"Cat," said Jameson, "Cat, I . . . I can't make . . ." He fell against her, then began to slip toward the deck. She let go of the wheel and the boat slewed wildly in a trough between waves. She put her arms around him and lifted, pushing his hips up onto a wooden seat built into the port bulkhead opposite the helm. She helped him lean back until his shoulders squared against the bulkhead, giving him support. She found the water bottle, put it to his lips, and watched him manage to drink some. The boat lurched and she threw herself at the wheel, controlling the swing until she had the *Dulcinea* back on the rough compass course he had given her. He watched her and knew they were two of seven, destined to serve.

She glanced at him and their eyes met. She knew he watched her, and she was comfortable in his gaze. She saw how pale his face had become, how his hand shook as he held the water bottle.

"John," she said. "John."

He looked into her eyes.

"The Lord bless and keep you," she said to him. "The Lord make His face to shine upon you and be gracious to you." She reached out with her left hand, he with his right, and their fingertips touched.

"The Lord turn His face toward you," she said to him as the day that was night howled around them, "and give you peace."

They were two, of seven, destined to serve.

ABOUT THE AUTHORS

Ken Abraham is the author of the #1 *New York Times* bestselling *Let's Roll!* with Lisa Beamer, as well as the author of *Payne Stewart* with Tracey Stewart.

Daniel Hart had a distinguished career in the U.S. Army and as a law enforcement officer. He now writes full time and lives with his wife and children in Florida.

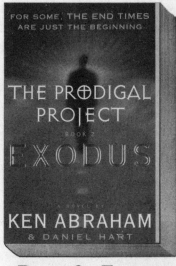
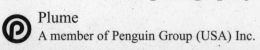